Unwinding Time

by

JAMES STODDAH

PUBLISHED BY OUTLET PUBLISHING GROUP
Bulloch House, 10 Rumford Place, Liverpool. L3 9DG.
www.outletpublishinggroup.com

This book is a work of fiction. Any resemblance to actual events or persons, living or dead, is entirely coincidental.

First edition.

www.jamesstoddah.com

ISBN – 978-1-9995965-0-7
eISBN – 978-1-9995965-1-4

Requests to publish work from this book should be sent to:
info@outletpublishinggroup.com

Printed by Lightning Source UK LTD

Cover design by Kyle Wilson

"The Rainbow comes and goes,
And lovely is the Rose,
The Moon doth with delight
Look round her when the heavens are bare,
Waters on a starry night
Are beautiful and fair;
The sunshine is a glorious birth;
But yet I know, where'er I go,
That there hath past away a glory from the earth."

WILLIAM WORDSWORTH.
Intimations of Immortality from Recollections of Early Childhood

CHAPTER 1

As the hammer comes down everything goes black.

Then there's the brightest of lights. There's an excruciating pain in my head and behind my eyes and it takes a few minutes to I realise I'm in hospital. I want to cry, scream… or die. A familiar face is silhouetted by the light above me. Grandad.

And all I can do is smile.

CHAPTER 2

I hate driving. I'm behind the wheel en route to Penrith, which will soon be my new home. Jared and Rosie are in the back arguing again and I scream at them to pack it in. It's hard enough driving in this weather without them two. Dad wakes up; my angry yell must be louder than their constant bickering.

'You're doing well,' he tells me. I'm not, I'm freaking out, but I nod anyway.

I can hardly see out the windscreen now the rain is turning to snow, the sort of snow the windshield wipers gather rather than clear. I wish Dad could drive. He failed his test three times when I was younger then gave up. He often talks about learning again but never does.

'Be careful,' he says a few miles further along, 'it's settling.' No shit, don't I know it? I'm barely doing thirty on the motorway, visibility is slim-to-nothing, everything is white and I'm following tracks from the van ahead. 'I think you're too close.'

At least my younger brother and sister have shut up. I'm not sure if they're mesmerised by the snow or fearful for their lives. I am too close. I ease off the accelerator but the car behind me is closer still. I hate having cars on my tail; I always feel guilty, as if I'm an obstacle preventing them from reaching their destination. I could think of better ways to spend my eighteenth birthday.

We're climbing as the road snakes through the mountains, not that I can see them, I just see a wall of white, and try not to be hypnotised by the driving snow. The car behind is still too close and I'm checking my rear-view mirror with increasing paranoia. Overtake me, you imbecile!

'Oh my God!' Jared yells, 'did you see that?' I didn't, but apparently there's a lorry on its side on the opposite carriageway. A stream of stationary vehicles bank up behind it and I hope I don't get caught like that. My little hatchback wouldn't cope; I could see us freezing to death, my first day of adulthood my last. Just my luck.

'You're still too close, Kayleigh, pull back.'

I don't want to do this. I panic, gripping the steering wheel so tightly my knuckles turn white; I'm dicing with death and not just my own. I suppress an onslaught of expletives and backchat and ease off again. I'm doing twenty and I swear that idiot behind is inches from my arse!

Still four miles from Shap Summit and everybody is steadily driving nose to tail. There are some cars on the hard shoulder and I pity them. I let out an involuntary moan which must have sounded terrifying because Rosie starts to cry.

'It's okay, Rosie, don't worry. Kayleigh's a good driver,' Dad says, taking out his phone. 'It must have been snowing here a while.' He calls Grandad Eddie; I can hear him on the speaker. There's an inch of snow in Penrith so far but it's not too bad if we can make it past Shap.

Eddie runs a shop in Penrith that sells books and gifts. If I make it there alive I'm supposed to be working with him in the shop and helping make things to sell. It's my ticket out of college and my mother's emotional chains. Eddie lives in a village outside Penrith, towards the Lakes; he has a barn conversion annexed to the house, which will be mine. I can have my independence, peace and quiet, and most importantly, distance from my past.

The blizzard is getting worse and the third lane is covered in about three inches of virgin snow. Nobody seems brave enough to go there. We're still a slow-moving convoy; I want to pull off the motorway at Shap but the slip road looks treacherous so it's safer to keep going.

A mile after the junction, the van ahead slams on its brakes. I do likewise but start to skid and, in slow motion, begin to close the gap. Rosie screams and my fight-or-flight reflexes kick in. If I do nothing I'll hit the van, so I quickly check to my left and there's space. I ease off the brake and turn into the lane, only for my back end to stay where it is and I start sliding sideways.

I shriek as I try to correct myself, gripping the steering wheel for life, and just manage to get in lane and brake again as I see the reason for the van's sudden stop. A car has spun to a halt and a woman runs across me as I'm slowing. I skid and my eyes lock on to the woman's. She looks terrified, but somehow my car stops inches from her.

The woman smiles and I let out a sigh of relief but a second later her face is pressed on my windscreen. I'm rammed from behind; somehow that idiot must have echoed my movements and not been able to stop in time. The woman rolls off my bonnet and on to the ground. I'm screaming as Dad gets out the car.

'Stay inside with the kids,' he says. I couldn't move if I tried. Rosie and Jared are whimpering and I'm no comfort to them. The woman's face flashes back in my mind as though it's on a video loop, reminding me of that scene in Jaws when that guy's head rolls through the hole in the boat.

I daren't look. Have I killed her? People are running around me but I'm shaking. The knock wasn't hard but it was enough to jolt the car forward and collide with the woman. An eternity passes before I see Dad standing up, covered in snow, with the woman. Her face is bruised and she's walking awkwardly, Dad helping each step. He brings her round to the passenger side, opens the door and she sits inside, her legs still on the ground. I repeat the word sorry, like a mantra through my hysteria. She leans back awkwardly and rests her hand on my knee.

'I'll live; it's okay,' she says. It's little comfort.

A man in a snow-sprinkled suit joins us. He looks like he's seen a ghost and I quickly realise he was the guy that hit me.

'Are you all alright?' he asks and I glare at him as if to say no, do we look it? His face drops and I see genuine remorse which makes me feel guilty. Dad takes control of the situation. An ambulance is on its way but the woman is more concerned about the traffic jam she's caused than the pain she must be feeling. Cars start to make their way slowly past in the right hand lane but another inch of snow must have fallen since the accident.

I hear the sirens get louder and panic. The police are bound to question me, maybe even arrest me. I had a couple of drinks last night when I went for my birthday meal with Mum, Jared, Rosie and Mum's latest boyfriend, *Seven*. I've given up naming them now. It's easier to number them; I don't get attached that way and I can't be hurt when they leave her. They always do.

The ambulance takes the woman as she might need an x-ray. Dad explains to the police officers what happened together with the guy in the snowy suit. I watch as he's breathalysed and worry in case the drinks from last night are still in my system. They seem to be jovial considering the snow and cold; I guess he passed. The police officer makes his way over to me with Dad.

It's my turn now. I don't think my lungs hold enough air, the perils of being five-foot three with a tiny frame. Eventually the contraption beeps and I inhale a lung full of freezing air and feel light-headed. Even as I'm told my alcohol level is okay, I feel queasy and need to sit back down in the driver's seat. Fortunately, Jared still has half a can of fizzy drink left and offers it to me; it does help. Dad does the paperwork and exchanges insurance details. They inspect the car; it has dents but luckily it seems driveable.

Dad must be freezing; he's covered in snow and I feel so bad for him.

'Follow the police van but keep your distance,' he says as he gets in the car, blowing in his hands. Personally, I never want to drive again and I'm in no state to, but I don't fancy a ride in that police van either or waiting hours for a recovery vehicle, so I brave it. I'm still shaking. Terrified of crashing into the police van, I keep a distance but can barely see the lights. Luckily the snow eases as we approach Penrith but there's much more than the predicted inch.

The road into town is slushy and the wheels spin on an incline. I'm chanting to myself as I go; my passengers are deathly silent. Eventually I pull up outside Eddie's shop. He comes outside to greet us.

And for the third time in my life, I reach out to my grandad in tears and hug him tightly.

CHAPTER 3

My back aches. I've finally got the barn looking the way I want it and am admiring my handiwork when there's a knock at the door.

'Here. All fixed,' Eddie says, holding up my car keys. It was a nightmare to sort it but the snow-suit guy paid for it, reluctantly. 'How about this too?' Eddie enters the barn and puts the newspaper on the table; the accident is featured on the front page. 'You've been here less than two weeks and you're already famous.' Oh, great. I get a nauseous dread reading the article. I'd much prefer a life of anonymity; I could happily live in the shadows. I still have flashbacks of that poor woman. I'm scared of falling asleep because her face on my windscreen wakes me in a sweat every night – and I'm no stranger to trauma.

'You've got it looking wonderful here,' Eddie says, looking around the open-plan kitchen-living room. I like it here. I now have framed artwork on every expanse of wall downstairs. There are oak beams on the ceilings that follow down to the ground, framing sections of the walls; it's modern but has that country feel. Upstairs is a bathroom and my bedroom; it's a perfect hermit pad for someone like me. In one corner of the living room there's a wooden desk, with ornate cupboards above for my art stuff.

Eddie leaves and I make myself some lunch. I've been eating breakfasts in here but having dinners with Eddie after work in the main house. The shop doesn't open on Sundays during the winter so I have a day off. I look out window as I eat, there's still snow in the fields and banked on the sides of the country roads. The thought of driving again terrifies me. The snow here is worse than in Penrith town. Thackthwaite is a tiny village about nine miles west of Penrith at the foot of Mell Fell, which is classed as a mountain but looks more like a big hill. Eddie told me that's because the house is already over a thousand feet above sea-level before the hill rises. No wonder there's so much snow.

I don't miss home at all but I miss Rosie and Jared. They had tales to tell their friends when they got home last week; they've got a namecheck in the local paper too, I'll have to tell them. I don't have many friends but my best friend, Lily, keeps in touch. She's always been my art buddy; she's into textiles and is a natural-born genius. Lily aces all academic and creative subjects and there's nothing she can't do. People call me a nerd, but I work hard and have no social life. Lily has a photographic memory - she could excel on lobotomy given a few hours practice and some instruction videos on YouTube – and still has time to party. I'm talking to Lily on video messenger when Eddie knocks.

'I've made some bread, do you fancy some while it's still warm?' You bet I do. That's always been one of the highlights of visiting Eddie when I was growing up. I end the call with Lily and follow Eddie into the house. The smell of bread and the open fire hits me, instantly triggering memories of good times. Eddie takes his apron off and rests it over the chair before he sits down. He's lean for his age and always active, and despite thinning, his hair has retained its rich brown, so he looks younger.

I'm eating my third huge wedge of bread when my gaze catches the small cupboard built into the wall next to the stove. It seems like a strange feature the way it's set in from the wall, and I mention it to Eddie.

'It's an old wages cupboard,' he says. 'The farmhouses in

this hamlet were all built in the late seventeen-hundreds by local gentry and they used to leave wages for workman, and later, servants, in the cupboard at the end of the week. When I first moved here the cupboard was buried behind the plaster in the wall. Back then, plaster was reinforced with horsehair and was strong. I was only fourteen and we were all really anxious watching the builder as he cleared away the plaster and tried to open it.' I always enjoy Eddie's stories; he's a hoarder of memories and even has a memory room upstairs full of boxes with old cards, photos, letters, scrapbooks and even his old school books. 'I was so excited and your Great-Aunt Rosanna was jumping up and down as if her feet were on springs. The builder had to force it open as the lock had seized.'

I'm hooked but he pauses to take another bite of bread and proceeds to chew it slowly, glancing at me sideways, knowing I'm not going to resist asking what happened next - which I do and he grins.

'When the door opened there was an avalanche of dust and horsehair, but there was that sketch.' Eddie points to the wall beside our table. It's a faded rough sketch of a castle on a steep hill drawn on what looks like a thin piece of wood about eight inches in diameter. I've noticed it there but never asked about it before. 'It's dated 1888. It's a French fortress, the sketch was wrapped in cloth. Your great-grandmother had a special frame made for it.' I ask if it's valuable. 'Sort of,' he says, 'more because of its age and originality and also the way it was stored, but the local antiquarian couldn't find an artist in their library who worked this way. It's rare for a sketch to be drawn on to wood; it looks like it's been sheered from the side of a big tree as it's slightly concave on both sides. We thought we'd keep it anyway. It obviously meant a lot to somebody at the time.'

I can't help but stare at it. Why would somebody hide it? Maybe it was stolen. At first glance it looks quite amateurish but my artist's eye can see there's good perspective; it's the sort of sketch an artist makes before they paint. My art teacher used to say the rough sketch is an artist telling themselves the story before they paint it. Eddie takes it off the wall and hands it to me. That's when I notice faint initials: PEM or maybe PEW. I ask how he knows it's French.

'There's writing on the back in French.' I turn over the frame but it's opaque. Eddie says he'll show me then disappears upstairs for ages. As I stare at the sketch I feel it stirring something inside. A pull, or maybe curiosity. Eddie returns with a handful of photos.

'We took some photographs before we framed it.'

The first thing I notice is how much the sketch has faded even over the fifty odd years since they found it, yet it's obviously been lacquered to preserve it. On the back, handwritten, it says: *La Forteresse de Mornas en soirée,* then underneath, *Le jour où le soleil brillait le plus. Sept 30 1888*. Other photos show the cupboard before and after it had been opened. Then Eddie unfolds a piece of paper and reads, 'The Fortress of Mornas in the evening. The day the sun shone brightest. Mornas is an old fortress overlooking the Rhone in Provence in France.'

I look it up on my phone and the photos online look even more impressive than the sketch. I ask Eddie if he's ever been there.

'I did eventually. Your grandmother and I had our honeymoon in Nice and we drove past it. We would have visited but the fortress was having a major renovation at the time and had closed access to the public. You can see it for miles.'

I'm fascinated. I can't believe anybody would want to hide it. My active imagination conjures up many theories from it being cursed or stolen, to being a cryptic treasure map. Either way, I have this overwhelming desire to go and visit the fortress.

CHAPTER 4

I was ten when my parents split up. Rosie and Jared were still babies, Jared being only fifteen months older than Rosie. We lived with our mother as Dad was supposedly the villain, having left us. I only found out recently that it was because of Mum's affair with *One*. I don't remember much about *One*; he seemed nice, he took us out to funfairs, arcades and the beach but within a few months he was gone.

Seven is here now in my barn with Mum, Jared and Rosie. They've been threatening a visit for weeks but kept cancelling at the last minute.

'You could do with new curtains,' Mum says, 'these don't match at all. Nor do the cushions, for that matter.' I shrug. I'm used to her criticism, it washes over me. She was never happy that I moved out at all. *Seven* is more complimentary and asks about my art and if I'm enjoying the shop and if I'm eating enough – questions he probably knows Mum should be asking. I've seen the signs before; I give it three months until Mum's forced to look out for *Eight*. At least Rosie and Jared are pleased to see me, though I doubt they'll ever get into a car with me again.

We go for a walk along the country lanes. There's a Z-bend in the road with a bridge at the bottom of a steep hill. Either side of the stream there are trees and it's beautiful. It's my favourite place in the world; everybody nicknames it Kayleigh's Corner. I spent many school holidays here and stayed for hours even on short visits. Before Christmas each year we always come for the holly; it's become a family tradition. You can follow the river up to Mell Fell; we've walked it many times but can't today, it's too muddy and cold for Mum, even though the snow has gone now.

I sit on the bridge with Rosie and Jared, catching up with their gossip while Mum finishes her cigarette and *Seven* stares up at the mountain in forlorn silence.

'They've been arguing again,' Jared says. I give him one of those looks that have become our secret language as if to say *nothing changes, just Mum being Mum.* There was always a tension at home, I'm so glad I'm out of it now. I can't wait until Jared and Rosie are old enough to get out. Maybe they can join me. I lighten the atmosphere and talk about my impending trip to France and tell the story of the discovery of the castle on the hill. 'Can we come?' Jared says, jumping down from the wall.

'Please! Please!' Rosie adds. I feel bad that they can't but I'm going with Lily.

We head back to the barn. Not a single vehicle has passed us. There are probably only ten cars a day that pass here out of season plus the odd tractor. I spy a pheasant and point it out to Jared who rushes towards it with his phone, only for it to take off. For the first time in my life I feel proud of myself as we re-enter the barn. I'm adulting in a way I had fantasised about for years; I'm independent, following my passions, and have family making the effort to come and see me. Even my mother's discouraging remarks don't faze me. After all I've been through, all the trauma and all the confusion, this feels good.

***

Lily was positively effervescent when I told her the story of *La Forteresse de Mornas en soirée*. She begged to come with me; I know her well, and I hoped she'd ask. I don't fancy this trip alone and I know her French is better than mine.

'Argh. Open these for me!' Lily says. I've been watching her fight a pack of shortbread with her long nails and it's set off a giggling fit. I take them and thank her, pretending I'll scoff them myself and she gasps. We're on the flight to Lyon from Manchester. We booked a hotel for the first night in the city and we have a bus trip to Mornas booked for tomorrow. I don't know what to expect; I just want to see the place and get a feel for the artist. It's nice to spend time with Lily, I've missed her.

'The fields seem exceptionally green,' Lily says as we start our descent and I look across her. I see what she means; it's early March, not quite spring yet but maybe it starts earlier this far south. I point at the Alps in the distance. I would love to travel more if I get the chance. Mum wasn't happy and threw a tantrum about this trip but Dad and Eddie were okay, especially about Lily coming with me.

'I'm glad we travelled light, I don't fancy that queue,' Lily says as we make our way past the handling area with our rucksacks. Outside we find a taxi and Lily gives directions. The driver tries to make conversation but his English is as bad as my French, though he's friendly enough. The outskirts of the city seem quite modern; if it wasn't for the French signs and driving on the wrong side of the road you would think it was any British town, with many industrial units and retail parks as we drive in.

The hotel is in the centre of Lyon. The city centre is pretty, there are quaint boutiques and coffee houses, most with seating areas outside, and older architecture with five-or-six-storey buildings.

'This reminds me of Edinburgh,' Lily says. It does, I expect to see another castle on a hill.

The hotel room is bigger than I expected for the price we paid and has an amazing view.

'It's a shame we're only staying here the one night. We should make the most of our evening,' Lily says. I'm up for that, feeling a surge of adrenaline as I look out the window and suggest we explore the city.

We stroll beside the Rhone, which runs through the centre of Lyon. Clusters of market stalls adorn the riverside, adding to the ambience. We stop at each one; many of the stalls have hand-crafted goods, and Lily buys a small leather purse for herself and we both buy a few gifts for family.

As evening falls, the city lights up. Not in neon, like London or New York, but a warm yellow-orange glow. It's a painter's paradise. We stop at the riverside and look out at the city.

'This is the life,' Lily says. 'You can understand how all those romantic French painters were so inspired.' She's right. We stand in silence for ages, our arms linked like the padlocks on the bridge below us – each one a promise; a symbol of hope.

We walk back to the hotel after eating at a restaurant then watch the city from our hotel room, talking into the night, wondering what tomorrow might bring.

CHAPTER 5

Croissants and orange juice for breakfast. We French in style. It's early though as our bus leaves at nine and we have to find the place first. I'm reliant on my phone to tell us where it departs so we leave in plenty of time and arrive early. The bus stops at all major towns on its way to Marseille, including Mornas. The three-hour journey is breath-taking with many vineyards, old settlements and plenty of greenery.

'I can never sleep when I'm away,' Lily says, resting her head on my shoulder. 'You were dreaming last night, it seemed violent,' she adds. I keep having nightmares about that woman's face on my windscreen. I've suffered from nightmares for many years. It's been an accepted part of my trauma; I've got used to falling back to sleep again quickly but I hate them, I feel guilty that I kept her awake. Lily's blonde hair curls down my shoulder. I wonder what my hair would be like blonde; I've never dyed it before. We're a family of blue-eyed brunettes. I don't have my hair too long either; it's thin and unmanageable, unlike Lily's soft and silky locks.

Lily is fast asleep and I try not to move but the motion of the bus makes her head bobble heavily so I lean in to steady her. I've known Lily since we started high school together. We weren't friends at first but we had a common enemy, Shelley Watson. Shelley is one of those girls who likes attention, gets popular by being a bitch and thinks she's God's gift to the boys. She wasn't pretty but she developed early and developed big. She flaunted her assets but they were the only thing she had going for her. She hated Lily because Lily is pretty so she made up lies and then became aggressive. I wasn't graced with Lily's beauty but I was teacher's pet. Mr Brady taught us art and we somehow connected with our ideas and humour. Mr Brady was hot too and Shelley didn't like it. Again, she fabricated lies and indirectly triggered the events that led to my trauma. Since then Lily and I have been best friends and have remained close since school even though we went to separate colleges.

Lily wakes when we enter Bolléne, the last stop before Mornas. The bus has been following the river for many miles now. We share a can of fizzy drink.

'I can't believe I can sleep on a rickety bus but not in a posh hotel room,' she says. I laugh; I'd been thinking the same thing. 'Look!' Lily yells, pointing ahead. I see it too. The castle on the hill. We're still several miles away but we watch it, transfixed, as we get nearer. The land around here is generally flat, gently rolling in places. The hill above Mornas rises steeply, a geological anomaly in the Rhone valley in Provence.

We're both animated as we get off the bus. The village is a shock; it looks as if it's been untouched for centuries. There are low-roofed cottages and narrow streets; many houses look in need of attention but are obviously occupied. Those that are painted on the outside are white or pastel colours. There's a feel to the place I almost recognise, it's warm and welcoming. I'm snap-happy with my phone and Lily livestreams a video of our walk along a narrow street in search of our hotel.

'This is like stepping back hundreds of years,' Lily says. We stop and look up the face of the huge cliff which dominates the village. You can't see the fortress from where we are, just the edge of a wall. 'Nobody could attack from here; it must be the safest fortress in the world.' I try to picture some deluded army trying to approach from the cliff. It's incredible to think that all this land was under occupation less than eighty years ago.

There seems little here in the village, only a café with a tiny gift shop and a small but quaint hotel. We think we might be a bit early to check-in so we get some lunch in the café. The door is so narrow we have to take our rucksacks off to get in.

'I'm glad I'm not obese,' Lily jokes. I look up to see a large woman inside serving and supress a giggle. 'Oh God, I hope she doesn't understand English.' I nearly choke. The chalk boards are all in French and the menu has pictures but they all look like light snacks. I recognise the word *poulet*, which I remember being chicken so we both take a gamble and order that.

There are only a few customers so our voices seem loud even though we both try to talk quietly. I notice a stand of leaflets behind our table and reach over to take one about the fortress. The writing is in French but I can make out the opening times; it looks like they do guided tours too.

The chicken meal arrives and it's amazing. I've no idea what it is but it's got some kind of sauce with peppers, onions, courgettes and pasta. There's plenty of it too; we're stuffed and it only cost ten euros even with a glass of orange juice. It might be our only meal of the day if the hotel only provides the breakfast we've paid for. Lily shares a photo on social media. You can never do anything in secret with Lily; her social media is her diary.

The hotel room is smaller than the one in Lyon. We place our bags between two small windows framing the back wall with views down the narrow street. The room has a low beamed ceiling and I wonder if the hotel has a height limit for guests. I claim the twin bed nearest the window, which is separated from Lily's by a small cabinet on which is a starry bedside lamp. The pictures on the walls are of the village and fortress, including a photograph from 1901.

'It's like time stopped still,' Lily says. I agree but then realise she's talking to the world, livestreaming the room from her bed. I poke out my tongue as the camera hones in on me. We freshen up then head back outside to start our adventure to the top of the hill to see the fortress for ourselves.

The narrow road winds steeply up the hill and we both struggle.

'God, I'm so unfit,' Lily says. 'I wish I'd done more sport at school.' I laugh. I was never into sports so could never claim to have been fit but I'm used to walking up hills. We stop every few minutes to catch our breath, eventually reaching a plateau above a mediaeval church and the road becomes a pathway. We look back on the town for a while and take a few pictures before embarking on our final ascent, which seems endless. When we reach the fortress Lily finds an energy boost from somewhere and is animated at our achievement.

The next tour begins at three but there's still plenty to see while we wait. We must be three hundred feet up or more and can see the Rhone snake in the distance and more mountains greying the horizon.

'You must be able to see a hundred miles,' Lily says, walking close to the edge; there's only a small wall and I tell her to be careful. She looks down and steps back sharply.

'Jeez! I never knew I could have vertigo,' she says. I laugh at her and she holds out her hand, it's shaking. 'It's like an overhang. I couldn't see squat over the edge, just a drop.' She starts to look pale and I offer her some of my drink and we sit on a rock for a few minutes. The ruins are fascinating; each inner wall must have been two or three feet thick. I wonder how the fortress would have looked when it was in use.

More people arrive and by the time the tour starts there must be a dozen of us, including three children. We hear a battle cry, then a male and female warrior arrive, reconstructing a mediaeval swordfight, pretending not to notice the crowd. The children are then given plastic swords and the fun begins. Unfortunately for us, it's all in French but we can make out enough to enjoy our expedition into the bowels of this ninth-century fortress. From the leaflets it's clear that its history was dark and the enthusiastic warriors shock the crowd with their stories. It's a shame I'm so useless at languages. The children love every minute. Rosie and Jared are probably still young enough to have enjoyed this too. At the end of the tour the warriors throw themselves over the cliff and we all gasp. A few seconds later a platform rises to the cheers of us all and the warriors take a bow.

Lily and I climb beyond the fortress to the high ridge viewpoint to see the whole valley. The spectacular outlook is awe-inspiring and I wish I'd had the foresight to think of bringing a sketchpad and pencil. We take more pictures and stare out, both of us in our own world.

'I wonder where that sketch was drawn,' Lily says, as if to echo my thoughts. I have a copy of the photo in my pocket and we look at it, trying to judge the angle. At first I think it must have been drawn from the main village but it looks different. Maybe the restorations have altered the shape a little. 'I think it must be from that direction,' Lily says, pointing across from where we are towards the river. I think she's right. It looks like there's a country road with scattered farmhouses. I suggest we investigate the area tomorrow.

***

The beds are surprisingly comfortable. I don't know if that's the reason we both slept well or if it was because we were shattered after our walk. My legs ache and I'm not looking forward to our trek later. I'm having breakfast with Lily; thankfully they serve coffee here, it might be the tonic I need to face the day. We're not the only guests but certainly the last down. The dining room walls are a dark red wood and there are old photographs of Mornas and the fortress on every wall. After breakfast we hang around and scour the images. There's one photo taken from a similar angle to our sketch. I take out the photo to make a comparison.

'Bonjour!'

We turn around to see a young man clearing the table we vacated. Lily kicks my ankle gently. I know what she's thinking.

'Bonjour,' Lily says timidly, but he doesn't look up.

The angle of the photo does seem similar to the sketch.

'I wonder where this was taken,' Lily says. I look closer to see if there's a caption.

The young man's curiosity must have got the better of him. He points at the picture above our heads and says something in French.

'Sorry... pardon,' Lily says, fumbling some French I don't recognise but the man must realise we're English, so he speaks to us in our tongue.

'My grandfather took that photo,' he says.

'Do you know where it was taken?' Lily asks.

'By the river, about half a kilometre on the old farm road to Le Lez. He liked to fish.' His eyes smile as he speaks.

'I'm Lily by the way, this is my friend Kayleigh,' Lily says. I was waiting for it. I just smile.

'Marcus,' he says, holding out a hand for us to shake. 'Pleased to meet you.' He must have noticed my sketch at that point. His eyes widen, and he starts talking French again before correcting himself. 'Can I see?' he asks.

I hand over the photo.

'We were trying to work out where this sketch was drawn,' Lily says. He seems transfixed. I show him the photo of the back and he becomes more animated and talks again in French. Lily and I exchange a glance and smile.

'Where did you get this?' he asks. For some reason I feel wary and hesitant to reply but Lily obviously doesn't share my thoughts.

'Kayleigh's grandfather has it. Do you recognise it?'

'Yes... no. Not exactly but I know somebody that might.

Can I show my father?' Lily looks at me and I nod, though I must look confused. 'Wait here,' he says and then disappears.

'He's cute,' Lily says, with a giggle. I laugh. 'I love his eyes; they're dark and smile with his lips.' I laugh again.

Marcus returns with his older clone. Distinguished laughter lines on his father's face show the Marcus you would expect to see in twenty-five years. They even share the same haircut, short on the sides but a fringe of dark brown swept to one side. They both have olive skin and smiling eyes.

'Hello again. This is my father, Louis,' he says. 'Papa, this is Lily and Kayleigh.' I've never heard my name spoke in a French accent before. I like how he pronounces it. Louis holds the photos in his hands. They speak with each other in French for a few minutes and it becomes awkward, standing here smiling, as if we understand each word. They could be plotting our murders and we wouldn't have a clue.

'Have you visited the fortress?' Marcus eventually asks.

'Yes, we went yesterday. It's amazing,' Lily says and I nod.

'Is this photo the reason you come to Mornas?' I guess it is. We both nod and smile.

'Would you like me to help you find where this drawing was made?' I look to Lily, again with apprehension, but she's smiling.

'Yes,' she says, 'if you don't mind, that is.' He smiles and nods and his father hands me back the photos with a matching smile. I wish I knew what they'd been saying.

'Meet you back down here in thirty minutes, is that okay?' Marcus says. We agree then head upstairs to get ready.

Half an hour later Lily's makeup is immaculate. I've put on some foundation, concealer, a little bit of mascara and have run the brush through my hair. There's no way I could or would attempt to compete with Lily. Marcus joins us; his open black leather jacket, jeans and white t-shirt make him look like he's stepped out of a seventies sitcom. I take another look to check it isn't his father.

We walk out of the village towards the main road, looking back every now and then to capture the view of the fortress. Lily and Marcus do most of the talking; I'm happy to play third wheel and listen in. We find out Marcus is twenty and helps his parents run the hotel. He did a foundation year at a university in St. Etienne but decided against his bachelor's degree. I interrupt, my courage and curiosity taking over my sonder, and ask Marcus if his father recognised the sketch.

'No. He didn't recognise the sketch but knew it might interest someone,' he says. I await more but he remains quiet. I look at Lily and she shrugs. 'There's a house along here, I think your sketch was drawn there. If the owners are in they might know more,' he finally says. I take a deep breath and feel a knot form in my stomach at the thought of talking to more strangers.

We cross a bridge over the motorway and continue down a farm path. There are some houses in the distance. I look back and can see the view of the fortress perfectly. There's no doubt that the sketch was drawn here.

We stop to take photos and Lily livestreams video again. I take out the photograph of the sketch and view it against the backdrop. There's more to the fortress now, extra buildings, but the angle is right; whoever sketched it must have stood within metres of where we're standing now. I think back to Eddie's discovery when he was just fourteen. He couldn't possibly have thought that fifty years later his granddaughter would be standing where the artist stood and looking up at the fortress they drew.

A little further along we see a large house nestling amongst trees, all in blossom of pink and lilac. It's like something from a fairy-tale. It's a large house with white walls, an orange-tiled roof and large round turreted bay, but it looks modern.

'Wait here, I'll see if there's anybody in,' Marcus says. 'Oh, any chance I can borrow your photos?' I hand them over and he thanks me.

'I could live in that house,' Lily says. I agree. Even the garden is beautiful; I'm sure the blossom will look like snow in another month. We watch the front door open and an older man with a mass of white hair gives Marcus a hug. They go inside and we wait around, taking more pictures. I'm so glad Lily is with me as my social shield; I can feel that familiar drum of my heartbeat in my chest.

'Are you okay?' Lily asks and links her arm in mine. I am, I think, I'm just annoyed with myself for feeling so pathetic. I smile and hope it looks genuine. 'You should have brought a sketch pad,' she says. She's right; I could emulate the sketch in the same style a hundred and twenty-eight years after the original. Hopefully I'll be able to do it from the photos I've taken.

I hear a whistle and look towards the house to see Marcus summoning us inside. Marcus stands at the door and introduces us to Didier Bernard as we enter. We're greeted with a kiss on each cheek and shown into a huge open room with a floor-to-ceiling window at the far side. I note the large rugs on the wooden floor – the type on which you would imagine Aladdin taking flight. Four two-seater sofas frame a glass coffee table, which is covered with magazines and place mats. On the far side of the room stands a white grand piano and on the walls hang massive canvas paintings, mostly music themed.

We sit down and a small woman enters with a silver tray. Didier takes it and brings it to the table. I can smell freshly ground coffee the moment he sets it down.

'Forgive my English is poor,' Didier says.

'It will be better than our French,' Lily says and we smile.

'This house was rebuilt after the war. It was once a stopping house for the old Roman road. My great-grandfather was a blacksmith; he had a workshop by the river but it was destroyed too.'

'It's a beautiful house,' Lily says. 'Beautiful garden too.'

'Thank you. And even more beautiful for having you two ladies here,' Didier says, pouring the coffee and offering it to us. 'So, this picture brings you to Mornas?'

'We wanted to see it for ourselves,' Lily says.

'I like your spirit of adventure,' Didier says. 'It is a mystery now, yes? Finding out who drew it?'

I guess it is. I'm still not sure what compelled me to come. I felt a pull to the picture when Eddie told me his story; I needed to see for myself that it was real. Now, I would love to find out the story of the picture itself. I don't know how much English he can understand so don't want to tell him the full story, so I just explain that my grandad found it hidden when he moved to his house fifty years ago.

Didier and Marcus hold a conversation in French for a while as I finish my coffee. Didier reminds me of those old pictures of Albert Einstein with his mad white hair. His face is animated as he speaks and his body language is confident yet relaxed; resting both elbows up on the low back of the sofa opposite us, he gesticulates with his forearms as he speaks. I try to make out what they're saying but they talk so fast it's impossible.

'You have helped me solve a mystery, but given me a new one,' Didier eventually says and then leaves the room, returning a few minutes later with an old wooden box. It looks battered and has a broken ivory seal on top. I can see that there are old letters and postcards inside as he opens it. He pulls up his gold-framed glasses, which were hanging on a lanyard around his neck, and starts reading a few, replacing them until eventually finding the one he's looking for.

'Ah,' he says loudly, reading to himself while closing the lid on the box. We all watch him, transfixed. 'Much was destroyed in the war but this box survived. It had many letters between my great-grandfather and his brother and niece. This letter was written October third 1888. My great-grandfather wrote that he was not happy that two artists had stayed over, vandalised the orchard during their stay and had left without paying.'

'Oh dear,' Lily says, looking at me. I start panicking that we're going to be held here as slaves to repay this debt to Didier's family. My overactive imagination is going to be the death of me.

'I will photocopy the letter for you to take back to your grandfather,' he says, looking at me. 'Could I keep or copy these photographs to store with these letters?' I tell him he can keep them as I can make more copies any time.

'The artist must have had a guilty conscience and hidden the sketch,' Lily says.

'Indeed. Possibly he vandalised the orchard for the wood to sketch on.' Didier hands me a scanned colour copy of the letter before we leave. 'I don't know who the painter was but I would be interested to know if you find out any information.'

'We'll let you know,' Lily says.

'Thank you, and you must visit us again.' We wave as we leave through the garden.

Marcus comes with us but is much quieter than he was on the way over as if he is deep in thought. He livens up as we get back into the village and tells us more about the fortress as we look up the sheer cliff face.

'Did you know, during wars of religion in the sixteenth century, the Catholics murdered all the Protestant women and children and forced the men and soldiers to jump off the cliff?' he says. I can sense the history lingering in the air. The dark mysteries of this mediaeval village still hold, spoken with reverence as if they are in the recent memory of all who live here. That must be why the warriors jumped at the end of the tour yesterday. 'This village has been treated badly but so many families have stayed here for hundreds of years. Everybody loves seeing the fortress on the motorway, it's a famous landmark,' he says.

We return to the hotel and thank Marcus, who says he will see us later. I'm itching to paint, I've never felt such a strong urge, but we're hungry so decide to go to the same café as yesterday. Thankfully they still have chicken on the menu, which is as enjoyable as yesterday. We both swipe through the photos on our phones afterwards. I keep thinking about which image would be the best to paint. The spring colours here look extra vivid; maybe it's the contrast to the sharp blue of the sky and lack of vapour trails giving extra clarity. We kill time exploring the rest of the village, even though our legs ache, before returning to the hotel.

The bus is early tomorrow so we plan an early night. I'm tired from so much walking, I expect to crash out quickly. There's a light knock on the door as we're packing our rucksacks. Lily opens the door and Marcus stands there, looking nervous.

'Sorry. I was wondering if you wanted to join me downstairs and share a bottle of wine,' he says. Lily springs to life but I'm tired so I decline but urge her to go; she's reluctant but I reassure her and she eventually agrees. I know there's already chemistry developing between them so it will give them an excuse to talk a bit more.

I fall asleep quickly but wake up when Lily comes in just before midnight and apologises for waking me. My mind drifts as I search for sleep again. I'm glad we came; we solved a puzzle for Didier if nothing else. I'm pleased with myself for making this trip even though I'm still nervous for the journey back tomorrow. I'm still unsure about Marcus and don't know why; maybe my distrust of guys is making me extra wary. I'm happy for Lily, but his silence as we walked back into the village seemed unnerving. I need to sleep and stop overthinking.

CHAPTER 6

I'm not sure if it's nostalgia or excitement that triggers as I step inside the art shop and hear a unique but familiar beep as I close the door. I smile and soak up the adrenaline rush as my gaze takes in the paints and canvasses. I squeeze past two younger teenage girls juggling supplies as they make way to the counter. I used to dream about doing this when I was younger. I had to rely on family to buy me art supplies for Christmas and birthdays. My bedroom was small so could never do as much as I wanted to, and Mum hated me making a mess, so most school projects had to be started and finished in a day.

I spend a fortune as I need some large canvasses and to refresh all my oil paints, brushes, pencils, knives and palettes. I hurry out as Eddie parked outside on yellow lines. His car is bigger and I'm not sure if the cavasses would fit in mine. He smiles as he sees me leave the shop laden down and immediately rushes to help me.

'How much did you need?' he says. I know. I got carried away, as usual.

I slept most of the day yesterday as we got back from France late the night before and I was up all night telling Eddie about the visit. Eddie was fascinated by the letter and wants to frame it so it hangs next to the sketch. All I can think about is painting.

Spring has yet to grace us here. There's still the barren shadow of winter hiding the colours, yet I can appreciate the rugged beauty of the Matterdale valley as we return home. As we pull into Eddie's drive we see a car parked next to mine. I don't recognise it at first but then I'm hit by a sudden panic attack. The face of my nightmares is at the door.

To add to my confusion, she's smiling. I'm too busy staring at her, trying to breathe, to realise that Dad's behind her. Eddie gets out the car to greet them, I'm still staring, trying to process the shock and ignore the flashbacks. My brain is tormenting me and my heart-rate must have doubled. Dad beckons me inside and I slowly open the door to greet him, leaving my art supplies in the car.

'You look like you've seen a ghost,' he says. Not funny. I say hello, and apologise again to the woman and ask how she is.

'I'm alright now, it took a few weeks for the bruises to heal but I was lucky. And stop saying sorry, it was an accident.' She smiles and I nod back and try to smile, but it's a feeble effort. I'm wondering why she's here. She's quite pretty without her bruises; she has long and wavy chestnut hair cascading beautifully against the black of her coat. She has small features; it wouldn't surprise me if she looks ten years younger than her age. I ask if I'm in trouble. Then I see the reflection of my confusion on Dad's face.

'Oh. No, sweetheart, no. Nothing like that. I've been seeing Polly regularly since the accident. I took the train up to see her this morning and we thought we would have a ride out to the Lakes and call in to see you.' It takes a few seconds for it to sink in. They're going out? My accident was Cupid's arrow? I think Dad can sense my bewilderment.

'You're not in trouble. If anything we should be thanking you, we're growing a good friendship. I miss this. I've missed the companionship.' He looks sad, as if he's realised I could be hurting. I'm not. I don't know how to show it; I'm not good at displaying true emotions. I want to hug him and tell him I'm happy for him but the flashbacks replay in my head faster and faster and I think I'm losing my mind. I muster a smile and excuse myself to the bathroom.

It's moments like this when I doubt myself most. On my own I'm a tower of strength. I can let my art keep me company, read books, listen to music and be at peace with my thoughts. Family should be my comfort but my mum has hated and resented me for years and all of her boyfriends left us. Dad has been my stability. He's never had another girlfriend or even spoken of another woman. For years we've stayed with him every other weekend – Jared and Rosie still do. I don't think I've ever thought about him having a new relationship.

I stare at myself in the mirror, leaning on the sink, and focus on my breathing. The only coping mechanism that works is to lecture myself and fight my mind. I tried self-harming when I was fifteen, which was a disaster. There was no relief in the sensation of cutting myself. It just made everything so much worse and it hurt like a bitch. *This is not a problem,* I tell myself. *Dad has invited his girlfriend over, that is all. Her face on your windscreen was a moment in time. It's gone. She survived. You're alive. Now go downstairs and stop being pathetic.* My eyes display my terror but I mustn't let them betray me.

I psyche myself up for a few more minutes and then venture downstairs, my smile and mask on show. Eddie's probably told them about my trip but I tell them anyway and explain about the letter and the history of Mornas.

'It would be good if we can get this letter translated,' Eddie says.

'I'm a relief teacher at the grammar school. I'll happily show it to one of the French teachers if you like?' Polly says.

'Yes. Good idea, if you don't mind,' Eddie says. 'I'm curious to know the full text. It might give some context.'

Dad and Polly stay for dinner. I help Eddie cook a makeshift roast; we have just enough meat and vegetables between us.

'You're doing well,' Eddie says and winks at me then carries on being his normal jolly self. Eddie probably understands me better than anybody, even though I don't talk to him in depth about things that trouble me. Usually he has so much energy, so much going on, the conversation rarely flows that way. He will have a heated debate about some political issue and talk about the injustices in the world and how he would help if he had the power or money. Yet he's good at showing both sides of a story too and doesn't hold grudges. Maybe the years have made him wise instead of cynical. I try not to hate, I've experienced what that can do. I feel sorry for my mother and love her regardless of what she feels for me.

The meal is a success but Dad and Polly don't stay too long afterwards as Dad has to catch the train back to Preston. I do hug him at last as he's about to leave and hug Polly too and tell her I'm glad I didn't break her.

After they leave I clear out all my art supplies from the car and take them into the barn. I had wanted to start while there was daylight but it's dark now so I'll have to start tomorrow. I look for the best photo to use for inspiration; there are so many good images of the fortress but I'd love to paint Didier's house and gardens. I can't help but stare at the photos of it - it's perfect, a painter's dream.

I'm settling for bed as Lily calls me on video messenger. I tell her about my weird day and panic attack, which she sympathetically finds amusing.

'Marcus is coming to stay with me for a few days at the end of the month,' she says. I'm amazed her parents will let him, though they do have a spare room. 'Marcus said he would love to see the original sketch of the fortress.' I know where this is going, and can't stop myself giggling. She knows as well. 'I haven't seen your barn yet, it will be good to see you again. I miss you already.' Her cute whine is adorable. I suggest they get the train to Penrith and I'll pick them up at the station and bring them here. I don't like the idea and I'm still wary of Marcus but it would be a good excuse for Lily to come over. I hope Eddie will be okay with it. It will be interesting to find out his thoughts on the guy.

CHAPTER 7

After *One* left there were about six months of just me, Mum and the little ones. It was a happy time and Mum was fun and gave us plenty of attention. I was wary of *Two* when she introduced us but he was good to me. He was creative and fuelled my passion for art. He moved in and I spent a lot of time with him doing crazy art projects. He would take us out on walks and we would stop and sketch, or collect pine cones, beech nuts and acorns. He would photograph toadstools and would draw them, often adding fairies and creating fantasy images. He taught me how to use watercolours and oil paints.

He became a father figure to me, more so than my own father, who I still resented for leaving us. We were spending every other weekend with Dad back then but I know I gave him a hard time and Dad must have hated me talking so fondly of *Two*. I often heard Mum arguing with *Two* but wasn't prepared for the day he would leave. It was the week before my twelfth birthday and he didn't even say goodbye. I cried for days and pleaded with Mum to have him back. Dad told me later that *Two* had broken the terms of his parole by spending time with me. I was too young to understand what that meant but I still feel Mum started resenting me from then.

I'm sketching the fortress. I don't want to compare mine to the original; I want to use my own photograph and my own memory while it's still sharp in my mind. Eddie's given me the day off as Mondays are quieter and we're still out of season for now. It's not coming out quite the way I want it to. I can be a perfectionist when it comes to my art but I need to be happy with the perspective and angles before I start to paint. I've been at it for a couple of hours now. The vision in my head works but my eyes aren't cooperating. I try not to get despondent but I can feel my frustration build so decide to have an early lunch and switch off for a few minutes.

I flick through my phone again while eating my soup and think about Didier's house and garden again. I'm tempted to try that and come back to the fortress afterwards. I'm excited at the thought as I finish my lunch. I could go to town with the colours on that painting.

I sketch rough, driven by my desire to start the painting. I paint all day, stopping only for dinner when Eddie knocks. By midnight it's starting to take form; I have to juggle drying time and map out sections with colour blending and layering as I go. I'm in France. I'm in a post-impressionist world, a time-traveller on the banks of the Rhone in 1888 capturing a moment in the future. Each brushstroke adds luminance and texture. Each shadow adds dimension. Every minute I paint adds nostalgia. The house and gardens may have been destroyed in the war but the sadness and hatred couldn't defeat it. New life grew new love.

I climb into bed at four-thirty, still in my alternative universe, happy in my creative flow and thankful for all the hardships that brought me to this point of euphoria.

***

I have an email from Dad. Polly had shown the letter to her colleague and attached a translation.

Dearest Brother,

It was a pleasure to receive your letter this week. It pleases me also to hear that young Madelaine is following her mother's passion for dressmaking. Please send her our love and encouragement.

The road has been busy. I find that I tire more these days but Frederick has been learning well.

The orchard is particularly healthy this summer; the fruit harvest will be abundant. Emily has tended the garden with love all summer. Emily was saddened by a blatant act of vandalism earlier this week when two artists, who stayed as our guests, cut from her beloved olive tree outside the meadow. Who would do such a thing? They left without payment, a mere promise of compensation on their return. Had I known about their vandalism at the time I would have branded their soles.

You must come and see us soon. A break will be good for us both and I can spoil you with food fit for a king.

Take care, kind brother.

Gerard.

I think Didier must be right. I would think the sketch does solve this mystery, given the dates. It's a strange thing for an artist to do. I would have expected an artist to be more respectful. Maybe he was so overwhelmed with the view that the compulsion to draw impaired his judgement.

I print out the letter for Eddie to read and take it through for him. I remember Didier saying how we had solved one mystery for him but given him a new one. I wonder who the artist was. I still don't understand why the sketch was deliberately hidden. How did it end up here in Cumbria? I'm amazed Dad or Eddie didn't investigate it themselves. I ask Eddie about it.

'It was a mystery for us at the time but after a few months of dead ends we just accepted it. I've told your father but I don't think his fascination aroused enough curiosity to investigate. I guess it's easier for your generation in the modern age of internet and smart phones.' He has a point but I think this mystery would have made me curious enough twenty years ago.

There was a vibrant art scene in France in 1888; this was the time of the post-impressionists. I covered basic art history at school but I've found out more spending the evening reading through articles tonight on my phone than I learned in three years of art lessons.

I guess I had to learn to create it first before I could understand more about it at college, had I chosen to study it. I hadn't. I had been persuaded that English, Mathematics and Economics would fare me better in real life by my mother and her boyfriend, *Six*, at the time. He was the wealthiest of Mum's men. Mum became the stereotypical trophy girlfriend; designer clothes and handbags, spas, facials and immaculate nails. It wasn't her. After the trauma with *Five*, Mum had eased her new boyfriend to us gently. We saw *Six* at the weekends and sometimes evenings, then he was around regularly and there was talk about moving into his mansion. He seemed nice enough; he had an ego and was sure of himself but was nice to me and Jared and Rosie. I had just got used to the idea when they split up. I've never seen him since. I would have begun to suspect that Mum had actually murdered them all and buried them in our garden if I hadn't seen *Four* after he left.

CHAPTER 8

Lily and Marcus are expected on the eleven o'clock train. I've spent all morning tidying up and cleaning round. I'm pleased with my painting of Didier's House. I've hung it on my wall as a centrepiece. I haven't painted the fortress yet but I'm happier with my sketch of it now. The shop has been busy this week now the Easter holidays have begun. Tourist season has started so I've been standing so much during the day that I've spent most evenings resting.

Lily is the first person off the train; she sees me and waves. Marcus follows and smiles; he has a bit of stubble and I don't think it suits him. They both stare at the ruins of Penrith castle opposite the railway station.

'No wonder you like the fortress,' Lily says.

'Can we visit?' Marcus asks. I hadn't thought they would be interested in the town. I'm happy for the suggestion as it passes some time and means less entertaining for me. We walk around the ruins of the fourteenth-century castle and read about the history. Being a Border town, Penrith had a few problems with the Scots back then. There's a steep grassy moat around the castle that I used to roll down with Jared and Rosie. Marcus is tempted, but stops himself, opting to run down instead and up the other side. Last time I did that my back ached for weeks.

I'm extra cautious driving them back to my barn and take the scenic route to avoid the big roundabout, even though it's a few miles longer. They're my first passengers since the accident. Lily doesn't stop talking, which is good in some ways as she's less likely to be focussing on my driving.

'This is beautiful,' Marcus says as we approach Thackthwaite. I see him in the mirror; his eyes look wide with wonder. I guess it's starkly different to Mornas.

I let them into the barn first so I can show Lily around my pad. Marcus gasps and goes white as he sees my painting of Didier's house. He looks as if he has literally seen a ghost. He perches on the arm of the settee, staring at it.

'Are you okay?' Lily asks, at first with a giggle, but then looking genuinely concerned.

'Where did you get this?' he asks. Odd.

I tell him I painted it and he shakes his head as if he doesn't believe me and I laugh. I grab my phone and find my inspiration. It's not perfect but then it's not supposed to be. He looks confused. I don't think he's blinked in two minutes and he's still deathly pale. I hope he doesn't throw up.

'Breathe!' Lily says, pulling on his arm in jest. It's enough to bring out a smile.

'Wow,' he says. 'You are a good painter. That's the best I've seen.'

I'm flattered. People rarely say nice things about my work. Eddie does but he's my grandad; I could draw squiggles with my left foot and he'd think they were amazing. I thank him. He moves closer to have a good look and Lily joins him.

'This really is excellent,' Lily says and I don't think my ego can handle this much praise so I thank her and offer them a coffee. I'm proud of my painting though, it's my best piece of work yet and my most passionate.

'Didier would love this. Can I take a photo?' Marcus asks. He still looks pale. I tell him to go ahead and he takes a few, even close up. I toy with the idea of giving Marcus the painting to take back to Didier but I don't want to part with it.

We drink our coffee, which brings the colour back to Marcus' face, and then venture over to the house. Eddie is still at the shop but I have the key. I show them the sketch; above it now is the letter from Didier's grandfather, together with the English translation that I printed out in an italic font.

'Wow!' Marcus and Lily say in unison. It's amazing to think how that mystery artist's work, on that day one-hundred and twenty-eight years ago, could cause so much excitement and intrigue after all this time. I remove the sketch from the wall and hand it to Marcus to have a better look.

'It's a beautiful frame,' he says. I tell him that my great-grandmother had it made especially. 'The sketch must have been preserved well. Softwoods rot more easily.' I show him the cupboard and explain how it was buried behind the plaster. I show him Eddie's photos at the time of the discovery. 'Real treasure,' he says.

'Is there a way of finding out the previous owners of the house?' Lily asks. Eddie would probably know. I check online to see if there are any historical references to the house. There's very little; it's mentioned that the area was owned by Lord Dacre at one time and that the Dacre estate was responsible for building most of the farms in the area. Whoever lived here back in the 1880s would have died long ago but it would be good to know.

We return to the Barn for more coffee. Lily and Marcus seem close now and comfortable in each other's company. I want Eddie to see Marcus for himself; I trust his instinct, so I suggest leaving early to show them the shop before dropping them off at the station.

I can't park near the shop and don't want to drive around for ages so have to brave parallel parking further up the road. Thankfully Lily and Marcus are having their own conversation about plans for the weekend so they don't notice my terror, or the mess I make of straightening the car. It's a relief to switch off the engine.

Eddie welcomes us as we enter. Lily has met him before

back home but she's never been to Penrith. Marcus is polite and mentions how nice his house is and thanks Eddie for letting me show him the sketch. He even praises my painting talents. I guess he's making a good impression.

I mention Lily's suggestions to track the former owners of the house.

'I have the deeds. All the previous owners are named. We tried to investigate many years ago but couldn't track anyone down, though it might be easier now with the internet,' Eddie says. Lily looks at me. I know what I'm going to be doing tonight. We spend a while in the shop as Eddie closes up. Marcus buys a book of the local area that has a picture of Penrith Castle on the cover.

I drop Lily and Marcus off at the station with ten minutes to spare. I can't park so we say our goodbyes in the car and then I head back to Thackthwaite, taking the scenic route. Eddie is back before me. He brings down a bag of old documents and places them on the table.

'There you go,' he says. 'Have a look through these while I cook.'

Most of the deeds are A3 sized and have beautiful calligraphy and are wax-sealed. Some documents have Georgian and Edwardian postage stamps on them. There are planning applications, receipts and builders' guarantees. I don't know where to begin.

I set everything in chronological order before I read them and finish sorting them as Eddie brings in dinner. I ask what he makes of Marcus.

'Trying too hard. Was he trying to impress me or his girlfriend?' I smile. 'Maybe he was just overwhelmed,' Eddie says.

I tell him about Marcus' reaction to my painting and he agrees it was strange. It was certainly over the top, if it wasn't genuine.

After dinner we both look through the deeds, writing out a timeline. The house was built in 1790 and the barns extended and the washhouse built in 1845. It was owned by the Dacre Estate until 1909 and let out to their farmers. In 1918 it must have had a major renovation and the pig sties built. It was sold again in 1955 and 1967, when Eddie's parents bought it.

'These people who sold the house in 1955 would probably be best to talk to but that's over sixty years ago now, I'm not sure anybody would even be alive,' Eddie says. 'I would think that the cupboard must have been sealed during the 1918 renovation.' The owner was a Roland Kimber Robinson.

I spend the evening with Eddie on various search and ancestry sites. We trace Roland Robinson and find he died in 1935 leaving the house to his son, John Roland Robinson, who died in 1989.

'Could be a dead end,' Eddie says. 'I don't know how much my parents followed this up or if they tried tracking John Robinson when he was alive.'

I'm reluctant to leave this mystery alone. I leave some messages on the ancestry forums to see if he has any living ancestors. They might have some old stories, diaries or documents that could help. Roland Robinson took over in 1909 but somebody lived here in the 1880s - there must be a way of finding out. I look up the Dacre Estate. The heritage goes back to the fourteenth century, where they also built a castle and moat, the ruins of which still stand. I find an online archive directory for Cumbria and there are hundreds of entries for Dacre; this will take a while because there's no chronological order.

My mind is fogged with names and dates and I need to sleep. It's almost midnight when I find a reference to Thackthwaite farmstead that seems interesting. There's a list of tenants dating back to 1845, one of which references George and Jane Kimber in 1889. Kimber is a strange name - if Roland Kimber Robinson bought the house from the estate in 1909, it's possible that he was related and maybe they had lived in the house for twenty years before they bought it. As fascinating as the theory is, it might give us the same dead end. Or does it?

CHAPTER 9

One of my earliest memories is of a visit to Cumbria to see Eddie. I was about four years old and we went for a picnic at Airaforce - a waterfall and series of woodland walks near Ullswater Lake. Mum, Dad, Great Aunt Rosanna and Eddie laid out the picnic in style on the grassy area between the river and woodland. I can remember running around eating my sandwich and watching the birds. Some came onto our picnic cloth to eat crumbs. I don't know quite how it happened but I think I mistook my family for another family and ran into the wood path to catch up. When I realised they weren't my family I panicked and ran away, further into the woodland - it all happened so quickly.

I'm not sure how long it was until I was found but it felt like hours. I remember my way getting steeper as I tried the river - I could hear it in the distance. I cried but I was away from the path and couldn't see any people. I was terrified and even the trees scared me and I tripped a few times in the brambles. I knew we had been close to the river but when I found it, it was a long way down and even my four-year-old self knew it looked dangerous. Eventually Eddie found me as I had started to make my way down. I felt such an overwhelming relief. I hugged him so tightly; I think he was crying too. I was scared of being told off so I even shied away from Mum and Dad when Eddie caught up with them and wouldn't let go of Eddie.

It was a long time before I went back to Airaforce. Now I love it. I made a painting once of the falls for a GCSE module as we had to emulate an artist so I chose Thomas Moran. Dad tells Polly about the day they lost me as we walk past the place we picnicked.

'The park had volunteers walking up the river looking for her and downstream too in case she'd been washed away. That river can be wild and she wouldn't have been the first to have been washed up lakeside.' Scary thought.

'You had an adventurous spirit even back then,' Polly says. No, I was just a stupid daydreamer even back then.

We look up at the waterfall from the bottom bridge. The spray from the fall forms a rainbow. I take photos. I've seen this happen before; I used to think it was magic, and this is the first time I've been able to capture it.

'To think that Sir Eglamore's Emma fell to her death there in mediaeval times,' Dad says. I had forgotten about that. Eddie told me the tale of Sir Eglamore; he had to leave his beloved Emma to fight in the Crusades and returned early to watch her tumble down the falls. He lived the rest of his life as a hermit and built a bridge over the raging waters so others wouldn't suffer Emma's fate.

'I'm dying!' Dad says after we ascend the one hundred and thirty steep steps, carved into the rock face, to reach a plateau at the summit. 'My body's not as young as my mind.' Polly pulls his arm affectionately and we make our way to the top bridge and look over to see the waterfall cascading beneath us. It's mesmerising. The sheer force of the water has carved a steep gorge over thousands, maybe millions of years. There are small buds on the trees; in another two weeks spring will transform this reserve into a blaze of colour. I must come back and get some inspiration for painting.

Many trees here are ancient; the trunks must be three or four feet thick and over a hundred feet tall. One tree has a thick branch that comes out at ninety degrees before bending skyward nearly as far as the main tree. I wonder how the sketcher of *La*

Forteresse de Mornas en soirée was able to shear the olive tree and remove any bark. He must have had a saw or an extremely sharp knife. Though there was a blacksmiths there - maybe he was testing out a new knife. I make a mental note to investigate the blacksmith online.

It still seems surreal that Dad has a girlfriend. I walk behind them, careful to watch my footing on the path. They hold hands or link arms spontaneously and it's so natural you wouldn't think they had only known each other for little over two months. We stop for a drink at the café next to the carpark. There are picnic tables outside and the chaffinches aren't shy. I update Dad and Polly on our investigations.

'It's wonderful that the mystery has sparked romance between Lily and Marcus, after all these years,' Polly says. This is what artists do, all artists. Even a songwriter or musician can create songs that bring people together through mutual appreciation and love of their work. How many relationships have begun at concerts, art exhibitions, book clubs, libraries and cinemas over the centuries?

Polly drives us back to Thackthwaite where Eddie is making us a roast dinner for our Easter meal. She drives through the narrow country lanes with confidence and I ask her if she knows the area.

'I live in Penrith now but grew up in Glenridding, a village further along Ullswater. I know these roads so well I could drive them blindfolded if it wasn't for other traffic.'

'We grew up in the same area but never met,' Dad says. 'Though Polly is eight years younger than me.'

I quickly do the maths, Polly must be thirty-five. She doesn't look it. I wonder if she's always been a single independent woman or if she has my mother's curse and all her boyfriends leave. She seems nice enough outside of my nightmares, which are thankfully becoming less frequent, but I still have regular flashbacks.

Eddie's roast dinners are a feast for my taste buds but leave my insides with work to do. I'm stuffed. Dad's spending every other weekend up in Penrith with Polly, alternating with having Jared and Rosie.

My phone pings an email notification. Somebody has replied to my message on the ancestry forum.

Dear Kayleigh,

I too have been tracing Roland Robinson and his family. Are you related? Maybe we can compare notes.

Oliver Hutton.

I reply as I wait for the water to run in the sink so I can wash up the dishes:

Hi Oliver, I'm not related but tracing the previous owners of my grandfather's house to help solve a mystery. Kayleigh.

Polly joins me and grabs a tea towel. I feel compelled to make conversation so ask what she teaches.

'English and English Literature,' she says. 'I used to teach full-time at a primary school but became a carer for my mother after she became ill. It was around the time I was separating with my boyfriend, also a teacher at the same school, so the time was right.' I ask if she had kids. 'No. I don't think either of us wanted to; we were surrounded by children every day. They were all our children.'

I'm tempted to ask what went wrong but maybe it would be rude. She's obviously a caring person so I don't feel so bad about Jared and Rosie spending time with her. I can't believe I'm vetting her suitability as a potential step-mum. My phone pings again and there's another message.

Dear Kayleigh,

That is very interesting to me. Does your grandfather live at Thackthwaite, Cumbria? We might be trying to solve the same mystery. I believe John Roland Robinson died in 1989 but can't track his movements after he moved out of Thackthwaite in 1955. Tell me about the mystery?

Oliver Hutton.

'Bingo!' Polly says. We tell Eddie, who is more cautious with his enthusiasm.

'For now, maybe we should just mention the find in 1967 and show him the photographs. We can omit the fact that I still have it in my possession for a while.'

Eddie is right. As much as I'm intrigued, the sketch was hidden for a reason and we already know that it was an act of vandalism. He helps me phrase a reply:

Hi Oliver, Yes he does. A wooden sketch of a fortress was found in the house, we've traced it back to its origin in France but are trying to find out who drew it and how it ended up in Cumbria. I would love to hear about your mystery too. Is it connected? Kayleigh.

'Your great-grandmother would love this right now if she was still with us,' Eddie says. I don't remember much about her; she died when I was about four and my great-grandad died the year before I was born. I think my generation take for granted how easy it is to get information and to find people with similar interests to connect with. It's hard for us to contemplate how different life was for our parents and grandparents.

Dad and Polly leave early evening to go to the station. I spend the evening with Eddie watching television and glancing down at my phone regularly, waiting for a reply from Oliver. Lily messages me to say that Marcus has left for home now and she's missing him already. I bring her up to date on the day's events.

I'm just settling for bed when the reply eventually comes.

Dear Kayleigh,

Thank you for your message, how interesting. Incredible. My parents once lived at Thackthwaite Farm so they must have sold it to your grandfather. Is the washhouse still there? The sink used to be a huge upturned bell. My father found a note in a tin under the bell mounting. It must have been left for Roland Robinson, but he probably never found it for some reason. The note mentioned that the "wood" was hidden and that the father had kept the painting, urging Roland not to tell "them" where he lived. He referred to them as "uncultured bullies, with no conscience or respect".

I would love to see the wood. Do you have it or know what happened to it?

Oliver Hutton.

CHAPTER 10

It's four in the morning and I still haven't slept. I had to stop myself from going over to the house to wake Eddie. I don't know if it's excitement or adrenaline that's keeping me awake. There's a painting! I'm piecing together the artist's actions. He was overwhelmed by the view of the fortress and had nothing to sketch on so used wood to capture the basic shape and perspective, then used the wood as a guide to paint. Then someone came looking for the painting? Why? Why hide the note as well as the sketch? The note must have been placed somewhere George thought Roland was likely to go. It's amazing to think that the previous owners had been trying to solve their own mystery as we have. I haven't replied yet; I need to talk to Eddie before I do.

The shop is open today and we expect it to be busy. I tell Eddie about the message in the car. I'm so tired. I don't think I slept more than three hours.

'Now, that's interesting,' Eddie says. 'I think we need to find out where he lives and meet up in a public place to exchange tales. I can suss out whether it's right to tell him that I have the sketch.' I use my phone to reply as we make our way into Penrith:

Hi Oliver,

Wow, that's fascinating. Yes we know where the wood is. Do you know what happened to the painting? The washhouse is still here but the sink has gone. Do you live locally? Maybe you can meet my grandfather and exchange tales! Kayleigh.

I help Eddie cash up and hoover at the end of the day. It was our biggest taking of the year so far; spring has delivered the good weather along with the tourists. There's been no reply yet from Oliver; I'm starting to think he lives in a different time zone. We celebrate the busy day with a trip to the chip shop. Penrith has the best chippies in England. Eddie drives up to Beacon Edge, which looks down on Penrith and over the valley towards the Lakeland Fells and we eat in the car.

'It's years since I've done this,' Eddie says, 'You kids used to love coming here and tucking into a bag of chips.' I did. This was always a treat when we visited with Dad. With neither Mum nor Dad driving and having to go everywhere by bus or train, being in a car was special. I was determined to pass my test; I always thought it would mark my freedom and ultimately it did. I just wish I didn't hate it so much.

Eddie takes the scenic route back and there's a car in the driveway as we pull in. This is becoming a regular occurrence. We see the silhouetted heads of two people at the front. Eddie looks concerned and my anxiety levels hit red.

'Just wait in here a minute,' he says, his gaze darting between me and the steering wheel. I'm in no hurry to get out but I shift to the driver's side and watch him walk over to the car. Before he reaches it both front doors open in unison. I drum the steering wheel with my fingers and watch closely and observe their body language. Eddie has left the keys in the car; I make a mental calculation of what I'd have to do to drive in an emergency and also get my phone out ready in case I need to dial 999. I can hear my heart thumping in my ears.

The man from the driver's side smiles but looks serious. He looks like he's in his late sixties, stocky, wearing a white shirt tucked into smart black trousers. The man in the passenger side is younger, early twenties with long brown hair and a swept fringe. He leans on the roof of the car with the door open, absorbed in the conversation between Eddie and the driver. I can't make out the conversation but they talk for about five minutes. Eventually they all walk towards the house and Eddie summons me out of the car. What's going on?

I have no time for my usual psyche-myself-up-to-be-sociable routine so hope that I don't look as petrified as I feel. Eddie introduces me to Oliver Hutton and his grandson, Caleb.

'I got your message so I thought we'd take a trip down memory lane and see the property again,' Oliver says. 'We were just writing you a note to say we called when you pulled in.' Oh. I hadn't thought of that.

Eddie shows Oliver and Caleb the cupboard and explains about the find. It's impossible to hold back the truth about the sketch; Caleb notices it quickly.

'Wow!' he says.

'Well, I'll be damned. All this time I've thought about what the letter meant by *the wood*, now it makes sense.' Oliver speaks with such a strong Cumbrian dialect that I struggle to understand. 'My old man always believed it was hidden here in the house. I don't know if they thought of looking behind the plaster. They checked the chimneys, barns, nooks and under flooring but weren't sure what they were looking for.' Oliver studies the sketch together with the letters. 'It's one hell of a mystery.'

'People must have wanted it for a reason,' Caleb says. He seems well-spoken compared to his grandfather. He has a strange attractiveness. His hair rest on his shoulders, similar to mine only it looks in better condition. He has an alternative look and wears Converse. 'Who would want the wood and painting so badly that George Kimber had to hide them?'

'They must either be valuable or were stolen, I reckon,' Oliver says.

Oliver opens the tobacco tin. The folded note inside looks

delicate and he opens it carefully to show me and I show it to Eddie as he comes back through with coffee.

'Maybe we can look for painters in the Mornas area of the time?' Eddie suggests. I wonder if I was right with my theory about the sketch being used as inspiration to paint.

There were many French painters at the time. Even Vincent Van Gogh was in Provence in those days. The sketch certainly wasn't by him. I look up other painters of the time and there's nobody of notoriety with the initials PEM or PEW but I notice Émile Bernard has the same surname as Didier. It's probably a coincidence and it wouldn't fit that the painter who vandalised the olive tree would have been a relative of Gerard Bernard.

I grab some paper and we all look through the deeds and letters to try and work out a timeline.

'I reckon George and Jane Kimber must have lived in the house while it was owned by the Dacre estate but bought the property for their son,' Oliver says. 'They must have moved out somewhere in 1909 or even 1918 at the time of the renovations and the interest in the wood and painting.'

'George Kimber must have had the painting with him when he moved. We need to find out where he went,' Eddie says.

'We tried tracing him but he disappeared. We eventually found his death certificate and he didn't die until 1932. Roland lived until 1935 leaving this house for his son, John.' Oliver says. It makes sense but how we would ever be able to find out, I don't know. He looks up at the oak beams. 'My old man told me these beams were made from ships, many of which were in the Spanish Armada. You can see from the random blocks carved out, they obviously hadn't been designed exclusively for the house.'

'I've often wondered about that,' Eddie says. Their gaze follows the beams as they speak. 'The washhouse had a bell you say?'

'Aye, the sink was an upturned bell. The mouth was about

two-foot wide and it was mounted on a brick casing. There was a mounting shelf high behind the bell about four inches deep. That's where we found the tin. It must have been a hiding place for tobacco. I reckon George Kimber left the note where he thought only Roland would find it. I've no idea if he ever did.'

'Maybe if his parents moved out, the son no longer had to hide his tobacco, so never returned to his hiding place,' Eddie says.

'Aye, you could be right. Roland's son died in 1989. We've been looking to see if he had any surviving relatives but we've not found any. Parish records have the death certificate in Carlisle. We've looked in obituaries but can't find a mention in local papers.'

'Any idea what happened to the bell?' Eddie asks.

'Aye, my parents had it restored and I still have it. We made a wishing well in our front yard.'

I'm fascinated by the tales. Houses can tell their own stories, hold their own memories and can snapshot the history and culture of their time. Modern houses seem soulless. It's maybe a sign of modern society - everything is disposable, designed to last until the next upgrade. If mankind looks back on today in 2200, what will they be able to tell about us? Will they look back with the same wonder that we do now? I doubt it. The washhouse is now Eddie's shed; he uses it for his gardening equipment and tools. The sandstone flags are still on the floor and the sink has gone but you can see where it was.

Caleb joins me in searching online with our phones while Oliver and Eddie talk over memories and theories. Oliver had already left messages on the ancestry forums about John Roland Robinson. With such a common name it's hard to establish the movements of everybody the search engines find.

'We need a list of cemeteries in the Carlisle area; we might be able to track down where he was buried and see if his gravestone mentions names,' Caleb says. I agree to check the

Penrith records.

'Okay, I'll check the Carlisle ones during the week as I live closer.' We exchange social media details and agree to keep in touch.

It's gone ten by the time Oliver and Caleb start to make their way out.

'Well that was fascinating,' Eddie says as they pull away, Caleb waves at me. 'Oliver remembers much more than I do about how the house was when we first moved here.' I think Eddie enjoyed reminiscing; he seemed to connect well with Oliver. I don't know what to think of Caleb or what he would think of me. It's teamwork now.

CHAPTER 11

I guess I gave Mum a hard time after *Two* left. A mixture of pre-pubescent hormones and blaming her for not making up with him gave me an attitude. Thinking back now, I was a brat. He was good to me so I thought he was good for her. He was the third guy who had walked out of our lives so I found it hard to build trust in anybody.

It was a year before we were introduced to *Three*. Mum really liked him and she became fun again. We started spending more time together; she would do my nails and show me how to put on makeup. We would cook together and, after a few months, *Three* moved in. By now I was thirteen and starting to develop and had spots and eventually braces. *Three* wasn't as exciting as *Two*; he didn't spend time doing art with me, he didn't take us places or wow me with his intelligence but he called me Beautiful. *Did you have a nice day, Beautiful? Dinner's ready, Beautiful. Pass us my lighter, Beautiful.* Jared was Trouble and Rosie was Smelly.

After a while Mum wasn't so well. She was looking pale and she lost weight, her skin was dry and her features looked harsh. She had a short temper and soon the arguments started. This was the first time I started to notice my own anxiety problems. I was scared he would leave. I started arguing with Mum again. Not long before he left I remember spending an evening with him. Mum had to go to a meeting so *Three* babysat us for a while. After the kids went to bed he made some special chocolate cakes; they were amazing. I remember the night well because I couldn't sleep even though I was so tired - I had to paint. I made an abstract with the most intense colours I could create. I could see myself nesting in the shapes and colours so called it "Self Portrait". Until I painted Didier's garden, it was my best work.

When *Three* left I was devastated again. How could Mum do this to all the guys? For this many to leave the problem had to be my mother but she would blame them. She referred to them as *Arsewipe, Shitface* and *That Twat*. I became more withdrawn; I spent time in my room reading or painting and crafting. If it wasn't for Lily dragging me out every now and then I would never have left the house. Mum tried to be kind to me but all that did was irritate me. She did sort herself out though. She started exercising and eating better and put on weight again and looked pretty. She even gave up smoking for a while.

I made up my mind that any guy that I felt truly loved me, I would do everything in my power to keep and, if we ever had children, we would never put them through what I had been through. The problem with that is that I don't let any guy too close. Love seems like a burden that society says I have to bear at some time in the future. I love Lily; I don't have any sexual attraction to her but I would live with her for the rest of my life if she ever suggested it.

Lily wants me to hook up with Caleb. I tell her about my day on video messenger and she can't hide her excitement. She's shipped us instinctively. He added me on social media this morning and sent a message tonight. Lily is trying to phrase the reply for me but there's no way I'll use her language. I keep it friendly but practical. I plan to visit the town hall and look at parish records tomorrow as the shop was so busy today that I didn't even have a lunch break.

'Chicken!' Lily says. Yes. She's right. I am.

We arrange for Lily to come up and stay with me overnight

for the weekend in a fortnight. I want to finish my painting of the fortress before then. I look up at Didier's garden; I'm so proud of it. It's almost as if I was possessed by the ghost of Gauguin, Seurat or Van Gogh and just let them take over.

***

That was easier than I thought. John Roland Robinson was buried at Beacon Cemetery in Penrith. It took me ten minutes to find him but all morning to psyche myself up to go into the council offices and ask. I'm still shaking as I make my way back to the shop and leave a message for Caleb.

'Well done,' Eddie says, 'We have the perfect excuse to buy a chippy after work, then we can explore the cemetery to find John's Robinson's grave.' I can't argue with that.

Caleb eventually messages back:

Good work! Let me know how you get on. I feel an idiot for not thinking of doing this years ago, maybe I missed the obvious by overthinking!

The cemetery is huge. The office is closed so we're going to have to search the entire area. It's a beautiful resting place with breath-taking views of the Lakeland Fells so I can understand why it's so popular. We ignore the very old graves but realise there are sections that tend to bias towards decades.

'Okay, these are eighties gravestones,' Eddie says as the fields become more open, away from the trees and main building, 'Let's alternate rows, it will take half as long.' I run ahead and find the grave of a seventeen-year-old girl who died; a faded photograph of her is embedded into the gravestone. It's scary to think how fragile life is. You don't think of mortality when you're young; you think you're going to live forever.

We spend twenty minutes walking along the rows. I've seen

two Robinsons so far but not the one we're looking for.

'We're well into the nineties here now,' Eddie says. 'I wonder if they've been separated by religion.' We walk along other sections of the cemetery and every once in a while see a stone that's not in keeping with the dates. 'If he was married, he might have been buried with his wife if she died before him.'

We work backwards from where we began our search. There seems to be fewer gravestones for the seventies. Did people die less often or was another burial site used before this one back then? The rows are steep as they bank up the hill and again we find nothing.

'I think we'll have to come back tomorrow and ask at the office,' Eddie says.

At the top of the hill we notice a small plateau dotted with gravestones. Eddie is out of breath so I tell him I'll take a look to save his legs. The first thing I notice is that these are nineties graves so I'm hopeful, and at the end of the first row I find John Robinson. His wife, Beverley, died in 1992 and is buried with him. The gravestone says they're survived by their daughter and three grandchildren.

I take a photograph before returning to Eddie. I virtually skip down the hill and Eddie welcomes me back with, 'You've found him then?' I smile and nod. I show Eddie the photo. 'At least we have a partner name now; we can narrow down our online search,' he says. 'This means there might be relatives we can talk to.'

I send the photo to Caleb and he immediately replies: *Well Done!* Eddie and I stand for a while looking at the view.

'When we first moved to Penrith we lived at a caravan site not far from here and this was my view for about four months while our house in Penrith was being renovated,' Eddie says. 'Even eleven-year-old me could appreciate the beauty of this town. Penrith has changed a lot over that time. You wouldn't recognise the town back then. Yet some family businesses go back four or five generations.'

One day I'm going to paint this view. I take a few photographs. The buds on the trees are starting to show life, the greens are lighter and the daffodils line the paths of this beautiful cemetery. The sun is low in the sky and will soon fall behind the mountains. Nature constantly paints for us; all we have to do is take the time to admire it.

I feel inspired. We take the scenic route home but I'm itching to paint again and I head for my oils the moment I get in. I need to finish the fortress. It's felt like a chore for the past few weeks, but now is the time. I can feel the passion and my focus and vision is sharp, so once again I let myself be possessed by the creative spirit and just paint. The greens stand vivid against the dark browns and greys of the cliff, the shadows more menacing still. They shade the plight of the soldiers forced over the top. They have been betrayed by their faith – the same God they devoted their lives to is now punishing them, their religion is their sin. Their sadness is embedded in the dark shadows of each stroke of my brush. The fortress stands powerful against the skyline and yet is in ruins. The colours below symbolise new life, forgiveness and faith in time and nature. I make the shadows slightly lighter towards the base of the cliff, as if the greenery below has an aura – a ghost of hope. Families who stand loyal to the town's history give warmth to the colours at the bottom of the painting. The blue sky by contrast seems cold. My painting depicts hope. The colours of nature will conquer the darkness of the evil in mankind.

And now it's six in the morning. The birds are already singing and the daylight is preparing the day's welcome. I have to be up in two hours. And I've never felt more awake.

CHAPTER 12

I let my guard down. It was a schoolgirl error, I know, but I'm cross with myself. I agreed to meet Caleb. We've been talking all week on social media and I've got to like him more. He's twenty-one, lives in a village called Durdar, which I find funny, he also DJ's the Rock Night at a club in Carlisle. We found out that John and Beverley Robinson lived in Askham, near Penrith, and found one of their granddaughter's family lives in the village of Caldbeck. We tried leaving a message on the granddaughter's Facebook but there hasn't been a reply yet. When Caleb suggested meeting up, I assumed it was to talk about our quest, but he's just told me I'm beautiful and asked if I would go out for a meal with him – a date.

I don't know him. I don't how to tell him that I don't want to, not yet, not this quick. Yes, he's good-looking and he seems kind; he likes decent music and has an air of mystery about him and most girls would probably be flattered. I'm scared. I know it doesn't make sense but I realise the reason isn't that I don't want to, it's because I'm already worried that if I commit myself emotionally, he'll leave me. I don't want to tell him the truth. I don't want to tell him that my only kiss has been with my mother's ex-boyfriend or that I was responsible for a murder. I'm eighteen. I don't want complications or emotional responsibilities or for it not to be perfect, and I don't want him to leave.

His face drops as I carefully ease him into the friend-zone and I blink back tears of guilt. I tell him that I like him and that

I'd prefer to build a relationship out of a friendship. That I have my reasons and it's not his fault and that I would like to spend time with him.

'I've been here before,' he says. 'I spent two years chasing an impossible girl. I was her first come-to after she had her heart broken by three other boyfriends. I was there for her all the time; we hung out, went to parties, watched the sun come up over Cross Fell and talked about our dreams. Then she found someone new and he didn't take to me, so now we're passing strangers. I don't want to do that again, that's why I'm asking you. I want you to trust me.'

I can only stare at him. Mum and Dad have told me I'm too trusting, I'm vulnerable and that I'm needy – a target for abuse. I've made mistakes. I've fought trauma and had an inner battle for years but for the first time in my life I feel like I'm in control. Yet here I am. My heart screams at me to let go while my head says no – if he's worthy of your love he has to accept it on your terms.

I tell him that the only way I can trust him is if he trusts me. I know I'm giving him hope but it isn't that I'm not interested in him. I am. I just don't want to commit myself emotionally to him too quickly, not until I'm sure of myself. I don't… feel it yet. I'm not a sleep-with-them-first-and-hope-it-works-out type of person. I'm not going to be my mother. I don't know if he's embarrassed or genuinely sad. I'm shaking with guilt, which seems to grip me from deep inside but I know I have to be true to myself. I don't know him well enough, I want to get to know him more, I'll be happy to spend time with him but as a friend.

'I guess we all have our demons,' he says, 'it'll be nice to get to know yours.' It won't, but I know what he's trying to say so I smile and nod before hiding my face behind my latte. I guess we never realise how complex people are as we grow up and don't consider what they're going through inside or why they do the things they do.

We go for a walk in Castle Park and spend some time at the castle ruins. Caleb seems to relax more as the afternoon wears on. He surprises me with his rationality and conscientiousness sometimes; he isn't particularly academic or creative but he is a thinker. We hear a little boy yelling from the castle archway and realise his mother is walking on with a stroller.

'I don't think she's realised,' he says. 'Hold on.' Caleb runs to help the boy down. It looks so natural you would think they were brothers.

'Thanks,' the boy says and high fives Caleb before running to catch up with his mother. I smile as he runs back to me.

'What?' he says. I say nothing. Maybe he's going to be worth getting to know more.

We make our way down to the shop before it closes as Eddie is taking me home.

'I'm glad we got to talk today. Sorry about making it awkward for you before. I'm bad at reading signals,' he says. I didn't realise I was sending out signals. I was just being friendly. We barely know each other. 'Thanks for your honesty anyway. I hope I can see you again soon.' A hug seems appropriate, though we're awkward and fumble to avoid arms. I promise him we will.

Lily's coming tomorrow; she's going to kill me.

***

Lily's train is due around two-thirty this afternoon so I drive in to Penrith with Eddie to help in the shop since I'll have the weekend off. The shop is busy, which is just as well as it stops me looking at my phone every twenty seconds. All quiet from Caleb. It's not that it should bother me but after yesterday, I don't want to be disappointed in him either. I told Eddie the truth and he agrees that I did the right thing by insisting I did things on my own terms but I question if I was being selfish by insisting we did. Where do you draw the line? Caleb's reasons for asking me were as valid to him as my reason for wanting to build our relationship through friendship, yet we both wanted to be with each other.

I'm feeling more miserable as the day goes on. There's a brief quiet spell in the shop at lunchtime so I go to the bakers to buy us a sandwich. While in the queue I message Caleb to say it was nice to see him yesterday and hoped he got home okay. I type that I'm sorry for… for what exactly? Nothing… so I delete that part and send it with an emoji smile.

My phone pings before I return to the shop and I smile, relieved that he's replied so quickly – but the message is from Lily.

Hey sweetie, the train's on time leaving Preston, see you in about an hour xxx

So much for being on time, the message board flashes that the train is expected in twenty minutes. I don't fancy waiting in the station so return to the car and listen to the radio. It will be nice to see Lily; I can't wait to show her my painting of the fortress. We must get a proper frame this week for both paintings in keeping with the era. My phone pings again, this time I expect it to be Lily but I see it's Caleb.

Sorry I couldn't reply earlier I've been helping out an elderly neighbour in her garden. She pays me in cakes and kindness. I got back OK. Hope you're having a good day x

I'm happy again. That's all I needed. I can't believe the emotional rollercoaster I'm on already. I know I'm not going to keep it secret from Lily but I'll try. I see the train approach so leave the car and wait on the platform as it slows to a halt. Lily's coach is directly in front of me. She waves before opening the door then gives me a big hug as she gets off.

'I missed you,' she says and I realise just how much I miss her too as we release our embrace. I help carry her bags to the car as the train pulls away.

We get home and I put the kettle on and Lily spies my fortress painting.

'This is amazing, Kayleigh babe. Knowing Marcus' reaction to the garden, imagine what he would make of this one.' We both laugh.

She takes a photo of the painting and sends it to Marcus. I bring her up to date on our investigation and tell her about Caleb's visit yesterday.

'Oh! Details! Details!' I laugh, I hadn't even hinted about anything that happened. I knew I couldn't keep it to myself. I tell her everything, omitting only my emotional rollercoaster today. Needless to say, she's hyped, but I wait for her to berate me for my insistence of taking control over the pace.

'No, you did the right thing,' she says, 'if he's worth his salt he'll play dice.'

I think she loves the idea of me having a proper boyfriend; she often joked about us hanging around together with our partners when we were older. She looks down at her phone with a shocked expression. Marcus has replied. *Where did you get that???*

'Didn't he say that when he saw the garden too?' she says. He did, I think.

Lily texts back telling him to chill, saying I had painted it and asked what he thought. Marcus texts back immediately. *Wow! That's unbelievable. She needs to make painting her career.* I'm still embarrassed by all this praise but it feels nice, especially from Lily, who is an amazing artist herself.

I show Lily the photos of Airaforce and tell her I want to go there tomorrow now the leaves are on the trees. The colours should be beautiful, I would love to paint that next. My phone pings and it's Caleb, much to Lily's delight.

I've been doing more investigations and managed to draw a family tree and timeline of the people we know of associated with the house. If Roland never found the note, it's not as if he wouldn't have spoken to George again in the fifteen years or so before he died so the family are bound to know what happened to the painting. If the wood was important it would have been easy to remove it when they sold the house to my great-grandfather and take it with them. So they knew it was there but chose to leave it. x

He's right. Maybe the wood was unimportant after all. Whoever was bullying George Kimber must have wanted it though. It would be good to find out what the bullies wanted with it. Maybe they got bored and it became old news and everybody forgot about it. I message Caleb while Lily talks to Marcus and updates him on our investigations.

Lily and I talk until midnight and plan our weekend. She's my first guest to stay over. When we were younger we had many sleepovers so it's nice we still can now we're older. I pull out the extension under my bed and make it up for myself so that Lily can have the more comfortable sleep and she feels bad for stealing my space. Not only don't I mind, I feel proud that I can. This is my home now. I've moved out first, before my friends go to university.

'I'll return the favour when you visit me at Brunel, if I get in,' she says. I agree. 'I'm still surprised you didn't hold out for uni.'

I could have, I know. I was doing the wrong subjects though; I would have needed to do a foundation course to do art. When Dad and Eddie were talking about the shop over Christmas, Eddie mentioned that he might have to close as he was struggling to cope but the shop wasn't making enough money to employ full time staff as overheads were rising.

I offered to help and make literary-themed art, crafts and decoupage to sell in the shop. I told them that I didn't want the burden of university fees around me all my life and convinced them that this was an opportunity an artist could only dream of. It spiralled from there. Instead of paying me a full time wage, he would let me stay at the barn rent-free, pay my bills, give me eighty pounds per week plus sell anything I make for the shop less a thirty percent commission. All I have to pay for is my food, petrol and internet. So far I've been averaging over one-hundred pounds per week in sales so it's working well and, more importantly, I'm earning money from my art.

CHAPTER 13

Airaforce looks even prettier than I imagined it would be. Lily and I have brought our sketch pads.

'We couldn't have picked a better day,' she says. We follow the path to the waterfall. With no wind we can hear the rush of falls in the distance getting louder as we approach. 'Though it looks like everybody's had the same idea.' It's busy, we move to an inlet to let strangers share the pathway as we make our way to a clearing.

'It's beautiful, I love this place,' Lily says. We stop at the top of a steep bank to catch our breath. We can see Ullswater Lake in the distance and Lily livestreams our walk towards the falls.

'Look at that,' Lily says, looking up at the waterfall, mesmerised. 'I could recreate this using textile cuts.' She snaps more photos and makes notes. 'Are there any fabric shops in Penrith?' I tell her there are and recount the tragic tale of Eglamore's Emma.

'Awe, that's heart-breaking. Those falls would have carried his tears along the river to meet her. Let's hope she could take them with her into heaven.' She's so poetic; my eyes well up at the thought.

We stand to the side of the main path and draw a rough pencil sketch. There's no rainbow today, there seems less spray where it hasn't rained for a while. After we've finished we make our way towards the café and I tell Lily about my adventure as a four-year-old as we go.

'Always a free spirit,' she laughs.

My phone pings when I'm in the queue at the café. I have a message from Colleen Baker, a surviving relative of John Robinson.

Hi Kayleigh,

Yes, I am John Robinson's granddaughter. Your message concerns me, if your mystery is anything to do with an art piece. Be very careful who you speak to about it. You could be opening up Pandora's Box. My great-grandfather was killed because of it. I don't want any more suffering, the mystery is buried, I'd rather it stay that way. I hope you understand.

Take care, Colleen.

'Woah!' Lily says. 'Maybe people know more than they let on.' That's my thinking too. I don't want to hold things back from Caleb but maybe I'll have to until I know more. I reply to Colleen.

Hi Colleen,

Thank you for your kind message and warning, I must admit I'm worried now. My grandfather found a wooden sketch of a fortress in France. My friend and I travelled to Mornas to investigate the artist and we met with people out there. I hope we haven't opened Pandora's Box!

Kayleigh x

She immediately messages back:

Oh no! Kayleigh, don't trust anybody. You say your grandfather found the wood? I need to tell you about it. You could be in danger and putting my family in danger. Could I meet you somewhere in public or your grandfather? Don't tell anybody about our meeting and try to play down your mystery as much as possible. The less people that know the better. I'm so sorry to be so negative. That picture is bad news.

Take care, Colleen.

I immediately phone Eddie and warn him.

'Okay, we need to think about this,' Eddie says. 'I'm worried what we've already opened ourselves up to. Don't mention anything to Caleb or Marcus until we find out more. Message Colleen and suggest we meet up, maybe in a café in Penrith or near where she lives. We need to find out more and we need to tell her what we know.'

I message Colleen and we arrange to meet the next afternoon at a bar in Greystoke, a village half way between Penrith and Caldbeck.

I feel deflated. I've lived this mystery for nearly three months so I don't want to let go of it. Surely we won't be in danger after all this time? This secret is over a hundred years old. The "they" that George Kimber referred to would be long gone by now. Maybe Colleen can tell us who the artist is or what happened to the picture and the mystery will be solved anyway.

'I should write a book about this,' Lily says. Now there's an idea – though Colleen would probably object. If "they" are responsible for her great-grandfather's death then it must have been serious.

We drive to Penrith discussing elaborate theories and Lily is as disappointed as me.

'I'll have to be careful with Marcus now but it could prove complicated.' I just hope we can solve the mystery tomorrow. We park up and head straight for the fabric shop.

'Look at this,' Lily says, showing me a green gradient fabric within moments of entering the shop. Lily's in textile heaven; it's just the distraction we need. I follow her around the huge shop and we spend a while looking through the off-cuts and line-ends and Lily chooses many then buys half a metre of various greens for a tenner. She's hyped about starting her project and I can't wait either; it's just like old times.

We return to the barn and immediately begin. I still have a couple of canvasses so we decide to create the waterfall using different mediums. We use our perspective sketches and phone photos for inspiration. Lily cuts out hundreds of leaf-shapes from her fabrics, sorting them into colours as I paint. I can almost hear the rush of the waterfall as I focus on the water. The persistence of the flow has carved through the rock. I think back over the years since the sketch of Mornas was made and wonder how much erosion has shaped this scene since. In geological terms that time is the blink of an eye. Geological history is as permanent and scarring as human history. I'm lost in my world of wonder as I craft the scene.

I glance at Lily's work as she glues each shape onto her canvas. The image is framed by the leaves of the trees in the foreground with only the waterfall and the bridge above it in greys, browns and whites. It's fascinating to watch her. The vision is in her head but with careful overlapping of colours you can see the shadows and reflections in the cascading water. Our only breaks are the occasional coffee and the pizza delivery courtesy of Eddie, who is impressed by our work so far.

Approaching three in the morning we're just about done. I'm pleased by the colours and array of vivid greens in my work and stunned by the effect of Lily's textile piece. Lily has developed a unique style to her work; you would think the image would be abstract but it isn't, she's recreated the scene perfectly considering the limited colours she's had to use. We both use a small fleck of pink about half way down the waterfall to represent Emma. It's been a good day's work. Lily's ignored Marcus' texts all night so takes a photo of her work and mine and tells him this is what she's been doing. He replies, despite the late hour of the day, full of praise for us both and seemingly relieved for the contact.

***

Greystoke isn't far; we usually travel through the village on our scenic route home from Penrith. It's a quaint village with a church, school and twelfth-century castle, which is still occupied. Eddie decided to keep the shop closed today after all. We arrive at the bar early and look around for anybody who might be looking for us. After a few minutes a couple in their forties enter and we somehow connect instantly.

'Mr Halsey?' The woman says.

'Yes, this is my granddaughter, Kayleigh, and her friend Lily.'

'Hello, this is my husband, Harry,' Colleen says. Harry smiles and looks down. I wonder if he feels as uncomfortable as me.

'Thanks for seeing us,' Eddie says. 'Kayleigh has told me about your messages; I'm sorry to hear about your great-grandfather.' He shows Colleen the photographs of the sketch together with the photographs of their find fifty years ago. Colleen and Harry study them in silence for a while.

'It's been a myth to us all these years,' Colleen says, 'It's strange to see evidence of all the stories I've been told after all this time.'

'I think this has been a mystery for many of us for over a hundred years.'

'My grandfather's great-uncle, George Kimber, was an architect and construction engineer. He worked on the Eiffel Tower and Blackpool Tower. I believe he was given this sketch together with a painting while he was working in France,' Colleen says. 'George always claimed it was given fairly but some men arrived from France during the war, over twenty years later. They were rude and threatening, returning a number of times and George, being a proud and stubborn man, decided they weren't going to have the artworks. George denied he still had them and the men didn't believe him so threatened to tear the place down.'

I get an uneasy feeling, guessing ahead that Lily won't like where this is going. I look up at her but she seems absorbed in Colleen's story.

'By then, the place had fallen into a bad state. George was injured during the war and his nephew, Roland, my great-grandfather, was growing up enough to take care of the farm and had recently met the woman he would later marry. The place was renovated and George and his wife moved out, leaving the farm to Roland and his wife-to-be. In that time George hid the wood and took the painting with him.' Colleen's hands shake as she speaks, cradling her mug of coffee.

'Why hide the wood? Why not take it with him?' Eddie asks.

'Nobody is sure, but the French seemed more interested in the painting. Roland continued denying he had the artworks despite being threatened many times. There was even a break in. He refused to tell them where George had moved and the men beat him up badly, but Roland genuinely didn't know where the artworks were.'

'What happened to the painting?' Eddie asks.

'After Roland was beaten up, George was going to let the French guys have the artwork after all but they went silent and they heard nothing for years apart from the odd letter. George's wife died of flu a few years later and his health deteriorated. He had been living in a village called Mardale but was forced to sell the house, eventually moving to Askham before passing away himself. He told Roland that if the French ever asked again, to give them his old address in Mardale.'

'Did you say Mardale?' Eddie asks.

'Yes. The drowned town.'

'So it really is buried then?'

'Yes. Roland was approached again in 1935, this time by two British men, both wealthy-looking thugs. They didn't take well to the revelation that the painting had been destroyed and my grandfather thought Roland had taunted them a little too much with the fact. My grandfather was still only a teenager himself. The next day Roland was found hanged. My family insisted it was murder but there was overwhelming evidence that he had killed himself. Apparently there were financial difficulties and mental health issues.'

'That's sad,' Eddie says. 'But you know it was murder now?'

'It should have ended there but during the drought of 1984 Mardale was exposed again and became a popular tourist attraction. Three Frenchmen tracked down my grandfather, wanting to know about the house in Mardale and asking if there was a cellar. In the conversation they mentioned how unfortunate it was that Roland had been uncooperative and had had the accident with a rope.' My grandfather couldn't help them, but the fact that people were still contacting the family after sixty-six years meant they weren't giving up. That's why you need to leave the mystery alone.'

I glance over at Lily and smile but she looks away; I sense that she's troubled.

'Did you ever find out who the artist is?' Eddie asks.

'During that visit in 1984 it was suggested to my grandfather that it might be Paul-Eugéne Milliet.'

'Woah!' Lily and I say in unison, staring wide-eyed at each other. The name is unfamiliar to Eddie and he glances over to us. 'His portrait was painted by Vincent Van Gogh,' Lily says.

CHAPTER 14

We spend the journey back to the house throwing ideas around. Were the artists who visited Mornas Paul-Eugéne Milliet and Vincent Van Gogh? Did Milliet paint the castle or did Van Gogh?

'If Vincent Van Gogh visited Didier's house it would have been known; the house would have been a tourist attraction,' Eddie says.

'True. It would have been documented in Van Gogh's letters too,' Lily says.

I'm online looking at Milliet's background as we talk. It's not as if he was a renowned artist. He was a French soldier, second lieutenant of the Zouves, stationed in Algeria. He befriended Van Gogh in 1888 and the artist taught him to sketch. Milliet was entrusted to deliver a series of Van Gogh's woodcuts to his brother in Paris. In this time, Van Gogh painted a portrait of Milliet he entitled *The Lover*, referring to both Milliet's declaration of being a lover of art and to his reputation with the ladies of Arles.

'Was the sketch an attempt at creating his own woodcut, do you think?' Lily asks. I guess it could be. I wonder if that's what the painting was in the end.

We told Colleen that we wouldn't pursue the mystery any more. We think we know what happened now. We certainly know why the wood was hidden, we know what happened to the painting and we think we know who the artist was. Why is it that I feel that there's so much more to know?

'What's a drowned town?' Lily asks.

'It's a town or village that was abandoned to make way for a reservoir,' Eddie says. 'Mardale was once a village and it's now underneath Haweswater Reservoir about twenty miles from here.'

'Oh, can we go there?' Lily asks, in a heartbeat and I see her eyes widen. 'Sorry! That was rude of me?' Eddie laughs.

'I can't see any reason why not,' he says. 'In 1984 there was a drought and it was so bad that the village became fully exposed again. The buildings had been flattened but the bridge was still standing until tourists took away all the rocks as souvenirs. I'm guilty myself; I visited three or four times during that summer. People came from all over the world to see it. Most of the rubble was cleared before flooding so the painting has probably rotted away in some tip by now; as glamorous as the idea is that it could still be there.'

'I wonder if some of the houses did have cellars,' Lily says.

'It's possible, I suppose, though I would think they would have been flooded.'

We might have owned a sketch by Milliet all this time without realising. It's a winding road to Haweswater; we're all quiet now. I look to Lily and her eyes seem full or close to tears. I ask if she's alright.

'Marcus knows more than he's letting on,' she says quietly. She could be right, as much as I don't want her to be because I've been pleased for her relationship. 'He has to know something otherwise he wouldn't have asked where we got the paintings when he saw them. He didn't react that way to our art of Airaforce; it was more of a natural reaction then. Makes me wonder if he likes me or of he wants a reason to stay in the loop.'

'There's no reason not to trust him just yet. If I were you I'd be normal with him but avoid conversation about the mystery or what we know,' Eddie says. 'If you find that he keeps pressing you for information then you know you'll have to back off. There's no cause to do that right now - he could be genuine.'

'I suppose so. I just don't like that he's holding out on me. If he knows more, there's no reason why he wouldn't tell me.'

I'm probably going to have to do the same with Caleb. I'll have to try to keep the conversation away from the mystery, as if I've lost interest. That won't be easy considering it's what brought us together and he's still making his own investigations. I need to find other things we have in common.

We drive alongside Haweswater, which is already pretty low considering the dry spring we've had. Eddie pulls over above the point where Mardale used to be. For now the village is still underwater. I feel the magic and mystery of the history lost. People fell in love in this village, their memories buried as secrets only told once in a rare, dry summer. Could there be a painting under there, so valuable that someone died for it?

Lily and I leave the car to take photos. The lake is beautiful, nestling so deeply in the mountains that the only way out is back from where we came. The spring greens give fresh life, their reflection disturbing the winter grey in the still waters, the season awakening new colour.

Is the mystery truly buried or have I already opened Pandora's Box?

***

Lily uses my old school case to carry her art home. She's so laden that we exchange an awkward hug before she boards her train home. I've enjoyed having her stay even if events didn't quite go to plan. I walk into town to join Eddie and pass the picture-framing shop. One day I'll get my paintings framed.

It's sad that the mystery is over, albeit not fully solved, but I feel inspired by it regardless. My old art teacher would be in awe of our original Milliet. I keep thinking about Caleb. He's been quiet over the weekend but he knew I had a friend with me. It will be nice to see him again.

The shop is quiet; the school holidays are over so there are fewer tourists. I help Eddie dust the shelves and notice a book from a local writer about Mardale. The book contains photographs from before it was demolished and during the great drought of 1984. It's fascinating to see the changes. Mardale was a small village with typical white stone-fronted farmhouses, a small church and primary school. The decision to flood the area was controversial at the time and many were opposed to it, especially since the reservoir was to supply the city of Manchester, eighty miles away. I can understand why the locals protested. I wonder which of these houses was owned by George Kimber. I can't see my heart letting go of this mystery even if my head insists.

Caleb messages me as we're ready to leave the shop.

Hi, I think I've found John Robinson's daughter, Lucille, in Askham. Maybe we could write her a letter as she doesn't appear to have social media. What do you think? x

I can't let him make contact, especially in light of the meeting with Colleen at the weekend, but I don't want to tell him about that either. I message back suggesting I phrase a letter tonight, trying to buy time. I tell Eddie as we drive back.

'It's a tough one. He'll make their family nervous if he approaches them,' Eddie says. Maybe if Caleb lets me write the letter I might be able to fake a reply and say enough to satisfy his curiosity. Maybe I can set up a dead end. 'I don't see why we can't actually tell him the truth and tell him that the original was buried under Mardale and that we believe Milliet sketched the wood. That does solve both mysteries, so I wouldn't see why he would want to approach the family even if he does turn out to be a bad egg.' My gut feeling is that he isn't involved but I'm a notoriously bad judge of character so how would I know? Caleb replies, saying it's a good idea and that he'll help me phrase the letter tonight.

I stare at Milliet's sketch as I eat my dinner with Eddie. As much as I've always been fascinated with art, I've never felt the same about history until recently. It's not the history taught in school, it's the personal history. People history. Places. I find it so inspirational lately that I'm overwhelmed with ideas. In the book about Mardale there was a story of a Swedish knight, Hugh Parker Hulme, and his entourage, that came to the village in 1209 en route to Scotland. They were hiding from King John, having been connected with the Canterbury Conspiracy of the time – monks and soldiers who had shown their allegiance to Pope Innocent III. After a storm, their supplies were washed away but news came of King John's death, so instead of continuing to Scotland, Hugh remained in Mardale. He became so popular with the village that they named his family the Kings of Mardale.

Caleb is in good spirits tonight. I show him my final painting of Airaforce and he doesn't hold back his enthusiasm. I used to be a scathing critic of my own work, but lately I've put so much more soul into my creations and it genuinely shows. We discuss the phrasing for a letter to Lucille – a letter that I won't send. I tell him that I'll send it in the morning. I wonder if she lives in the same house in Askham that John Kimber moved to after Mardale. I nearly mention it by mistake and go hot and cold at the thought of it.

Lily phones as I'm getting into bed. I tell her about my day and my dilemma with Caleb.

'Yeah, I nearly landed us right in it too with Marcus. I accidently told him we went to Haweswater and he laughed, thinking I said Whores Water. Luckily I corrected him telling him I said Ullswater and that he just had a dirty mind and heard it wrong.' I laugh; that was close. 'Surely we have to trust people after all this time,' she says. 'It's been over thirty years since any contact was made over it. Nobody could be in any danger, it doesn't make sense.' I do agree with her. It's absurd to think there could be anything sinister about this. I just love the whole mystery element; it's not a treasure hunt for me.

CHAPTER 15

I thought I loved *Four*. I don't know if it was the terror of him leaving, the fact that I got overly protective of him or puberty messing with my hormones, but I did fall in love with him. He was the first of Mum's boyfriends to treat me like an adult. He listened to me. He talked to me about everything from the environment to the music I listened to and we discussed creative ideas.

Mum was happy too. We found him at the same time, so it wasn't as if he was somebody she introduced us to. There had been uproar locally because of plans to start fracking on our doorstep. Big oil companies had applied to dig up the land and drill to extract shale gas in the area. Nobody in the community wanted it and Mum and her friend agreed to join the rally and we came along. It was an excellent day; we made placards and marched the streets and then had a picnic. *Four* was there and we got talking. He was just a nice, friendly person who cared about humans. We invited him for dinner and he just stayed and chatted to us. Mum's relationship grew from there. I don't know if I was jealous; I was happy that he was in our lives.

As the months went by he spent more time with us and eventually moved in. I started repairing my connection with Mum slowly. It suited me; I didn't want my crush to tell me off so I made an effort. Every time she was snappy or moody with him, even if it was over something trivial like leaving his coat on the back of a chair, I had a panic in case the argument would blow up. I know now that I went out of my way to steal his time. I spent less time in my bedroom, more time downstairs talking. He helped me with my homework and with art ideas for my school projects. Maybe Mum started feeling smothered by me. After a few months the big arguments started. They got worse and eventually Mum couldn't be civil with him at all and there was that familiar tension in the air. I couldn't stand it and if anything it drew me closer to him. He once told me he was unhappy but staying because he cared about me.

I felt good about that. Maybe my fourteen-year-old fragile ego liked that I had this power over him. I had started telling Lily about him and maybe I was too transparent with my excitement. Shelley Watson found out and started spreading rumours about me sleeping with my mum's boyfriend. The accusations were horrific to me at the time and the rumours escalated to the point where my form teacher called me in after school to ask if they were true.

Now I wish I had just said no; but I hesitated.

***

My literary-themed art gifts are getting more popular. I have ten custom orders for my paper flowers. I cut out pages of books that we have duplicates of and fold the pages to make a rose-style paper flower. I mount these on a stick and add lace for decoration. I've been selling them steadily for fifteen pounds each but Eddie's started taking orders for custom books, including many for self-published authors. I've also been selling a lot of boxes, decorated with torn book pages, and bespoke notebooks. Lily sent up an Alice in Wonderland-style dress that also sold quickly. All week I've spent the day in the shop and the evening making stock.

Caleb is on video messenger with me as I make a paper flower; it's become a routine this week. He's often on his computer games while I work away and the conversation can be sparse but it's as if he's in the room with me. I've not mentioned about any reply from Lucille and I avoid the conversation about the mystery as much as I can.

I've seen his parents a few times now in the background. They have a staunch Cumbrian accent, like Oliver; it's surprising that Caleb's accent isn't as strong. He does have some dialect but it's tame by comparison. I ask, and immediately regret it, as I'm met with a wall of exaggerated Cumbrian gibberish spoken at pace. I stare open-mouthed and he laughs.

'I'm fluent when I'm in company,' he says. 'Otherwise I'm trying to make more of an effort to curb it. Not just for you, but for work as well.' I guess I'm honoured.

I finish my paper flower and twizzle it in my fingers to show Caleb - *Ta da!*

'That's amazing,' he says, 'and adorable.' I'm sure I'm blushing, but I grimace at him and poke my tongue out. I can be childish when I want to be too.

I keep thinking of new ideas for shop gifts. I'd love to do some literary fine art too. Maybe scenes of somebody reading a book with the magic happening in the distance or fantasy imagery coming out from an open book. I sketch ideas down and before I know it hours have passed and Caleb's offline. He leaves a message: *You're on planet Kayleigh so I won't disturb you, but sleep well, Morisot x*

I laugh to myself, how would he know about Berthe Morisot? He's either more knowledgeable about art than he lets on or he's been looking up female artists online to impress me.

It's gone one in the morning when I settle. At least I have my customised orders ready for the morning in the shop. I'm pleased with myself. I've come a long way in the past few years. I think back to how I was at fourteen and the drama I caused and the trauma that followed. I would have given everything to be in this position now. I still hate my social anxiety, I still hate the person I was and I sure hate driving, but considering where I could have been, the life I was determined to escape, I'm doing better than I ever thought I would. Many artists have used their pain to inspire them but I'm finding you can't create art from pain alone. You need joy, you need wonder and passion. You need to be *The Lover*.

CHAPTER 16

The back of the shop has a small store room. At one point Eddie was going to turn it into a reading area but it's full of boxes of books yet to put out for sale. The room has shelves but they've been used to dump supplies. Eddie has had a brainwave to put all the books in the main shop and turn the room into my work room so that I can make crafts while I'm here, on view to the people in the shop. I can then help to serve customers while the shop is extra busy. I've spent two days unboxing books and shelving them and the floor space is growing. I like the idea, it will free up my evenings. I can't believe how popular the craft stock is getting.

I'm loading European travel books onto the bottom shelf when I look up to see Polly.

'Hey!' she says. I smile and stand up, my knees cracking as I straighten. 'I've come to ask a cheeky favour for your dad.' I laugh. 'He hasn't mentioned me yet to Jared and Rosie but wants to introduce me properly and he's worried how they'll react. He wondered if you could test the water a little when they come up tomorrow.' I can see why he's worried; they also witnessed Polly's face on my windscreen. 'Maybe just say that you've seen me and that I'm Dad's friend. You don't need them to know it's anything serious yet.'

I agree and she hugs me. I do get the feeling that she's serious about Dad. I still wake randomly from nightmares but that's not her fault.

'Thanks, Kayleigh, you're a star.'

Eddie and I are in the shop until late, choosing which books to put out and which to keep in my craft room. My muscles ache from all the reaching and stretching and I'm struggling to find space on any shelf now. Eddie must have thirty-thousand books or more.

'How about this?' Eddie says. I look over and see he's made a couple of hammock style shelves for some of the books we keep on display behind the tills. I'm impressed; he can be quite inventive at times. 'This will free up an extra unit we can use on the shop floor.'

If I had all the time in the world I'd be imaginative with the shop layout and turn shopping here into an experience - maybe paint a dragon mural and let its jaws be shelves for fantasy books, maybe the fire breath could be lower shelves with children's books on them. Maybe we could have a heart display for romance and the grills of a police car for crime books.

We finally finish at nine and I'm starving.

'Pizza?' Eddie offers. It sounds too good to refuse.

We eat in the car before heading home, looking out at the night view over Penrith from our usual place - the Lakeland Fells are silhouetted by the stubborn embers of daylight until they surrender as we eat the final pizza slice. The curtains close on another day.

Back home, I put the kettle on. I could do with tidying up a bit and running the hoover round the place before Dad and the kids arrive. Eddie knocks.

'We've had a visitor,' he says, handing me a piece of paper. "Edward Halsey" is written on the fold, and when I open it up the message reads: *I know where the painting is.* The note isn't signed. 'This is a mystery that doesn't want to be left alone,' Eddie says. I ask if he's told anybody. 'I've only spoken to your father and Rosanna about it. It won't be them.' No it wouldn't be, he's right. 'We just have to hope they come back soon and explain.'

I don't know what to do. If I question Caleb and it isn't him then I'll have to tell him the truth. It can't be Marcus; I'm sure Lily would have warned me. That only leaves Colleen but that doesn't make sense.

After Eddie leaves, I message Lily to see if she's still up. Thankfully she is. I explain what happened and ask if she's heard from Marcus today.

'I've had a quick natter with him because he had to go out with his father but he was definitely at home, I recognised the surroundings.' That narrows it down to Oliver and Caleb or Colleen, but since Colleen was telling us to leave the mystery alone, it would have to be Caleb. 'It's likely to be, Kayleigh, I hate to say,' Lily says. 'You're going to have to play it cool but you need to find out.' I look at my phone; the last message from Caleb was at 2.49 p.m. asking how I was getting on with the craft room. Could it be that he was checking that we were out and made the visit knowing the house was empty?

I can't bring myself to contact him now. It's late and I feel deflated. I get ready for bed while talking to Lily. The note states the writer knows where the painting is. Does that mean it still exists? Lily can sense that I'm upset.

'We might be wrong, Kayleigh babe. Caleb might not know anything. Maybe Colleen held back information. Maybe her husband knew more - maybe there were things he couldn't say with his wife present?' That's a thought. Colleen was obviously distressed by it so I don't think she held anything back. Unless it was all an act, I suggest.

'It could be. Colleen might have called the meeting to try and work out if we were genuine or connected to the French baddies of old. Maybe the family had discussed it so she went to yours to tell you the truth.' I prefer this theory. 'So be natural with Caleb,' she says. 'Say nothing and see if he stumbles over himself probing you for information.'

***

I have my customary twenty minute wait and existential crisis in the car outside the station as Dad's train's running late. This will be the first time they've been in the car with me since the accident so I would imagine Jared and Rosie are as nervous as me. It's another sunny day and warm enough to wear shorts and a tank top. The January snow of four months ago seems a distant memory now.

The tribe arrive and I greet them on the platform. I joke about their bravery for getting in the car with me. Rosie's big blue eyes look at me with irrefutable fear and I feel awful, bless her. I lighten the mood, putting the radio on asking about their week, while taking the scenic route home. The relief is clearly visible when they reach Thackthwaite in one piece.

While Dad tends to the garden, I sit with Jared and Rosie. Jared carefully tears out pages from books while Rosie folds the pages in quarters. I bring up the accident as a way of bringing Polly into the conversation. I tell them how I've seen her a few times now and how Dad's been a good friend to her.

'She sounds nice, maybe she can be Dad's girlfriend,' Rosie says. Right on cue. I smile.'Dad doesn't want a girlfriend,' Jared replies quickly, and my manipulative bubble bursts.

I tentatively suggest that he might one day. He's been lonely for a long time.

'She's too young for him anyways, she won't like him,' Jared says.

'She might…' Rosie cuts in. I mutter that she's thirty-five. Not too young.

'Whatever,' Jared says, ripping out the pages with less care and more venom. I'm surprised at Jared. I thought it would be Rosie who would protest, being Daddy's girl. I need to somehow warn Dad so I put the kettle on and make an excuse to go outside and ask if he needs a cuppa.

'How's it going?' he asks. I tell him about Jared and warn him to take it slow. At least I've done enough for them not to freak out when they do see her.

'Ah, okay. Thanks for letting me know. I'll tread carefully. At least you've put the idea out there for us. And yes, I could murder a drink, thank you.'

I notice how Jared is nearly as tall as me now. They've had it hard too with Mum and her boyfriends. They were too young to really know what was going on much before *Four* and it was impossible to shield them from the dramas that followed. They must feel like I do; it must be hard to get attached to any father figure. Maybe Jared doesn't want to think that Dad is about to become unstable too. I ask how Mum and *Seven* are getting on. I'm surprised they've lasted this long.

'He goes out when Mum starts; it makes her cross but he doesn't like to argue,' Jared says. I joke that he's a clever guy. 'He's out a lot, but when he is home, it's cool.' I tell them both that they will have to come up and stay a weekend in the summer holidays.

'Can we go to Airaforce?' Rosie asks. Of course we can.

The kids love my paintings. I've been thinking of painting Haweswater. It's scenic and rugged but not too colourful. I've been thinking of how to add colour considering its colourful history. Airaforce is Rosie's favourite painting.

I've only had one message from Caleb today, asking me how I am. I replied saying that family are up and that I'll catch up with him later. I'm half on the lookout for the return of yesterday's visitor. I mention the note to Dad when he comes in for his coffee.

'The note doesn't sound threatening; it seems like whoever it was is trying to help and was unlucky that you were out,' he says. 'My guess is that it's connected with your meeting in Greystoke last week.' I buy that theory more now. I just can't rule out Caleb and Oliver.

We all help Dad in the garden; team work. Dad turns over the soil, Jared rakes up the weeds and Rosie and I bag them up. Some of the perennials edge the garden but the bushes have been neglected or have died back. Eddie doesn't have the time to look after the garden properly. He mows the lawn sections regularly but it's hard to maintain it.

'Do you fancy a trip to the garden centre?' Dad says. 'It would be nice to buy some plants and surprise Grandad when he gets back.' I quickly calculate the route in my head and potential traffic and parking situation before agreeing. We look a state but for once I don't care.

We make it in one piece. Dad grabs a trolley and Jared immediately takes over, nearly knocking over a stand of birdfeed in the process. Dad pulls him in line quickly. There's a beautiful array of colours in the plant section, it's hard to know what to choose. Dad's more knowledgeable on the hardiness of each species. Left to me, I'd choose solely by the colours. After half an hour we have twenty or thirty plants so head to the checkout and Dad pays.

The garden is beautiful by the time we've planted them all; we all take a moment to stare at our efforts.

'Not bad at all,' Dad says. I look at Jared and Rosie; they're covered in mud but then so am I. I look down at my grubby hands and reach out to Rosie's nose and she ducks and then shrieks, 'Grandad!'

We hear Eddie's car pull into the driveway and all rush to greet him. He beeps the horn and waves. We must look a state. Rosie grabs his hand the moment he gets out the car and leads him into the garden.

'Wow!' Eddie says. I can't believe the transformation in just a day. The colours look so vivid. My mind goes to my palettes, subconsciously thinking of creating these colours.

'I'll put you in charge of watering these every night, especially this week while they take hold,' Eddie says to me. I don't mind at all. The garden breathes new life into the house from the back; I rarely see it from this angle. The large slanting roof hangs low over the kitchen. The garden is raised as the house was built in to the bank, the gravel driveway leading to the front of the house is lined with sycamore trees and they continue to the back, guarding the house from the prevailing winds. I still love hearing the rush of the wind in the trees when I'm awake at night.

After dinner, Eddie drives us all to Penrith station. An emptiness burns through my stomach as I say goodbye to Jared and Rosie; I never realise how much I miss them until they visit. I promise them that they can stay for a while during the summer holidays and wave them off as the train departs.

We're both quiet when we get in the car. Eddie rubs his face before he starts the engine. It's been a long day for him in the shop on his own; I offer to run it solo tomorrow so that he can have a rest. Sundays are never usually too busy.

'I'll be fine,' he says. 'I can help you get the craft room finished. I'll be in good fettle after some sleep.' I squint at him, unimpressed. He does need to rest.

I check my phone as we return in case I have a message from Caleb but it's quiet.

'Thanks again for helping with the garden; it looks beautiful,' Eddie says as we park and I head for the barn but before I'm through the door he shouts, 'Kayleigh!'

I look across to see him waving a piece of paper at me. No way! I run over to him. Again, it's a handwritten note on the same lined paper as yesterday. Eddie opens it up and reads out, '"I can't come again, it's too dangerous. Sorry I missed you. I know where the painting was, you might still have it. Don't tell anybody about this note and be very careful who you tell. Does Edgeworth ring a bell?"'

CHAPTER 17

Eddie and I take a walk along the road before we head to the shop. The fresh morning air awakens nostalgia; the dew adds something to the smell that disappears during the day. I would bottle it and have a constant feed into my craft room if I could. We leave the road, open a gate and walk up a steep track, overgrown with weeds; no cars have driven here in over thirty years. Eventually we come to a derelict farmhouse. It has a huge hole in the roof. Dad once told us that an aeroplane landed in it and I always believed him. The truth was less glamourous. Brandon Edgeworth, an eccentric of old, moved out of the property when his family had grown up and he had to move into town. The local council charged him rates on the empty property, which he objected to. The only way he could avoid payment was to remove the roof, because then it wouldn't be considered as a liveable dwelling. The house has been untouched in all this time and a huge tree now grows out of its kitchen. You can still see ceramic kitchenware and the stove.

'He was a funny old man, Brandon; he was grumpy and arrogant and yet always an entertainer. The villagers loved him and hated him. He was always friendly but brash with it. He would do anything to help anyone, would care about your health but at the same time comment on a spot or bad hair, moan about the noise of a lawnmower and get irate if you walked past the house and set the sheep off.'

It's dangerous to go inside, other than the kitchen part, and there are big notices everywhere to keep out. Not that it stops

Eddie.

'Wait here, I'll go inside. It should be okay,' he says. I'm not so sure but do as he says. I take pictures. It's incredible to think that a building like this has been left abandoned; it's beautiful and has views to die for.

I wonder if the painting is here; I hope not, it must have surely rotted away by now if it ever was. Eddie emerges with cobwebs in his hair and wipes them away with a tissue.

'I can't see there being anything here unless it's been hidden under the flooring or something,' he says. 'Brandon got on well with my parents and came to our house often when I was a teenager. He moved out around the same time I went to university. I've been here with your father and Rosanna at times but it hasn't changed much in thirty years, other than the tree getting much bigger.' I ask if Brandon could have left the painting with my great-grandparents.

'I don't think so. They would have told me. Brandon was a handyman mind; he did some building work for people and plastering jobs, fixed walls – that sort of thing. I'm not aware that he did any work at ours.'

The mystery deepens. It was hard to sleep as my mind teased me with it all night. At least we know the notes weren't left by hostile baddies and there was a reason for the anonymity. Why it would be dangerous to come again is still a worry though.

'Maybe we can rule out Mardale now,' Eddie says. 'Was that a story just to close the case for the bullies?' If they returned in 1984, they must have believed it was still there.

We walk back to the house, load up the car with my craft supplies and drive to Penrith. I'm looking forward to setting up my workspace now. I ask Eddie what we should to about Caleb.

'I think we should still be careful for now. I'd be interested to know how well Oliver Hutton got on with Brandon Edgeworth, mind.'

I suggest that I mention to Caleb that we had a walk to

the house this morning and say Eddie was curious to know if Oliver remembers Brandon. I won't need to mention anything about a connection to the mystery. It will be interesting to see if there's any strange reaction. If nothing else it will give us a clue as to how much they know.

It takes most of the morning to get the art stuff into my craft room and make it ergonomically friendly. I still have four custom orders for my paper flowers to do and it's lunchtime before the shop is quiet enough for me to start working on them. Not that my mind is on my work. If the painting wasn't destroyed, what would be the point in keeping it where nobody could see it? If it was worth something, then better to sell it. At the very least take it with you. You wouldn't leave it in the house you sell, not when people are willing to kill for it. Was Roland really that stubborn to let nobody have it rather than let the bullies have it? How much would a painting by Milliet be worth?

A regular comes into the shop, Mrs Ruskin. She's a local author who has written three books that sell steadily; I hear her talking to Eddie about restocking her latest book and she spies my paper flowers in small glass vases on the counter. Eddie does his regular sales pitch then points in my direction and she comes over.

'Oh my, these are beautiful,' she says. I thank her, blushing. 'Are you making custom orders?' I nod and hand her the one I've just completed, twizzling it in my fingers as I pass it to her. 'Would you mind if I take some photos? I wouldn't mind featuring these on my blog.' I don't mind at all. I show her the boxes and notepads too with some new ideas I've been working on. 'These would be unique items I could give away as prizes or perks on my crowdfunding page,' she says. I offer her a discount and agree to make fifteen flowers, nine boxes and six wired hearts. She leaves happy, and I'm going to be busier than ever.

'I wonder if we'll have any surprises waiting for us this time,'

Eddie says as we drive home. I'm thinking the same thing. 'I honestly don't think I have the painting and I doubt it will be within the grounds of the house. The place was renovated when we bought it in the sixties and over that time we've practically rebuilt the barns.'

I wonder if the painting might not be framed; it could be on rolled canvas, which would be easier to hide.

'The more I think about it, the more I think Oliver and Caleb know very little. I think this has been a mystery to them because of the note they found and they've investigated online out of curiosity, the same way we did. It doesn't make sense for them to leave notes for us. Now it's more about their feeling of entitlement should we ever find the painting. I don't think we could be looking at anything too valuable; I think it's purely about solving the mystery,' Eddie says.

I hope this is the case. I would prefer not to hide anything from Caleb, but all these warnings of not trusting anybody are alarming. So much has happened now that I don't know how best to tell him; he's likely to be hurt that I withheld so much from him. I can only tell him the truth.

There's no note waiting when we get home. I stay for dinner and help Eddie clean up a little; the house is still dirty from us traipsing in and out during our gardening marathon yesterday. I look over to the washhouse from one of the front room windows and notice the door is open slightly. We must have left it open when we replaced the garden tools yesterday. I go across to close it. It's messy inside – Eddie has been using it for storing stock. One day, when and if I ever have time, I'll tidy it up.

Lily phones in the evening and I tell her about the note.

'I think it's safe to say you can rule out Caleb,' she says. I'm glad she thinks that too. 'Lucky you,' she adds quietly and I detect sadness and ask if she's okay.

'Yeah, it's just Marcus. He's been distant lately. He's asked after you a few times but only mentioned the mystery once, nothing to make me suspicious. I think he's losing interest in me though.' I tell her it's his loss. 'Yeah, I know. It's just disappointing. He was talking about coming here in a few weeks but when I press him, he has excuses and little enthusiasm. I told him I'd come and see him but he hardly jumped with excitement.'

Lily's love life has always been complicated and I've no idea why. She's stunning, intelligent and creative; she gives her all and yet carries a mass of broken hearts. They've not all left her, sometimes she's had to end it, but she has a trail of three-month relationships. She remembers them by season: spring 2015 was Josh, summer 2015 was Liam… She's never short of attention but I don't know how she attracts all the non-committals. I try to express sympathy but in light of the latest developments, maybe it's not a bad thing. Lily will find someone else quickly, I've no doubt.

Lily shows me two more dresses she's made for the shop; they're a vintage design, in the style of Pride and Prejudice and Jane Eyre. She sends me the photographs and they're incredible; I'm sure they'll sell quickly. I'll pick them up next weekend as I'll be down for Jared's birthday. I talk to her most of the evening to keep her company while tearing out pages as I'm going to need hundreds. I feel guilty desecrating these books. The printed words alone have no meaning without context; each story, each character, each sub-plot meaningless, the new art merely hints at what could be. Lily loves the beautiful chaos in my shame.

It's late by the time we settle so I won't attempt to talk to Caleb tonight. I leave him a quick goodnight message and apologise for being quiet and say that I'll catch up with him tomorrow. He replies immediately: *Sleep well, Morisot x* I laugh, he's obviously waiting for me to pick up on his clever pet-name for me. Shall I message him back? Nah, I'll let him wait.

CHAPTER 18

My form teacher obviously didn't believe me when I told her that I wasn't having an inappropriate relationship with *Four*. I remember her sitting on the edge of her desk while I stood beside her, my messenger bag over my shoulder and books tucked under my arms. Her smile was unnatural and her questions were loaded, as much as she was being gentle and tactful. Even though I denied the rumours of sleeping with him, the questions were still direct.

'Has he touched you in any way or made you feel uncomfortable?' No, he hadn't.

'Has he kissed you or attempted to?' No, he hadn't.

'Do you like him?' Yes, I did. I couldn't tell her how much or why it meant so much to me that he was in my life. I thought I'd done a good job. Then Mum got a visit from social services.

I came home from school the next day and Mum had been crying. She told me about the visit and I told her about the teacher questioning me and that Shelley Watson had spread rumours. I don't think Mum believed me either and I don't think she believed *Four* when he came home and she confronted him. I couldn't look him in the eye that night and the tension was so bad that I ate my dinner in my room and avoided all conversation. My biggest fear wasn't the shame, it wasn't that nobody believed me. I feared him leaving.

The next day *Four* knocked on my door after school. I knew what was coming. He told me my worst fear; he was leaving. He had no choice. I broke down and threw myself at him, hugging him tightly in streams of tears, begging him not to go.

'I'm so sorry,' he said, and held me. 'I do love you but not in the way I love your mum, if anything, it's deeper. I care for you, I admire your spirit. But I can't stay; I can't make your mum love me so I have no choice but to leave.' I wouldn't let him go; I told him I loved him, I told him I would run away with him and leave Mum. I don't know why but I kissed him, fully on the lips, and for a few seconds he reciprocated, I know he did.

I think he realised then why I was so devastated. Maybe he'd thought I loved him only as a father figure, which, as much as I did, I wanted to love him more, maybe not sexually, but to feel and be loved. He changed. He backed off; I could see fear in his eyes. This made it even worse for me. He remained nice but became more confident, less emotional, less the caring father figure that he had been at the start of the conversation.

'You can't love me like that, Kayleigh. It's dangerous to even think like that,' he said. 'I don't want to hurt you, I thought I was doing the right thing by staying the past few months and trying to patch things up with your mum for your sake. I know how hard you've taken all of your mum's boyfriends leaving. I've done everything I can.' He had, I know, but he was still leaving me.

He was kind to me when he left the room and I saw he was fighting back his tears. He packed up his things while I was still sobbing and wailing, savouring the memory of his lips against mine. I never wanted to see Mum or speak to her ever again at this point so when she came in my room to try and console me, I threw my mug at her. It shattered against the wall next to her. *Four* knocked on my door later that evening to say goodbye and again I pleaded with him not to go; I told him I would rather be dead. I'll never forget the look he gave me; it was the sort of fear you see in horror movies. I stared at him and said that I meant it.

'I'm not worth it, Kayleigh,' he said. 'You take care of

yourself, I'll see you again soon, okay?' I was crying too hard to answer. He pulled me to him with one arm and gave me a brief but intense hug, and for a moment I felt like all my troubles had disappeared. But two minutes later he was gone.

That day still replays in my head regularly, no matter how hard I try to change the subject or distract myself, and it triggers memories of all the things that happened afterwards; the things that I came here to run away from. I'm beginning to realise, though, that you can't run away from a memory.

***

I'm on a roll. I don't yet know if I've torn enough pages to make everything I need but by lunchtime I've made six paper flowers, and that's despite helping Eddie serve customers. It's amazing how so many people like to stand and watch me work. It's awkward and I'm prone to making mistakes when they do, but they're always full of praise.

We found a printing firm that make customised pens. We scanned in some book text and I highlighted the word "Love" in yellow. We received the order first thing this morning and we've already sold ten of them. I tell Eddie it's about time he got himself a website to sell stock, but he doesn't want to.

'I'd rather people came in to the shop,' he says. I remind him that Penrith is in the middle of nowhere. 'No. Not at all,' he says. 'Its location is perfect, it's a tourist town, it's close to all major roads from every direction and it's on the main West Coast Railway route. It's a beautiful town to visit. So let them come.' I admire his optimism but I think he would sell more literary gifts online.

Mid-afternoon and I'm focussed on my crafts. There are people in the shop but I'm leaving Eddie to deal with them. Suddenly I'm aware of being watched. I ignore it for a couple of minutes before looking up, only to see Caleb standing there.

He can tell I'm startled and he laughs.

'I didn't want to disturb you,' he says. 'I was bored, so thought I'd come and see you.' I smile and instinctively apologise for the mess and he laughs again. 'I'm impressed. You've got yourself a proper workroom here. It's cool that people can watch you.'

I'm ready for a cuppa so ask Eddie if I can leave for half an hour and go for a drink with Caleb. We walk to the nearest coffee house, overlooking the churchyard in the centre of town. I know this is the ideal opportunity to tell him everything but it's hard to know where to start; how can I justify not telling him sooner? I take the angle that I've been so busy the past few weeks that I've not had a chance to update him fully and blame the rest on Eddie.

Caleb takes it well, thankfully. I tell him about the meeting with Colleen and about the notes at Thackthwaite from the visitor we missed.

'I can understand why you were forced to hold back on telling me,' he says. 'That does put a new spin on everything.' He fidgets, tapping his fingers on the table, his shoulders bouncing. 'Wow, I can't believe the can of worms we've opened. Oliver's gonna love this.' I tell him that it's okay to tell Oliver but for them both to be careful who they speak to, especially as it's worthy of local, if not national press. 'No, that's cool. I don't think my folks would want to risk being caught up in any danger either. I wonder where the painting is though, and what happened to it.' I tell him about our search of Brandon Edgeworth's house.

'I can't remember Oliver mentioning about Brandon Edgeworth. What a card though, imagine removing the roof to avoid taxes, that's insane!' I don't think Brandon thought it through properly. 'It's hard to tell if your visitor left a clue to solve or was actively telling Eddie where it is. Either way, it does seem cryptic.' We both come to the conclusion that the mystery visitor is Colleen's husband, Harry. It would be wrong to go round there and ask more questions, especially if he's made the journey without Colleen's knowledge.

Before we know it, we've been an hour so I'll have to get back to help Eddie. We awkwardly hug goodbye outside the coffee shop.

The shop's been busy too, but Eddie's okay.

'I've another three orders in for your paper flowers. Your work has been featured on a major blog that's been shared on social media, apparently,' he says. It's so strange to be recognised like that for my work. It's inspiring. I have even more work to do now but it's good and I hope Eddie's shop takings are up over previous years. I'm proud that I've been able to help. It defends my decision to come here too.

I update Eddie on my conversation with Caleb on our way home. I hope I don't regret telling Caleb; so far he's remained nice to me and given me space and I feel sorry for Lily with Marcus. Maybe the distance has been too much for them after all. Marcus' family have their roots embedded in Mornas and the area; maybe if he's thinking long term, the idea of him leaving for England is daunting. I can't see Lily giving up on her university studies.

We pull in to Thackthwaite and I join Eddie for dinner. We're getting a routine now where I help him cook and wash up afterwards and I end up with a free meal. As much as I embrace my independence in the barn, I think it suits us both this way.

'Did you shut the shed door in the end?' Eddie asks as I'm peeling potatoes. I did. I know I did.

'It's open again.' I join him outside and we go over to the washhouse. Eddie slows and puts his finger to his lips. I pull up and can feel my heart thundering. The door is open slightly, as it was last night. Eddie holds out his arm to keep me behind him; we can hear a scraping. He opens the door gently and a startled cat scampers out and I shriek.

Inside is still a mess; it's hard to tell if anything is missing. Eddie looks at the bolt and it seems to pull securely.

'There's no way the cat would have been able to open it,' he says. I retrace my movements. I definitely bolted the door; someone has been here. I head for the barn. It's locked. I go inside and it looks untouched; it doesn't seem as if anybody has broken in. I re-join Eddie and we scour the rest of the outbuildings. The woodshed seems normal, even Eddie's axe and saw are where they should be. The main barn is virtually empty anyway; eventually Eddie wants to do it up like he has with my barn but for now it's only used by the nesting swallows.

'I don't like this,' Eddie says as we return to the house. 'I might have to invest in a CCTV camera.' That's a good idea. I shudder at the obvious conclusion my mind makes. Did Caleb come here after our meeting? If it was him, what was he looking for?

After dinner I have to venture back into the washhouse to get the watering can. The flowers look beautiful; I'm pleased with our work over the weekend. I make a personal vow to keep on top of the garden and weed it every week to stop it building up. I have another look around the washhouse after I've finished in the garden. It's a small building on a single story; you can see up to the slate roof from inside. The walls are bare and there's a window looking out to the house. Under the window, you can tell where the sink used to be as there are still the mountings and wooden supports that have worked themselves free from the plaster over time. To the right of that is a stone shelf that runs across the full length of the wall. Eddie has tools on it and boxes of God-knows-what. There are sandstone flags on the floor. I look to see if there's any obvious tampering but there doesn't appear to be. Did I really close the door last night? Maybe I'm losing my mind.

CHAPTER 19

I still hate driving. The traffic is busy. I wish I had set off later now; it's the weekend home rush for many and there are major roadworks so it's stop-start and clutch control for miles. I listen to the radio but it does little to calm me. Eventually the traffic starts to move again but I'm exhausted by the time I get to Mum's, over two hours later.

It's Jared's birthday tomorrow. I've been in the shop all day trying to catch up on my orders as we're getting a steady stream of new requests. I've had a lot of people contact us having seen my work posted on social media. It's surreal when strangers enter the shop and speak to me by name, as if I'm supposed to know them. The local newspaper is featuring the shop and my work tomorrow so it's maybe a blessing that I'm away. Dad and Polly are going to help Eddie as it's likely to be busy, so I don't feel too bad.

'Kayleigh!' I hear as I open the car door. Jared and Rosie come rushing over to greet me and I hug them, holding each in one arm. We go inside the house and I can't keep up as they tell me their news, both talking at the same time. I've barely as much as waved at Mum; she mimics a drink and I smile and hold up a thumb to accept.

'Look,' Rosie says, sitting on my lap and showing me the prefect badge pinned to her purple school jumper. It's nice to see everybody. I've been dreading coming back all week. I always feel the tension in these walls but I miss Jared and Rosie so much. The atmosphere seems better though today, even

Seven is jovial, thankfully. We have dinner together.

'I went to London last week,' Jared says, handing me brochures of the National Portrait Gallery and Tate Modern. I remember that trip when I was in year eight; it inspired me. I've never considered Jared an artistic type, he's always been into sports but he enjoyed it; maybe he'll follow his big sister.

After the kids settle I drive to Lily's as she only lives about three miles away. She's as excited to see me as Jared and Rosie were and gives me a big hug. We go to her room, which is nearly as big as the downstairs of my barn. The room has a large expanse of floor for her textiles and artwork, her bed is to one side and opposite is her desk and sewing machine. The walls are white but there's colour everywhere. Two mannequins display the dresses she's made for the shop, which look amazing. The textile piece she made of Airaforce is above her bed.

'I'm working on another dress,' she says, showing me a floral print of purple, white and blue. She also shows me a patchwork quilt design she's attempting. She's tiled many coloured strips that look like books in a bookcase. They all look good; Eddie's going to love them. It will be extra money for Lily too. She seems more upbeat than the other day.

'I'm not chasing Marcus. I'm replying to his messages and texts but I'm not making the first move anymore. He keeps asking me if I'm okay but I'm giving him the *fine* treatment.' I laugh. If he's getting complacent, maybe it will make him think. I tell her about my conversation with Caleb. I think she would love to talk as openly to Marcus but his ways are so strange she knows she can't.

It's late as I leave. I take the dresses with me and hug her.

'I'll come and help you in the shop after my A-Levels, I can stay for a few days then,' Lily says, releasing her embrace. It would be great if we can both work in the shop. I do miss her, and I'll see her even less when she goes to university. I think of how good she's been to me, how she brought colour to my darkness; the days we shared and the secrets we keep. Some memories you don't want to run away from.

***

Jared's chosen a day out in Blackpool for his birthday. He had fun opening his presents first thing and was spoilt rotten, he's appreciative though. I did offer to drive but *Seven's* car is less of a squeeze. Not that I'm complaining. At least we have decent weather, even if that means it takes ages to find somewhere to park.

We take a slow and steady trek along the promenade dodging a river of people. Rosie spies a Minions grab-machine.

'Wait! I want a go!' she says. We watch as the arm lifts the toy agonisingly close to the edge before dropping short of the tray. It's addictive, we all have a go. Rosie jumps up as I tease it closer still. But no luck.

'Come on, let's get some doughnuts,' Mum says, ending Rosie's disappointment. It takes us an hour to reach the Pleasure Beach, a huge funfair with terrifying rides. Jared looks up at the rollercoaster with wide eyes.

'I'm not going on that!' Mum says. Jared tugs on my sleeve and horror surges though me. I'm saved by *Seven.*

'Come on, I'll do this!' he says, grabbing Jared's arm. They leave us to join the long queue, snaking through a maze of barriers. They could be there hours.

Mum's in good spirits for once and we go on the Dodgem cars. Rosie and I take one car and Mum takes another. Rosie shrieks as a car hits us but I take the wheel and aim for the side of our collider and smack them back. Rosie loves it. It's hard to hear her over the loud music. She points at Mum and we chase her round, eventually bumping her car at the back. Rosie is red-faced with giggles and disappointed when the ride ends.

'Can we go again?' Rosie says as we get out and join Mum.

'How about candy-floss instead?' Two young children walk past with rainbow candy-floss and Rosie runs over to the cabin to join the queue. Mum and I laugh.

We sit down on a bench with our sugar clouds to wait for Jared and *Seven*.

'You probably don't remember coming here with your father before Jared and Rosie were born,' she says. I'm not sure if I do. 'You must have been about six. Your father won a huge tiger; it was so big it was hard to carry round with us.' Oh, I do remember, I didn't realise that was Blackpool. We came by train, eventually Dad gave the tiger away, as it was impossible to carry it round with us. The little girl who he gave it to was so happy and even though I was disappointed that we couldn't keep it she promised to look after it so I felt happy for her. I liked that feeling. 'You were such a good girl,' Mum says. 'You were so happy he had won it and yet even at six you could understand why we couldn't keep it.' Is that a compliment? I raise my eyebrows and wait for the *Look what happened* but Mum stuns me by putting her hand on my shoulder and saying, 'You've always been a good girl, and more than ever now.'

Luckily, I'm saved by Jared, who runs up to us asking if we saw him. We didn't but all three of us say yes. *Seven* looks like he's been dragged through hell and we laugh.

'Well, that took me back to my teens. I know why I stopped doing that now,' he says.

We stay for a while and I take Jared and Rosie on some of the smaller rides and we buy ice creams. I'm still shocked by what Mum said. I'm so used to disapproval of all my decisions: my choices for my GCSEs, my personal choices for college, my choice of friends, music, clothing, makeup, hairstyle and of course, my decision to leave. I've been careful not to tell her much about the Mornas mystery; I know she disapproved of my trip to France. Has she changed, or has she always thought I was a good girl?

The kids are full of their day as we head back towards the car. I look up and see the huge tower. To think that one of the construction workers of both the Eiffel Tower and Blackpool Tower lived in my house five generations ago. I take some photos of it; you rarely see it from this angle, you become so aware of its height when you're this close.

It's been a surprisingly good day. I've not heard from Caleb but he knew I was with family today. Oliver remembered Brandon Edgeworth but never got on with him so they couldn't shed much light on the note but Oliver is more curious than ever. I'm still confused about the washhouse, wondering if I'm already going senile in forgetting to bolt the door.

We have birthday cake when we get back, and although I'd planned to go home tonight I'm too tired, so I decide to stay.

'You're growing up fast,' Mum says, after I help put the kids go to bed. We venture to the sitting room with a glass of wine. The room feels warmer; I'm not sure if it's the floor lamps or the atmosphere. Something's changed. 'I always feel bad about what you went through. I know I messed up with relationships and you've always resented me for it, but I've had my reasons. Every time.' It's awkward because on the one hand I'm glad she recognises it and on the other, I don't want to say, *That's okay, no damage done*. I am damaged. I say that it was hard for both of us.

'Yes, but you had no choice, I did. I wanted a father figure for you as much as I wanted a lover for myself. I became drawn to people who treated you well instead of treating me well. I could never find one who loved us both.' I don't believe that. I remember *Four* telling me that he wanted her to love him. I remind her.

'He knew you were my priority. He knew the way to make me happy was to treat you with kindness, and he did. He didn't understand that he also needed to focus on me too. I wasn't hiring him as a nanny. I wanted him to blend in, to be my partner but treat you kids as his own. He treated me more like a boss, using the way he treated you as his barometer for our own relationship. He never made the same commitment to me emotionally. The arguments started because I was desperate for him to see that. I didn't realise he was infatuated with you until it was too late, or that it was mutual.' I can feel my stomach churn and I try to focus on the photo on the wall above Mum's head to avoid the flashbacks.

I ask if she still resents me for that.

'Oh, Kayleigh,' she says, 'I didn't resent you. This is a lie you've been telling yourself for years. All I've ever done is try to protect you. I just failed. I think you've often seen my sadness as anger.' I'm stunned again. Have I? She's never told me this before; she's never openly encouraged me or even paid me any compliments until today. She's always been cold. I'm still staring at the photograph but my eyes are filling. I tell her that she never told me before.

'I'm flawed when it comes to expressing emotions. I'm cold and seem heartless and I know it. I can't excuse it, I always have. Your father couldn't take it anymore. I fly off the handle at trivial things and I ignore the big problems because it's easier that way. The trivial nonsense becomes magnified to mask the bigger issues. Maybe our bad communication became a habit. The love has been there all the time though.' I notice she's buried herself deeper into *Seven's* arm as she talks and he squeezes her gently. This is a revelation. Has *Seven* finally tamed the beast? I'm stuck for words but manage a smile. There are so many questions I want to ask. I still find it hard to believe what she's saying, but then have I really ever thought about it from her perspective? I've always considered that she's just compulsively selfish. I remind her I went through hell.

'We all went through hell, Kayleigh. Me, Jared, Rosie; we were all going through the same things but we had you to worry about too. You screaming in the middle of the night, you trying to take your life and that terrifying wait at hospital.'

I turn away. I know that was bad. My one and only attempt at self-harm, never again. I wasn't trying to end my life; I was trying to find sensation, to overwhelm the bitter sadness. It went wrong and I nearly died. All it did was add to my trauma. For years afterwards I wished I had died. I was stupid. 'The thing is, Kayleigh, you thought it was all about you. It's been so hard to talk to you, all these years you've convinced yourself the world is against you, and it's been so hard to assure you otherwise. This is why I'm so proud of you now. You've become the person I always knew you could be.' My eyes overflow. I wasn't prepared for this at all.

I catch her eyes and they're flowing too. *Seven* must be feeling awkward but he cuddles her and looks towards me. No bitterness on his face, a silent mediator. I wonder how long Mum has been waiting for this moment. It's obviously no surprise at all to *Seven*. I say that we've both grown up a lot then this year. Mum gives a half-smile and I tell her I'm sorry. I mean it too. She might be right, maybe I read her wrong, maybe I was selfish, but I was a kid. I needed her, I needed guidance and assurance and I needed encouragement. I've wronged them all and I didn't know it. And I realise now how much I've wronged *Five*.

CHAPTER 20

I'm out of bed later than I planned and phone Eddie to apologise. The shop was busy yesterday after the piece in the local paper so I have lots more orders. I tell him I'll head back to Penrith after my breakfast. I didn't sleep well at all. Last night's conversation replayed and rewound constantly in my mind.

Jared and Rosie are up and *Seven* is in the kitchen making a fry-up while Mum has a shower. I join him and sit at the breakfast bar. I apologise for last night and thank him too; it must have been awkward for him.

'I think your mum needed that as much as you did,' he says, turning over the eggs. 'I can tell that you love each other; you've had a breakdown in communication for so long it's become routine.' He's probably right. 'She does love you. You grew up faster than she was prepared to accept. She didn't know how to protect you, or help you grow. She didn't want to control you but then she didn't want to restrict you either. In the end I think she did neither and you were left to find your own way, blindfolded. She didn't realise until it was too late.' I guess so. There's no set of instructions for parenthood or fixed rules to having children and how to bring them into adulthood. The transition is hard enough as it is, and Mum and Dad were both young when they had me. I tell *Seven* that he's good for her and I hope she sees that.

'I'll do my best to make it work. I don't plan on going anywhere,' he says. I reach for the plates and set them out ready for him. 'I think your talk last night will help a lot. She's been worried about you and worried about how far apart you've drifted.' I need to make more of an effort myself now. It will be easier if I don't end up fearing my visits and it will help Jared and Rosie too. I promise to play my part too, then call Jared and Rosie to the table.

Mum's upbeat when she comes downstairs and we eat breakfast together with no mention of the night before. It feels strange as I leave. They all come outside and we exchange hugs.

'Safe journey,' Mum says quietly, holding on to her hug for longer than I can ever remember. This must be the first time I've ever left the house ever without feeling relieved. I pip the horn and wave until they're out of my rear view. I'm still too numb to know how I feel, but I I'm genuinely pleased I came down.

It's late morning by the time I arrive at Penrith. The shop's busy and a customer watches as I show Lily's dresses to Eddie.

'That's beautiful,' she says as I hold up one of the Pride & Prejudice designs. 'Could you keep that by for half an hour so I can show my daughter?'

'Of course,' Eddie says. I've no idea what to charge for it yet. I take the dress into my craft room. Lily will be pleased.

'There are another two orders for customised paper flowers today on top of all those orders from yesterday,' Eddie says, pointing to a stack of books and notes on my desk. I notice he's already framed the large article from the local paper and displayed it behind the counter. 'You're becoming a bit of a celebrity; at least it's for happier reasons this time.' He winks at me. Very funny. Not.

I help Eddie serve the customers for an hour or so before working on the new orders. There's a steady flow of people all afternoon and many are entertained by watching me work. It was such a good idea to put my craft room on show, so many people want custom orders from their favourite books. Often they buy the book then leave it with me to make flowers, notebooks and boxes from the same book. The blog post circulated on writer's groups on social media so we've also been getting authors ordering their own books.

I'm shattered by closing time, especially having driven this morning. We celebrate with a visit to the chippy and park in our favourite place to eat.

'I was talking to Rosanna last night; she's going to come and visit in a few weeks,' Eddie says. I mumble and nod as I have a mouth full of battered fish. There's no way to eat elegantly in the car. 'She'll bring down some of our parents' journals and photographs when she comes. She seems to remember your great-grandfather writing about Brandon Edgeworth at one time. She's going to look it up.'

I haven't seen Great-Aunt Rosanna for years. She lives in Newcastle with her cats, now that her family have all grown up and left. Her husband disappeared when her children were young. She's funny, I like her; she's larger than life in every way. I haven't had too much time to think about the mystery for the past week; it's like the pace of life has accelerated all of a sudden. I'm happy for Eddie though; I've helped turn the shop around and I must have made over five hundred pounds for myself this month in stock I've sold.

My phone pings. Lily has split up with Marcus. I phone back immediately and ask what happened.

'I heard nothing all day yesterday so video-called him today to see if we could talk as the whole thing's been bugging me for weeks. I could just tell he was different so I told him it's not going to work. He said he doesn't want to split, it's just things are complicated. I could understand that if he was still being normal with me but he's changed.' I tell her that I'm sorry. 'He hasn't taken it well but I don't know what he expects. I can't live this emotional rollercoaster.' I feel guilty that I'm relieved. I love Lily and I want her to be happy but it makes things less complicated for me. Maybe I am still selfish after all. I offer for her to come up this week and revise here but she still has an art project to finish.

Eddie heads back while I'm still on the phone. I tell Lily about my conversation with Mum. I hadn't told Eddie so I assume he's listening too.

'About bloody time,' she says. 'That's going to help you both lay your demons to rest. I'm so happy for you, Kayleigh babe.'

We end the call as Eddie returns to Thackthwaite.

'I'm pleased you were able to talk with your mother. She's had a tough time too over the years. Her heart is in the right place even if her head isn't always,' he says. 'If nothing else it gives you some closure.' That's true. I do still feel numb; I don't think the reality has kicked in yet. Maybe I'm scared that it could trigger a breakdown if I think about it too hard. Or worse, I might start to feel demotivated if everything I thought inspires my independence turns out to be a lie.

***

'Can I steal your granddaughter for a few hours?' I hear a familiar voice say. I look over to see Caleb in the shop.

'You can borrow her. I need her returned in good condition,' Eddie jokes, waving me in.

I've been busy in the shop all week. I've hardly had time to do anything else. I've spoken to Caleb every night on video messenger but only as I've been working. I'm not sure I like the idea of being stolen. I ask where we're going.

'You'll see,' he says, as if I have no choice in the matter. I wash my hands as they're covered in print and glue.

We leave the shop and Caleb unlocks his car. I hesitate.

'Trust me,' he says. I squint at him as if to ask, why should I? 'I'll have you back safely in three hours. You won't regret it.'

I give in. We drive in the direction of Askham and I worry in case we're about to land at Lucille's house but he turns towards

Haweswater. He plays rock music quite loud and bounces his head to the beat as we drive. The conversation is trivial; he's DJ'ing all next week at the Rock Society student bar and I tell him about the shop orders.

Haweswater is low. I realise how much water it's lost in the month or so since I came with Lily. We've had a dry spring but I'm surprised it's this low. The shoreline looks like a crime scene; the edges have been drawn with white chalk. I've worked out why we're here before Caleb pulls over. Mardale Village is visible. You can tell where the bridge was and how the streets forked.

We get out the car and walk down. The mud is drying fast; we leave footprints but the mud doesn't cake to our shoes. I take photos as we go.

'Amazing,' he says. 'It's not been as low as this since 1995 apparently.' I tell Caleb the story I read about the Kings of Mardale. 'It's a very remote place to hide; there can't be a more isolated place in England. It's nowt but a dead end.'

We walk over where the bridge once was. I twirl around with my arms out over the bridge looking in all directions around me.

'As soon as word gets out, this place will be busy as hell,' he says. I realise he's videoing me so poke out my tongue at him. I was expecting to see a lot of building rubble but there's mainly mud and the edges of walls that once were. 'We could never tell if there were cellars here,' he says. He's right; it's hard to tell where any houses were.

'I can't see the painting being left here,' he says. 'I don't think those French dudes would have bought that story either, especially when they came back in 1984. If George Kimber didn't leave it here, he must have taken it to Askham with him, but then Colleen would know about it. It's bound to be with her mother, Lucille.'

I'm thinking the same thing, unless George brought it

back to Thackthwaite for Roland after all, but why would John Robinson then leave it behind?

'I still think Colleen knows more than she lets on,' he says. He might be right but there's no way we can ask her.

We walk towards the water's edge but the ground becomes muddier so we don't go all the way. We turn to face the ghost of the drowned village, the mountains rising high above it and I take a photo.

'Can you feel another painting coming on?' Caleb asks. He's getting to know me well.

We head back to the car and sit inside for a while looking over at the vast emptiness now created by the receding waterline. This used to be so green; lush fields of Mardale valley with a river, farmhouses, trees and hedgerows. We think of how the world has changed with technology but even this secluded valley isn't immune to changes we place on the Earth.

'Woah!' Caleb says as a Tornado fighter rips through the valley with a deafening roar. Another stark reminder of how the world has changed in the ninety years or so since these waters rose. We watch the jet turn on its side before rising over the fells and disappearing from view. 'I guess it's the ideal valley for training exercises, there's no one to complain about noise pollution.'

We head back to Penrith. The music is on and the windows are down, and I love the feel of the air brushing my arm; not that we can travel at any speed on these country lanes.

'You should come to one of our rock nights next week. I'm DJing but you can join me in the booth. Or dance, if you want.' I laugh; I don't dance. I do love rock music though but I don't think I could handle a rock night. 'It will do you good to get out and let your hair down. You live like a hermit.' Cheers. It won't do me good either and I definitely don't have any desire to go clubbing or let my hair down. The thought terrifies me, though the idea of seeing bands live appeals to me more. I tell him that I'd rather not but I'd maybe enjoy going to a gig. His face lights up.

'Deal!' he says. What have I let myself in for?

We get back to the shop, technically half an hour later than the promised three hours, not that Eddie notices as the shop is busy and I feel a bit guilty. I say goodbye to Caleb and help Eddie serve.

'It's been quiet,' he says, after the current round of customers leave. I'm surprised. 'We've only got those orders in today.' He points to my desk. There's a huge pile of books and paper. Not so quiet then. He laughs.

I work in the craft room until closing time. Eddie looks tired again and I offer to cook tonight, which he gladly accepts. I tell him about my afternoon in Mardale.

'I'm not surprised it's low after such a dry spring. I might take a ride out one evening.'

After tea I return to the barn and begin to paint. I look at the photograph I took looking back on Mardale with the mountains in the distance. I can see where a waterfall would be, given normal weather conditions. It's lined directly over the bridge. I can visualise the flow bringing life to the valley in the days before the flood. I start there, the focal point of my image, depicting the flow of time. The vivid greens of the mountain, the yellow and purple heathers that begin with the trees half way down; the darkness at the bottom of the painting – the sparse nothingness of a dead valley; a valley with only memories – a partly submerged bridge the only *anything* in the foreground. Only the sides of the green valley on the picture frame the scene like curtains on nature's stage. Curtains that can never close and a play people can never again see. I add a small yellow flower at the base of the bridge, maybe a dandelion, or a buttercup – the King of Mardale, attempting to reign again, until time brings the flood again.

CHAPTER 21

It amazes me how easy it is to zone out when I'm in the craft room. Often Eddie will call me to help behind the counter and I realise the shop has a dozen or more people inside. I've been working on orders all week; I'm often aware of people watching me and sometimes I'm not. I know Eddie is talking to someone but the conversation is ambient noise, like the passing traffic. I hear a cough close by that brings me back to reality. I look up to see Marcus. Stunned, I drop my scissors and apologise out loud. Marcus smiles. I think he's been watching me for a while.

'We've come to see you,' he says. I look over to the counter to see Eddie talking to a man with a mass of white hair. Didier Bernard. Wow.

'He wants to see the sketch with his own eyes. I've known about this visit for a few weeks but I didn't want to tell Lily. I've felt bad, it's torn me apart but I couldn't say.' I ask him why not?

'It's complicated. I like Lily; I want her to give me a chance. I've been dreading this trip but it's been out of my control.' I'm not sure I like this. My mind frantically tries to update itself on the mystery. How much does Marcus know? At what point did we keep him out of the loop. Why is he here? Why would Didier come all this way? The more I think the less I think this could be a social visit. I get up and walk past him towards Eddie and Didier without making eye contact; he follows me.

'Kayleigh. Nice to see you again,' Didier says, greeting me with a kiss on each cheek. 'I was telling your grandfather how talented you are. Marcus showed me the photographs of your incredible paintings.' I thank him and join Eddie behind the counter, faking a smile and tugging on Eddie's sleeve out of sight to let him know I'm suspicious.

'Would you let me see the sketch?' Didier asks Eddie.

'Did you come all this way to see it or were you just passing through, taking a chance?' Eddie asks.

'The sketch has been a mystery in my family for over a hundred years,' Didier says. Then he turns to me. 'I haven't been totally honest with you. There was another letter I didn't mention, I have it with me. I want to show you.' He goes to his pocket of his blazer jacket and pulls out an old envelope. 'Please. Let me explain at your house.'

All I can think of is Colleen's warning and the note saying not to tell anyone. Maybe it's too late. Maybe we would be in danger by being stubborn and could suffer Roland Robinson's fate. They're probably wondering why we're hesitating considering they won't know that we would know about the French baddies of old. I know where they live, as does Lily. I think Eddie has worked this out too.

'Yes, of course,' he says. 'I don't finish here for another hour. Have you a car or did you come by train?'

'We drove, yes.'

'Come back in an hour; you can come with us and I'll drop you back off afterwards.'

'That's very kind, thank you, sir.'

'There's a tea room opposite the church, maybe you can have a drink there while you wait.'

'Thank you, we will.'

They smile and leave and we serve customers before we can speak about it.

'I don't think they would have come in person if they were going to be a threat to us,' Eddie says. I'm glad we're on the same wavelength. 'I'm curious about the letter. What are the chances it mentions a painting?' High, I would think.

I text Lily and explain what's happening and about my conversation with Marcus. She texts back immediately, deeply concerned. I tell her that I'll keep her updated throughout the evening.

Didier and Marcus return and we leave right away. I sit in the back of the car with Marcus and Eddie takes the scenic route home to avoid the big roundabout at rush hour.

'You live in a beautiful part of the country,' Didier says as we approach Thackthwaite.

'Thank you. Did you drive from Southern France in a day?' Eddie asks.

'No, we drove as far as Kent yesterday and up to Cumbria today.' They must be shattered.

'Where are you staying tonight?' Eddie asks.

'We've booked a hotel in Penrith for two nights. We will stay locally tomorrow to have a rest before driving back on Sunday.'

We get to Thackthwaite and I show Didier the sketch while Eddie goes to the kitchen to feed the stove and put the kettle on.

'So strange to hold this in my hands,' Didier says quietly, as if he's the only person in the room. Marcus sits next to him, watching Didier's obvious wonder. Both of them are smiling and for a moment I forget Pandora's Box.

Eddie joins us with a tray of coffee and explains the story of the discovery fifty years ago. Didier listens, enthralled, and gets up from his chair to look at the cupboard.

'Incredible,' he says. 'It must have been an exciting find. Something of fairy tales.'

'It was. My mother had the frame made especially for it.'

Didier sits back down and pulls out the letter he mentioned earlier. 'A few weeks after the vandalism incident, my great-grandfather mentions in this letter that a horseman arrived with a delivery of art, including the sketch on the wood, taken from the olive tree. My great-grandmother, Emily, a proud and stubborn woman, rejected them. She gave them to an Englishman who had been staying there. He was working on the tower of Paris and his wife loved art. He was very grateful and stayed another day to help fix problems in the smithy.'

'Interesting,' Eddie says. 'Strange to think it's been hanging on that wall for fifty years. This begs a question though, why was it hidden?'

'My grandfather had a fascination with the story. He was never pleased that his mother had given them away. He wasn't a nice person and his English wasn't good; I think the Englishman had been scared by him.'

'Did your own parents ever take up his search?'

'My father did for a while. He hired private investigators, but he was a lazy man who threw his money at things and delegated. He soon gave up.'

'Is he still alive?'

'No. He died thirty years ago.' I quickly do the maths. He would have died after 1984, the last known approach to Colleen's family. This mystery probably was buried after all, until I opened Pandora's Box.

'You mention other artwork,' Eddie says.

'Yes. I was going to ask you if you were aware of any other artwork found here.'

'No. The entire place has been renovated in the past fifty years. There were people who lived here before we bought the property, they might have found something.'

'My grandfather tracked down the owners of the time. Apparently they did find something, but then they destroyed it.'

'Why would they do that?' Eddie asks. He's an impressive actor.

'Your guess is as good as mine.' Didier laughs. 'I suspect out of spite, knowing my grandfather, had he pressured them too hard.'

'So why ask me if I had found anything, if you knew the previous owners had already destroyed it?'

'Because I don't think they had what my grandfather was looking for.'

'Which is?'

Didier hesitates and reaches into his jacket pocket and pulls out another envelope, this one thick. 'Mr Halsey, I would really like to buy the sketch from you and take it back with me. I have ten thousand euros here. I think that's more than you would ever receive by auctioning it. The sketch is valuable to me, personally, rather than of any value to anybody else.' I bite my lip, itching to tell him that we know who sketched it but I remain quiet.

'That's a generous offer, but the sketch is also sentimental to me and my family.'

'Let's just say I want to succeed where my family failed. It's not so much sentimental, as much, it's more that I want…' he pauses as if he's trying to find the word, 'closure, I suppose. I loved my father but he wasn't a nice person. It would give me great pleasure to succeed in something where he failed.'

'I can understand that but I also have my own reasons to keep it. There's also no way that I can accept your offer without speaking to my family too. You say that you're in Penrith for a few days, maybe I can give you an answer tomorrow.'

'I respect that,' Didier says.

Eddie goes to the kitchen and returns with baked potatoes for everybody and a choice of toppings. We all seem to opt for butter and cheese. Conversation is light for a while and Didier looks around the room as he eats. I text Lily to tell her I'm still alive but don't tell her yet about the conversation.

'These are wonderful old English farmhouses,' Didier says. 'So much character and so many buildings. Do you keep animals?'

'Not any more. My parents kept chickens for a while but no

livestock. We rent the two fields opposite to the farmer down the road.'

'You should see Kayleigh's artwork,' Marcus says to Didier. My eyes widen and a knot in my stomach rips through me instantly, and it must show as Marcus looks at me. 'If that's okay? I should have asked you first. I just love your work.' I wonder if I should bring the paintings through or take them to see them in the barn. Did I tidy up? I don't think it's clean. I'm aware of all eyes on me and involuntarily nod and agree.

'Do you remember the paintings in my music room, Kayleigh?' Didier asks. I do, they were music-themed, almost fantasy, and some were on massive canvasses. 'My great-grandmother painted them all. She was taught and inspired by Berthe Morisot.' Weird, Caleb calls me by her name. Are they in this together? 'She regretted giving away the vandal's paintings after she had done so. She knew the effort and passion that would have gone into the artist's work but her resentment of the vandalism caused her to act irrationally.'

I tell him that she was a very good artist and that I'm surprised she wasn't renowned, especially considering her friendship with Morisot.

'She was. She held an exhibition in Paris once but her style was seen as retrospective at the time and she didn't get the respect she deserved. I think she had a unique style, personally.' She did, her subjects were so different to those of the impressionists of the time even if the style was the same. 'It would be good to have the wooden sketch back in the house. It would help close the book on the story and history of the house.'

He's appealing to my artist's conscience. He knows how I think. It's clever too, because it's probably working and I do want him to have it. Still, there's a niggle in my head that warns me not to trust him. He does seem honest; he certainly hasn't come here in any aggressive manner, but the sketch is so old it's part of our heritage too.

I apologise for the state of the place twice before I open the barn door. Thankfully it's not as bad as the vision in my head. Didier looks at the paintings with a big smile.

'I've never seen my house look quite this beautiful,' he says. 'These branches in the foreground belong to the olive tree.' I never realised. 'This is a passionate painting too,' he says looking at the fortress. 'You've captured its dark history and yet made the village bright, it's alive.' He definitely understands me.

My pride turns to panic in an instant. There's my painting of Mardale. It's going to be obvious that it's a drowned town; if he knows the history he's going to realise I know more than I've let on. There's no way I can hide it if he asks. I feel sick. He compliments me on Airaforce and my self-portrait before looking at the painting of Mardale. I watch his face rather than follow his gaze, hoping my panic doesn't show.

'Interesting,' he says. Oh crap.

I tell him that it's my latest work and that friend took me to a local reservoir last week, because it's dried up so much lately where we've had no rain. I felt inspired to paint it. I tell him a village once stood there and now all that remains is the bridge. He listens, still staring at the picture. His smile doesn't seem to falter but he studies it in detail, moving closer as I speak.

'You're a very clever girl, Kayleigh.' I'm not sure if he means that as a compliment or as a threat. 'You paint like a poet.' My eyes well, I can't help it. I thank him. For somebody to understand that, that I express my passion through visual metaphor, is the highest accolade I could ever have.

Didier puts his hand on my shoulder as we turn to leave. 'You're going to go far. You have a very special talent.' I smile; I'm too stunned to speak. I catch Marcus' eye and he winks.

We return to Eddie, who's clearing up in the house, and Didier continues his praise for my work to Eddie. I still don't know if I'm in trouble. I decide not to travel with them back to Penrith so say my goodbyes outside the car. No doubt I'll see them again tomorrow.

***

Dad and Polly come into the shop early. Eddie and I were talking until late last night. He's wary of Didier but also respects that he turned up personally. He reckons that since his family's aggressive tactics failed he might be trying the opposite.

'The sketch must mean a lot to their family, regardless of who drew it. Do you really think he wants it for personal reasons or because it's worth a fortune?' Dad asks.

'I don't know. The question really is that if we found out it was worth a fortune would we keep it or sell it?' Eddie says. 'In other words is there a price, or would we keep it anyway?'

'It's been on the wall for fifty years, would we have enjoyed it any more had it been worth something or would we feel the same?'

'That's my point,' Eddie says. 'If we accept Didier's offer and it turns out to be worth a fortune, would we feel duped? It's a matter of deciding whether it's potential value and sentimental value means more to us than Didier's offer.'

It's a lot of money to me but it's not so much to Eddie and Dad. Not that I would expect it to be shared with me anyway.

'Nothing will take away our memories of it, or the story of its discovery,' Dad says. 'What did you think of him, personally?'

'He's highly educated, very smooth and extremely confident. He was kind to Kayleigh too. His family have a history of violence though. It's hard to know whether he has the potential to turn.'

'And you, Kayleigh?' Dad asks.

I tell him that he knows his art and that his language has improved considerably in three months. He excused his bad English before.

'Hmmm. I guess he's still holding back information,' Eddie

says. Though so are we, and Didier probably knows it too. 'I'd love to be able to talk to a professional and work out how much the sketch would be worth if it can be verified that it's Paul-Eugéne Milliet's work.'

'Okay. Leave it with me, I'll phone around and see if I can find out,' Dad says. 'What time are they coming back?'

'Four o'clock.'

'I'll be back before then.'

CHAPTER 22

I'm making mistakes with my work today and had to scrap some rather than hand out substandard orders. It's hard to focus with so much going on. I texted Caleb to ask why he calls me Morisot and he replied to say she was the first French woman artist on the search results online. I haven't told him about our visitors; I'm not sure who I trust right now. I wonder what Colleen would make of this. Would we be selling out? Is it blood money? Was her great-grandfather killed to prevent the sketch getting into the hands of the French?

On the other hand, it's water under the bridge. Does it matter now? The sketch is only as valuable as what anyone is willing to pay for it. I can hear Eddie on the phone to his sister, Rosanna. From what I can make out of their conversation, she's willing to let Didier have the sketch.

It's three o'clock when Dad and Polly return.

'I've spoken with a couple of people, an auctioneer and an art dealer and they both say similar things,' Dad says. 'The artistic value alone, without any verification or provenance would just have antiquity value, possibly in the hundreds of pounds. It's the story that gives it value, if things can be verified. A collector could pay anything from one to one hundred thousand upwards. They said that it would be worth much more alongside Mr Bernard's letters than it would alongside the story of our discovery.'

'It makes sense,' Polly adds. 'It's worth more to Didier than it is to you, that's why he's willing to pay higher than you're ever likely to get for it yourself to have it in his possession.'

'This brings me back to my original question,' Eddie says. 'What is it worth to us? Is the sentimental value more important than the physical value?'

It's a dilemma. I know I'll miss it but in the end it's just a sketch; we have plenty of photographs of it now. I could make a collage and include the old photographs. Maybe it's the mystery I'll miss more. What if we never find out what happened to the painting?

This becomes a general thought. Dad and Polly remain in the shop to wait for Didier and Marcus, who arrive just before we close.

'Hello, again,' Eddie says. 'This is my son Peter and his friend, Polly. Did you enjoy your day?'

'It's a delightful town. We visited the castle, saw the giant's gravestone and enjoyed a wonderful English pub meal,' Didier says. 'Did you discuss my offer?'

'We have. My son's spoken to some professionals and we do understand that the sketch would be more valuable to you than us. We're trying to balance the physical and sentimental values.'

'You've done your homework. It's true, it will be worth considerably more to me than it is to you. The difference is, I have no intention of selling it,' Didier says. 'I just want it back in our possession. Rectify mistakes made by my family. I'm a proud man, Mr Halsey. I've been spoilt, I was born into money and I'm lucky, I have plenty and therefore I'm used to getting my own way. I don't want to go home empty-handed. If you let me have the sketch now, I will double my offer. I won't again. It's my gamble on its physical value eventually but it's more than you would ever sell it for. I will give you twenty thousand euros for it right now, to take it back with me.'

This is interesting because I know Eddie was going to accept ten. He hadn't got that far and Eddie continues the act, looking down at his hands in silence.

'It's up to you, Dad,' my father says to Eddie, softly.

Didier leans in towards Eddie and mumbles something to him; I can't hear what he's saying. I look over towards Dad, who shrugs. He pulls back again and there's no change of expression from Eddie.

'It's a generous offer,' Eddie says. 'I can understand why it means more to you than it would to me. I'm going to miss it.' Eddie reaches under the counter. He has already wrapped it in bubble-wrap and placed it in a bag. 'I brought it in with me in case.'

'Thank you, Mr Halsey. Of course you can come to France and see it whenever you wish. It would be a pleasure.' Didier hands Eddie the envelope and counts out another ten thousand euros. Eddie doesn't ring it in the till but writes from an old receipt book, as Didier counts.

'In receipt of wooden sketch, as discovered at Thackthwaite Farm in 1967 and purchased this day in 2017 for the sum of twenty thousand euros. Cash paid. Will that be okay?'

'Perfect, Mr Halsey, I appreciate it.'

Eddie hands over the sketch and Didier accepts with a handshake. Didier thanks us all personally with a hug or handshake. Marcus smiles as he approaches me.

'Thanks, Kayleigh. Please explain my visit to Lily. I don't want to stop seeing her; I couldn't tell her about this visit and she finished with me before it happened.'

I tell him that I will, then wish them both a safe journey home as they leave.

'I hope we don't regret this,' Eddie says as we watch them walk away. 'I hope we've done the right thing.'

'Time will tell,' Dad says. Polly hugs his arm.

'Did he threaten you, before you agreed?' she asks.

Eddie looks in my direction, and then says, 'No.'

***

I've been bringing Lily up to date all evening. I don't know how I feel about it all. I think it was genuine, even Didier's offer to come to France any time if we wanted to see the sketch.

'There's no way you can tell Colleen's lot, if she ever asks.' I know. That's where the majority of my guilt lies, and Eddie's guilt too from what he was saying in the car on our way home. I tell her about Marcus' closing words.

'I'll give him another chance. It was strange that he went along with Didier; they obviously know each other well, but I didn't think well enough for a two thousand mile road trip,' she says. That's true. He must have come to personalise the positive approach. Didier succeeded by creating as much honesty as he could, even if it was an illusion. The psychology worked.

I'm working on a photo collage as we talk. I've taken many photos recently of all the places connected with the sketch. Maybe we can replace it with a photographic story. I need to think of the layout. An idea hits me, but I'll need daylight.

'What will you do now?' Lily asks. Good question. Maybe we have to leave the mystery alone. I don't know what I'm going to tell Caleb yet. Eddie's right; Oliver might feel entitled to some of the money even though they wouldn't be in law. I don't think it will go down well when he finds out what we've done. I tell her that I don't know. I don't want to give up the hunt for the painting either.

'The wooden sketch must have been what they were looking for all along, if he wasn't too fussed that George Kimber had destroyed the painting.' I guess so. I still can't believe it was worth killing for. There's no doubt Didier knows his art though - they are a family of artists.

Caleb's been quiet this week as he's been DJing until late and sleeping most of the day. How things have turned around in two days: Lily could be back with Marcus and I might have to cool things with Caleb. I hope not, but this will be the big test for him.

I say goodnight to Lily and settle early for bed. I set my alarm early. I have a plan.

CHAPTER 23

The scene is perfect. The morning dew forms droplets on the leaves and petals that glisten in the low morning sun. The flowers are awakening to the new day. It's worth the early rise to take pictures of the garden with the house in the background. I've also brought my sketch pad and folding chair. I'm not good at painting outside but I can sketch the shapes and get perspective. I'll need to buy new canvasses today.

I finish up and have breakfast with Eddie in the house.

'I'll have to go to the bank first thing and get this money in,' he says. The thick envelope is in front of us on the table. 'Whatever balance it works out at I'll split four ways with you, your father and Rosanna. Though you should really be entitled to more, considering the work you've put in to it.' I don't mind; I wasn't expecting a cut at all and I've never had any serious money. I'll save it for now. I keep getting a wave of nausea every time I think of telling Caleb but really this has nothing to do with him and it's Eddie's decision in the end.

I would prefer not to work in the shop today. I'd much rather paint but there are still so many orders I don't want to fall too far behind. I hold the shop while Eddie goes to the bank. I have an uneasy feeling in case Didier paid in Monopoly money instead of euros. That would be our luck. Eddie is a long time too, which doesn't make me feel any better. I serve a steady flow of customers while he's out.

'Well that was an eye opener,' Eddie says when he finally gets back. My sense of dread grows. 'The bank told me I'd get a better exchange rate if I bargain at the travel agents. I've been to all of them in town. The problem is, where it was so much I had a whole load of security forms to fill out and explanations as to how I got the money.' He hands me a paying in slip for just over sixteen thousand pounds. 'I think we should have fish and chips tonight to celebrate.' Too right.

I still can't believe it. It's amazing how the value of art can grow with context. Every painting you see has a story, whether it's a local artist or an established master. And there's value in that story over centuries, regardless of how good the art is. I would never have considered the sketch would hold any real value. It's been there as part of the fabric of our lives for generations, hanging on the wall, barely noticed.

'I'll transfer the monies tonight. You deserve it,' Eddie says. I tell him that I'm going to give a thousand to Lily, she helped a lot, and none of this would have happened without her.

'No, I'll give her a thousand, you keep yours. I'll transfer the extra into your account for her.' That's so kind. I give Eddie a hug and thank him.

We see out the rest of the day in good spirits, I catch up on many of my orders and manage to get to the art shop mid-afternoon to buy more canvasses and oils. I can't wait to get started with my painting. We're eating our fish and chips at our usual place looking out over the fells from the roof of Penrith.

'This place has changed a lot. I used to come here with your father and eat from the same chippy,' Eddie says. 'People fear change but it's part of life. The town is so different now but those changes have made it better.' I hear this resistance to change a lot in the shop, especially among Eddie's generation. Eddie dips his chips in ketchup as he speaks. He's one of the few northerners who doesn't smother them. 'People my age don't like our memories to be damaged; we want to remember things how they were so that we can revisit memories with nostalgia. But that's not how it works.' I must be too young to recognise that feeling but if this view changed and the town built high-rise flats to spoil it, I would be upset too. 'What we crave is not the town the way it was before, we want our youth back. We want to relive those memories the way we experienced them back then; undamaged and uncorrupted by the passing of time.'

I shudder at the thought of Eddie's mortality. He's a fit and healthy man on the edge of retirement age but I can't bear the thought of him not being around. These memories are priceless to me. Maybe that's what his generation are so protective of ultimately; the mortality of memories.

I start painting as soon as we get home. I use the photo from this morning, alongside the one I took after we planted, for inspiration. For our family, the mystery started here fifty years ago; to think that my grandfather was younger than I am now. This house has been loved all those years, it holds memories and secrets. The garden is the latest new life. A piece of the old has now returned to its origin and I bring new hope and new art to the place, keeping the cycle of love and creativity inside these walls.

The dew represents a new dawn, a new chapter in the house. The sketch has gone but there's new art to replace it. Yet the memories remain, uncorrupted by time as I'm the latest generation who can share the stories. Home-grown art will now stand in place of the sketch, telling the story of what once was. The garden looks alive with colours of summer. The sloping kitchen roof shelters and protects, like a slate umbrella, impenetrable to anything that would spoil the hunger for the love the house maintains. The window in the centre of the frame upstairs is Eddie's memory room. It's only fitting that the sun's early rays should be reflected there, scattering photons of wonder back to the artist; to the new observer. Timeless stories, captured on canvas, and spoken in the oils.

I crawl into bed at three in the morning, alive, content and wide awake.

***

Rosanna doesn't change. She's larger than life with a big heart and sense of humour to match. It's hard to tell when she's joking or being serious. It's good to see her again. Eddie's baked a fruit loaf especially. She likes her food.

'Four generations have lived here now,' she says. 'Not bad going for a house that Dad's solicitor called *That heap of rubble*.' How could anybody call it that?

'It was in a bad state. The Huttons didn't have the money to modernise it properly so the house just got worse,' Eddie says.

'You're certainly the most talented out of all of us,' Rosanna says to me, looking up at the space where the sketch used to be. My collage is hanging there now. In the middle is the photo of the front and back of the wooden sketch. Coming away from those four corners are the large photos of my four paintings: The fortress, Didier's house, Mardale and our house. Between them are smaller photos of the discovery and other photographs I've taken connected to the mystery as well as photos of the letter from Didier's grandfather. The collage is placed on a canvass which looks as though there should be a post-impressionist's style painting behind it with blues on the top, rich greens on the bottom and coloured gardens on the sides. I sealed it so that the photographs wouldn't ruffle over time and Eddie bought a box frame for it to keep it all together. It turned out as well as I hoped.

'Kayleigh's done remarkable work there,' Eddie says. I'm glad he likes it; I was pleased with how well the painting of the house turned out too.

'Have you heard from the rich Frenchman since the weekend?' Rosanna asks.

'No, but Kayleigh's friend has heard from the young guy, Marcus. He said how happy Didier was with the sketch.'

Lily and Marcus have been talking all week. I think she's forgiven him now and she's planning to visit him soon. I transferred the money to her and she was ecstatic. Her family are well off but Lily never has much personal money. She's been spoilt throughout her life because she usually gets what she asks for but she rarely has money to spend on herself. What she has usually goes on fabrics and art supplies.

I've avoided Caleb as much as possible but he knows I've been busy. He said he'll come to Penrith soon and kidnap me again. I've been friendly to him but he probably thinks I'm being how Marcus was with Lily. I don't feel ashamed of the decision we made; I'm scared of being disappointed in Caleb if he reacts badly to the news.

'My conscience is bugging me for taking an equal share of the money from that sketch. I didn't exactly contribute,' Rosanna says, pouring herself the third cup of coffee in a row. How does she sleep? 'I think I should at least take Kayleigh out for a big spend-up of art supplies, from my share.' I laugh and tell her it's fine, I'm making money from what I'm selling in the shop too.

'Don't argue with your great aunt, my girl. Nobody does that. I can at least keep you stocked up in paints, cloths and messy stuff.' I laugh. I don't know how she thinks I work though I do make a mess; I lay down a sheet in case I drip paints on the carpet, it happens. 'What else do you need?' Rosanna hasn't seen my book gifts yet in the shop. She will tomorrow. I tell her that I need an extra pair of hands. She looks at me perplexed. Eddie laughs.

'I guess I'll be making a mess too then!' She might regret that.

Rosanna's keen to visit the Edgeworth house again but it's getting late and light is fading.

'I remember the old fella, I think he had a thing for our mum,' she says. Eddie laughs.

'He was smitten for sure, even if he was twice her age.'

'He was that. He used to walk down the lane in the summer if the milk had been left out too long in case the birds got to it first and leave it in the porch or washhouse if the porch was locked.'

'Oh, I remember that,' Eddie says.

I listen to them, watching their body language as they talk. Every now and then Eddie cuts off another slice of bread, breaks a part off, scrunches it to apply a small amount of butter then eats it, hardly looking away from Rosanna. Rosanna has her elbows on the table, hugging her mug lovingly in both hands. Both of them are in the late autumn of their lives yet both so alive. Their memories are a bond that connects them more strongly than their blood. I'm terrible at painting people and yet this image before me - the cupboard behind them, the dark beams overhead, the small farmhouse window letting in the dying light of the day, the orange glow of the wall light behind, the bread and the white coffee pot with primroses for decoration on the table - there's nothing at all to indicate this is 2017. It could as easily be 1888. I carefully raise my phone and discreetly take a picture.

CHAPTER 24

Mum and I didn't speak for many weeks after *Four* left. I floated about the house. I ate my food without engaging in conversation. I spoke to Jared and Rosie and laughed and joked with them as if nothing was wrong but ignored everything Mum said. Thinking back, she tried, but I was so repulsed by her for not loving *Four* the way I wanted him to love me, the way I thought I loved him. I wanted nothing to do with her. I spent a lot of time at Lily's house, most of that time I would be crying. She was good to me and in fairness blamed *Four* rather than Mum. I was having none of it.

When I kissed *Four* I could have sworn for a few seconds that he reciprocated. Over the weeks that followed I convinced myself that he loved me as much as I loved him. Mum had torn us apart. There was something electric about that kiss, something in the moment that connected our souls. And then remained with us. Was he lying in bed crying every night like I was? Was he recalling those few seconds repeatedly like me? He was my soul mate.

In my mind that was enough to fake the healing - knowing he was thinking of me like that. I told myself stories, programmed my own memory to believe that the things in my imagination were real. We could go anywhere together. Do anything. That was the start of the big lie. I didn't mean to cause harm, I didn't mean to damage people. I wasn't a nasty person. I didn't want to hate Mum but then I didn't want her to hate me. Eventually I spoke to her, answering yes and no questions. I'd wash up the dishes without being asked. Tell her about my day. But she seemed to remain cold to me. Detached. Maybe she was playing me at my own game but I became convinced she resented me.

After two months, feeling miserable at home and at school, where I was still being churned by the rumour mill, I reached out to Mum one evening. I was desperate for her to befriend me again, to be my mother. The conversation never got close to where I hoped.

'Well,' she said, 'you'll be glad to know the arsewipe that gave us so much heartache is happily settled with a twenty-one-year-old floosy. So at least someone's happy.' At first I thought she meant Dad. Then I realised she meant *Four*. I felt the world crash around me in that moment. I still don't know to this day why she thought that telling me would make me feel happy. I left for my room and cried harder than at any other time in my life. The pain inside was so bad; that gut-wrenching feeling of heartbreak and betrayal. I needed a release, anything to distract me from the pain ripping through my soul.

At first I teased my wrist. I was in the bathroom, despising the eyes of that girl in the mirror. I didn't recognise her. I felt sick. I felt the pain of betrayal and I took the razor and rested it on the flesh and swiped, just enough to cut. I felt a slight sensation but more adrenaline than anything. I was still in tears, the scene was blurry. Then I did it again and made what I thought was a gentle slit. It hurt more than I thought it would and at first the blood welled like my tears but then it gushed. I screamed and grabbed a towel as the pain intensified and I panicked and slipped, colliding with the sink unit. I screamed again, trembling and saw the towel around my wrist turn red quickly. The family were downstairs. I could hear the television on and Jared and Rosie arguing. Mum must have been in the kitchen. I made for the door but felt light headed. I remember screaming again and then nothing.

I awoke in a hospital bed two days later. There were monitors and wires everywhere and I was in pain all over. Mum looked so sad; Dad looked like he'd aged overnight. The pain was nothing compared to the crippling guilt I felt. And my love for *Four* instantly turned to anger.

***

'It's all Kayleigh's wonderful work. There she is, go and say hello…' Oh God, not again. Everybody that comes into the shop gets to see me at work and Rosanna sings my praises and elevates me way higher than I deserve. It's hard to work knowing I have constant red cheeks. She's loud too; I can usually focus on my work and zone out of the customers and Eddie when he's here but Rosanna's bellowing voice makes it impossible to switch off. There's only the two of us in the shop today. Eddie's having a day off. He's going to a book festival tomorrow in the hope of picking up new stock so we've convinced him to have a rest today.

Rosanna's sales pitch is certainly successful; that's the third order in this morning. I've also had a request to make a paper flower out of the inner sleeves of classic rock vinyl records. I realised I could still make them in the same way as long as they were cut and folded properly.

'That's Lily's remaining dress sold,' Rosanna says, joining me in the craft room after the shop empties. 'She'll have to make some more. It's exhausting work this.' I laugh. She must have had sales experience. Lily was planning to come up at the end of next week after her final exam and bring new stock but Marcus has convinced her to go to France instead. I joked that she cares about him more than me and she took it seriously so I've been feeling guilty all day. I would hate her to feel under pressure to see me or prioritise me over her boyfriend. At least I have a positive reason to message her again.

The author who wrote the blog about my work and this

shop made a slide-show video of my work and shared it on social media writers' pages and it's gone viral in the writing community. The video now has over ten thousand views. I created a page for the shop last night, since Eddie refuses to have a website, and messaged the author who has added the link to her post. As a result my phone pings every minute with a new notification for followers. I've had over two hundred likes already and the page isn't even a day old.

'Are you playing a game on that thing?' Rosanna asks. I tell her what I've done. 'That's clever. I think the entire generation of Halsey brains were dumped in your head, girl.' I don't know about that, Jared's not far behind. 'As if you weren't busy enough.' She has a point.

When we get back to Thackthwaite, Eddie greets us with food fit for a king – as Gerard Bernard would have said. He's made a roast dinner, apple crumble for dessert, more bread and prepared food for us to heat through tomorrow. So much for resting.

I need to rethink the workspace in the barn. Rosanna spent nearly a thousand pounds on art supplies for me yesterday. I have enough to keep me going for a while, including a dozen large canvasses. I shoved four on top of my wardrobe, two beside the cabinet, and two behind my desk but the rest are leaning against the wall next to my easel. It's all tempting me and enticing me but I know if I start I'll not want to stop until I finish, which will probably be breakfast time. I take another look at the photo I took at the table of Eddie and Rosanna. I'll never be that good.

I climb into bed and message Caleb quickly. More excuses for being quiet today but I tell him about my social media page for the shop and about my order for the record sleeves. I start watching video tutorials online on how to paint people, especially in the way the post-impressionists did. I also find a documentary on Berthe Morisot. I love her work; she shares my passion but it's Vincent van Gogh's work that I admire the most. I watch two documentaries, one of which curates his work in Provence. I respect his eye for colour and the context of his vision. I'm forced to stop as my battery runs out just after midnight, but I just have enough time to read Caleb's reply. He's coming to Penrith tomorrow. There goes my sleep.

CHAPTER 25

Eddie leaves early. I'm still in bed when I hear his car start up and crunch the gravelled driveway as it makes its way out. I only slept for three hours; partly because of the heat but mainly because I was preparing my speech for Caleb. At least I can't be kidnapped today as Rosanna will need me in the shop. This time I'll get Caleb to help me in the craft room; he'll love it, I'm sure…

I prime Rosanna on the way to the shop and warn her not to mention the sketch, explaining about Caleb's connection to the mystery. The morning is quiet at first so I manage to get a productive start. I'm defacing the inner sleeves of Led Zeppelin and Black Sabbath albums when Caleb arrives. From the horror in his face you would think I was mutilating babies. I feign an evil face as if I'm enjoying every second.

'I knew you were a psycho,' he says. 'I hope the God of Rock has mercy on your soul.'

I tell him that I'm turning Satan's music into something beautiful.

'You didn't just say that! I should walk out of here and never speak of your name again.' Oh, the irony.

I joke that he might do that anyway when I tell him my news. I look up at him, the horror on his face increases. I point at the chair and motion for him to sit down. I resist the urge to hand him a book just yet and order him to start ripping the pages. There's no point delaying. I tell him that Eddie's sold the sketch.

'No way! Who to?'

I tell him about Didier's visit and explain about Didier's stories. I don't mention what price he sold it for. It's none of his business. I tell him the wood is back in its rightful place, it's gone home. Caleb doesn't say a word. In fact his expression lacks any emotion at all. I can't tell if he's angry or amused. I look back down at my work, my heart rate increasing with his silence. After thirty seconds, I look back up and joke that I had a feeling he'd take it badly.

'No. I'm just shocked,' he says. 'I wish you'd told me.' He looks down. I expected anger but I'm getting sadness. I wasn't expecting this, I'm not prepared. I tell him it's been manic here, I wanted to tell him to his face, not on messenger.

'I just thought.' He hesitates. 'I don't know, I thought we were in this together, that's all. Oliver would have bought it if Eddie was going to sell it. Probably at a fair price too. We're also part of its history. Oliver made a wishing well from the bell in the washhouse after all.' It never once occurred to me that Oliver would be interested in buying it. With all these dire warnings and people hurt, I had thought anybody interested in it might steal it or worse.

I tell him I'm sorry. We were caught off guard by Didier's visit and had to make a decision quickly.

'What's done is done. We'll have to find this other painting instead.' I ask if he's mad at me.

'Why would I be? It's not your fault.' I don't know if I feel relief, sad or excited. On the one hand, he's passed a major test. On the other, I've hurt him. I'm making a habit of doing this; a guilty conscience and social anxiety create a vicious circle. I pass him a book and ask if he fancies helping me by carefully tearing the pages out. I see the first smile of the day, albeit brief.

The final Classic Rock flowers look good. I use black lace rather than the usual white and consider painting the stick black too but don't have my paints here.

'It would look cool in black. Maybe you could get a silver pen afterwards and vine some dots like leaves up the stem.' Good idea; that would look effective. I'm impressed at his creative contribution. We work in silence for a few minutes but I can tell he's still digesting my news.

'Dare I ask how much Eddie got for the sketch?' I was prepared for this question and always thought best to play the innocent card. I tell him I don't know and that was between Eddie and Didier. I don't think he believes me for one moment.

'Fair enough, I get it,' he says.

The shop is busy for a while so I help Rosanna serve customers while Caleb continues ripping pages but there's a lull mid-afternoon so I ask Rosanna if Caleb and I can grab a late lunch. We go to the tea rooms by the church yard again. I deliberately pepper him with questions about his DJing and gardening and try and get him to talk about himself more – anything to move the conversation away from the mystery and the fact that I've let him down again. He must hate Eddie right now.

'I'm not looking forward to telling Oliver the news,' he says. Obviously my distractions aren't working. Does he have to tell Oliver? I suggest he doesn't.

'I guess not. I'll feel bad if I tell him and guilty if I don't. I never thought your grandfather would sell it; I didn't see him as a money type.'

It's strange when the situation is presented in black and white. Eddie isn't the money type; the decision was based on his conscience more than money. The sketch was more valuable to Didier's story than it was to ours. However, when you erase all the sentimental attachment, Eddie did sell out. Didier made a monetary offer, Eddie deliberated and accepted. That doesn't make him the money type; it just means that the opportunity value of the money was more than the value of his sentimental attachment to the sketch. I could explain this to Caleb but he would never understand. So I just shrug and suggest he had his reasons.

'Don't tell the Robinsons whatever you do,' he says. I instinctively wince. I hope whoever left the mystery notes never turns up again. Caleb's logical reasoning is refreshing in some ways because he obviously has empathy. Often, those who see things in black and white are cold, arrogant and lack compassion. It's rare for them to find any colour. I'm glad that Caleb's showing his own colours. I like him more as I'm getting to know him.

We return to the shop and it's busy so I need to help Rosanna. Caleb tactfully motions that he'll head back so I smile and wave him off as he goes. I don't get much more done in the craft room but I bring back the Classic Rock paper flowers with me to finish off at home.

'No wonder Eddie needed help,' Rosanna says, 'I'm exhausted after two days.' He does well. Maybe he can afford permanent staff now the shop is extra busy and I'm also on hand. Eddie can rest more and be more selective in his buying.

After we eat I go to the barn and finish off the flowers. Lily had her last exam today so I video call her and tell her about my conversation with Caleb.

'He's a keeper, Kayleigh babe. Maybe it's about time you upped a gear. Suggest a date or something.' The thought terrifies me but maybe she's right. He didn't disappoint me, he's taken the relationship and friendship on my terms and I genuinely like him. I can only respect that. I tell her that I will.

'Yes! About bloody time,' she says. I laugh.

'I'm off to France this weekend. Marcus is picking me up from Marseille. I wonder if I'll get to see the wooden sketch in its new home.' That will be surreal.

I show Lily my finished paper flowers with the silver vine up the stem. Caleb was right, it looks effective and Lily is impressed too.

'You should send a picture to lover-boy so he can see what you've done.' Arghh, don't call him that.

I'm tired. After such little sleep last night, the day is catching up on me. I end the call with Lily and get myself ready to settle. I hear Eddie return as I get into bed and the day ends very much the way it began. Only instead of feeling anxious, I feel excited. I text a goodnight message to Caleb and thank him for not being mad at me and apologise again for not telling him sooner.

***

It's Rosanna's last full day. I think she'll need a rest after this week but it's been good for Eddie to have her help. The shop is well stocked again. Eddie returned from the book festival with twelve boxes of new books as well as a line of diaries, notebooks and some bookish jewellery. I bought a bracelet with delicately painted clay book beads on it; I'd probably be able to make something like that.

The customer loved their Classic Rock paper flowers. I posted a photo of them on the shop page on our social media and we've had tons of enquiries. The page has reached a thousand followers in under a week.

'The shop is becoming well known among the literary community. Many people have heard the shop mentioned in the past few months,' Eddie says. 'It's strange considering I've been running it for twelve years.' I'm pleased for him.

I haven't spoken much with Caleb as I've been busy. He tried to get me to go over and see him but I'll have to do that next week. Eddie's keen to give me some time off too now. I don't mind being busy, I love what I do so I don't really think of it as work, but I really want to paint again. I found some books in the shop about painting people in everyday situations. I keep looking at the photo I took of Eddie and Rosanna at the table. They were either side of me with the table in the middle so I don't know whether to make them the focal point of the painting or the table, or maybe the wages cupboard in the background.

Rosanna's helping me in the craft room while Eddie serves. There's been a steady flow of customers but we're not too busy. I'm chatting with Rosanna when Eddie comes to us, looking agitated.

'I need to go back to the house quickly. Could you look after the shop for a couple of hours between you? I won't be long.'

'Yes, sure,' Rosanna replies. 'Is everything okay?'

'Yeah. I just need to go back quickly.' He turns to leave and Rosanna and I look at each other.

'I'll go and man the till then,' she says.

At first I'm okay but as the afternoon wears on a feeling of dread takes over. I feel clumsy and my folding isn't accurate; it's out of character for Eddie. I hope he's okay. Every time the door opens I look up in case it's him. I'm not making my best work so I abandon my crafts for a while and help Rosanna.

'He's been gone for four hours now,' she says. 'Maybe he had to meet someone? I'll give him another half hour then phone.'

I wonder if he'd heard from Oliver; maybe Caleb told him after all. I take another custom order for a notepad and box, half looking out the window. It's another sunny day so the town is busy and school children make their way home, adding to the numbers. I don't miss school, or my daily walk home in all weathers. When the shop empties Rosanna phones Eddie but there's no answer; hopefully he's on his way back.

As closing time approaches, he's still not back.

'I guess we're going to walk home,' Rosanna jokes but her gaze is constantly out the window. For once, I wish I had my car. There's still no answer when we call him.

I call Dad as I know he'll be up this weekend to see Rosanna off. Maybe Polly can take us home. It's unlike Eddie to be out of touch for so long, and thoughts of him lying at home ill or having had an accident cross my mind and I fight them off. I'm mid call when I see Eddie pull up outside.

Rosanna opens the door. 'About time too!' she yells. I end the call with Dad and join them.

'Sorry,' Eddie says. I notice a change of clothes. 'I had something to do then spent over two hours on the roadside. Both left hand side tyres blew, must have been a sharp pothole or something. I only had the one spare, so walked for ages to phone for help.'

'You not have your mobile? We've been calling.' Rosanna says.

'I forgot to pick it up before I set off.'

'Typical.'

'Friday fish and chips?' he says, as if we could refuse.

We go to the chippy then drive to our usual place to eat. I can't tell if Eddie is faking his jovial mood. There's something that seems different. I'm not used to him being anything but transparent and I'm dying to ask why he went home. Maybe it's something he doesn't want to discuss in front of Rosanna and he'll tell me later. Rosanna doesn't seem bothered or even curious.

It's a glorious summer evening. I can't think of the last time it rained. I wonder how Haweswater will look now. There's been hosepipe bans for over a month all over the country. I get a message from Lily to say she's at the airport about to board her plane to Marseille, lucky girl.

We get back to Thackthwaite and I join Eddie and Rosanna for a coffee and chat before going to the barn. I notice a rarely-used mug in the sink. Eddie's had a visitor but I don't ask. I'll prime him tomorrow after Rosanna's gone.

I'm tired. I'm not sleeping too well with my busy mind and the summer heat. I guess evening coffee won't help. I leave just as the daylight is beginning to fade. I say goodnight and as I leave the outside light comes on. I look back and see Eddie and Rosanna still at the table. Usually you have to manually switch the light on. I look up and notice it's a new casing too. Eddie's fitted a security light. I look to my left, and notice Eddie has put up the CCTV as well, focussed on the driveway in front of the house. What's going on? Why do this now?

I return to the barn but I'm nervous. I remember Didier whispering something to Eddie before he accepted the offer. Could that be connected? My phone pings as I get into bed. It's Lily; she's arrived safely in France. I shudder. God, I hope my paranoia is unfounded. I message her back:

Glad you arrived safely. Take care, if there's anything to give you any cause for concern, get out of there quickly. Love you Lily-pops x

CHAPTER 26

Dad arrives with Polly to see Rosanna for an hour or so before she leaves. I'm at home as Polly will drop me off at the shop to help Eddie later. I show them the CCTV and security light.

'I think he's just being safe, especially where you've had visitors lately,' Dad says. 'Maybe he got somebody in to fit them and that's why he came back yesterday.' I never thought of that. It's possible, but why be so secretive about it?

'I'm pleased. It's about time this place had some security,' Rosanna says. Dad agrees. I've never felt unsafe here before but with those notes and warnings and the washhouse door being tampered, Rosanna is probably right.

The postman arrives as we're about to leave and there's a letter for me in a handwritten envelope. I open it as I make my way to the barn to get my phone.

Hi Kayleigh,

I thought I'd write you a letter since I can't get to see you lately.

You were right when you suggested we should build a relationship out of our friendship, I think we would have struggled to maintain it. I don't think we could be together. It's not that I'm not attracted to you, you're beautiful, but you're so self-absorbed. You prioritise money over everything. I'm not talking about the wood, even though money played a part there too. I'm talking about priorities. You're working all hours to meet your orders, and that's great for your business and getting recognition – you deserve it. There's just no time for anybody else.

You used to talk to me while you worked, now you don't. You can't find time to come and see me and when I see you, I have to kidnap you and get permission for even an hour. You held back on me about the Robinsons and again about Didier. Even when you apologised, it was more about you and about how my reaction would affect you.

I know you were worried about us having a relationship in case I left you. I understand now that it would have happened as you feared.

I'm sorry if I upset you now by this letter. It's just I wanted more. I wanted a friendship that meant something: trust, respect and mutual terms. I can't spend every day wondering when I'll get to see you, or wondering if I'll even be able to speak to you tonight. I've done everything I can but I can't cope with the friend zone. I just hope you understand.

So good luck with all you do. I think you'll be a millionaire one day and be recognised for your art all over the world.

Maybe see you again in another universe, Caleb.

I run upstairs to the bathroom and the sobbing starts. I didn't see this coming. And what's more, he's wrong.

I hear Polly call downstairs but I look a state, I can barely see myself in the mirror as tears blur the image. She's obviously heard me as I can hear the concern in her voice as she walks up the stairs. I don't want to see her or anyone right now. I'm lying. I want Mum.

'Are you alright, Kayleigh?' I've left the bathroom door open. I open my mouth to speak but nothing comes out, just the tears again and my face scrunches and I can't control it. My usual mask won't fit. Polly hugs me to her and I show her the letter, which she reads while holding me. I feel such a failure. I can't do anything right with relationships or friendships.

'He hasn't got to know you well enough,' she says. 'He sees in black and white.' I've thought that too in the past. How the hell can I be broken-hearted when I wasn't even in a relationship with him? I didn't want a relationship because I didn't want to be hurt. I didn't want a guy to leave me, but now Caleb has left me anyway and I'm still hurting. I can't win. Why do guys do this? All the time.

'Do you want me to come back and get you in an hour or so?' It's probably better but I can't leave Eddie. I shake my head and wipe my face on a towel. I quickly reapply some eye makeup and fake a smile in her direction. 'You'll pass. Come on.' She takes my hand and leads me out of the room.

I get into the back of the car with Dad and I apologise for taking my time. I really did need the bathroom but not for the reasons they would think, but at least it's a conversation killer.

I've never been obsessed with money. Most of my money goes on art stuff or presents for birthdays and Christmas. I don't work late for the money, I work late so that I can meet the orders and not let people down. I feel a responsibility to them. Caleb is right about not having time for him in the evenings lately but that's also because I've had people with me. I've not had time for myself either, to paint. I'm trying to be sociable. It wasn't as if I didn't want to talk to him or to meet him.

I don't know how to reply. If I tell him he was wrong he'll think I'm being aggressive. I don't want to beg for his friendship either or he could take control of our relationship. He's right that we need to have mutual terms but he doesn't know that he had done enough for us to negotiate those terms. Am I really self-absorbed? That's the worst letter I could have received. I'm always thinking about others. I'm always questioning my motives.

Did Mum feel like this when her boyfriends left? Did she kick them out or was she left feeling this pain and lack of self-worth? This time yesterday I was as happy as I could be. Life sucks.

I hardly speak in the car. We get to the shop where I take over so that Dad, Eddie and Polly can take Rosanna to the station. Within a few steps inside the shop, Eddie asks if I'm okay. I might fool Dad and Rosanna but there's no fooling Eddie. I scrunch up my nose and say that I'll tell him later.

Alone in the shop I feel deflated. I'm desperate to reply or acknowledge Caleb's letter but don't know if I should. I want to phone Mum but I'm scared customers might come in. So I wait. Eddie returns with Dad and Polly after half an hour; I assume Polly will have told them what happened. I really wish I wasn't in the shop today. I just need thinking time. I go to my craft room when they get back and eventually Polly escapes to joins me. I ask if she told them.

'Eddie asked,' she said. 'He noticed you were down. I didn't say I'd read the letter, I just told him you had a letter from Caleb that upset you.' Fair enough. 'He was wrong, you know, Caleb.' As much as I'd like to think so, he wasn't. Not when you look at it in black and white, how he sees it. He was wrong about the money but I can understand why he would think it. I'm a terrible friend. I let him down, I kept important things from him and was too wrapped up in my work to realise he wanted more from our friendship. He wanted us to be friends. I like my own company. I enjoy having time to myself to just do what I want, even if it is work. I'm not cut out for a relationship. I hope Lily doesn't see my friendship like Caleb does.

I thank her and ask for advice on how I should reply.

'Do you like him?' I nod. 'Then tell him. Leave the ball in his court and if he returns it you can explain yourself. If you give it a shot and it doesn't work out then you have nothing to lose. But if it does, then you have everything to gain.'

I guess so. He's already gone. I don't want to beg or be seen as begging. I compromise.

Hey Caleb,

I got your letter. I respect how you feel but you're wrong about the money. I work so that I don't let people down. I was wrong in not finding time for you and I apologise. I do want to see you again. Yes, as a friend, but I've grown to like you too and enough to want to spend time with you and get to know you more. I won't message you again. It's up to you. I can't guarantee I won't let you down again but I can guarantee I'll try my best. Kayleigh x

I show Polly before I hit send.

'Perfect,' she says.

It's lunchtime before Dad and Polly leave. The shop is steady with customers but I join Eddie and talk between serving them. I tell Eddie about the letter and he laughs.

'He really doesn't know you, does he?' My fault, I guess. Do I really know him either? Apparently not, considering how he's been feeling over the past few weeks. No quick reply from Caleb but at least my conscience is clearer. I mention to Eddie that I noticed the CCTV and security light.

'There was no way I could set that up myself; I'll have to show you how to use it. The CCTV is connected to the Wi-Fi and records in twenty-four hour cycles. You can watch it on any device connected to our Wi-Fi and there's a separate monitor with memory in my room if I wanted to extend the recording, say if we went away for a week.' The shop is quiet, and Eddie continues talking, walking towards the door. 'I got professional advice in the end and had it properly fitted. It was worth doing it anyway and it will bring my insurance down in the long run. I'm hungry now; mind if I dash to the bakers and get us something?' I smile and give him a thumbs-up as he leaves.

As much as Eddie knows me well, I know him well too. I still get the feeling he's acting out of character. He's usually laid back even when busy. Lately he's been on his feet more, always seems occupied and makes more excuses to leave the shop or have time off. Even getting the security fitted professionally without telling anybody seems strange. Maybe I'm just being paranoid in wake of the letter. I've lost my ability to read people and I'm not sure if I should trust my intuition.

I message Lily saying that I hope she's having a better day than me. I get a message back:

I'm in Arles. Loads to tell you. What's up, Kayleigh babe? Hope your day gets better x

I'm glad she's okay. I smile and just text back that I've had one of *those days* and that I'll be fine. Still no reply from Caleb.

Eddie returns with food and I escape to my craft room to eat. As the hours go by and Caleb doesn't reply, part of me hopes that he doesn't. When I think of the emotional energy involved in devoting myself to a relationship, I don't think I have it. I want to be loved and I want to love but there's so much I love about my life and the world. I'm not lonely, I'm not miserable any more. I'm never bored. Some people can't function outside of their social circles and have to binge-watch television to fill their time. I don't even have a television. Maybe I want to be loved for what I do rather than who I am. Maybe I'd rather hide in obscurity and let my art represent me. Banksy has got it right. I want to paint so bad.

There's still no reply by closing time. Caleb must have made up his mind, or moved on already, which wouldn't surprise me either. Eddie drives back and my thoughts turn to the CCTV camera. It's not that we'll sit and watch nine hours of footage every day, it's more a case of knowing we can, should we notice any disturbance. Not that there appears to have been one as we pull into the driveway.

We get out the car and Eddie pauses, looking over to the washhouse.

'I could do with sorting that shed out. There are books in there to go through as well that will need dusting down,' he says. 'Do you think you could man the shop on your own tomorrow?' I don't mind. Sundays are usually quieter. 'I'll give you the day off Monday to make up for it.' Sounds perfect to me, I can paint.

I help Eddie make dinner and afterwards we both head to the washhouse. I grab the watering can and give the garden its usual evening soak then help Eddie lift all his stuff out of the washhouse. The stone walls are painted white inside but it's dry. It seems to maintain the same temperature summer and winter, always cooler in the summer and the stonework seems to radiate enough heat in the winter to stop it getting too cold.

By the end of the evening, as light fades, everything is out of the washhouse. Eddie takes the boxes of books into the house to go through. Many can probably be used for paper flowers. I'm tired so decide to have a shower in the morning early and settle at a reasonable hour. I receive a message from Caleb as I'm getting ready for bed.

I've spent the day wondering if I should reply or not. Maybe we shouldn't give up on each other too quickly after all. When can you have time off?

I reply that I'm off on Monday and suggest I go to his – which was always my plan to do at some point during this week. He replies with a smiley face emoji, *Thanks!*

So much for painting.

CHAPTER 27

'I think there's another painting,' Eddie says at breakfast. 'I've been thinking about it for the past week or so. Didier already knew I had the wood and he knew the painting had been destroyed. So why ask me if I'd found any other artwork?' Yes, I remember now. I had just assumed it was the wood they were looking for. 'Maybe the note we received was for a different painting?' He could be right; I try to process Eddie's thinking. 'But if the painting was here, then why didn't Colleen know? Did her grandfather not tell her or did he not know himself? That made me think; maybe Roland gave it to Brandon Edgeworth?' That would make sense. If he left his house in the seventies because he was too old then he will be dead by now, maybe even his children too. Why would the note suggest it could still be here?

I like that Eddie's still thinking about it. I don't like the idea of letting the mystery go just because we've sold the wooden sketch. I drive to Penrith deep in thought. No wonder Eddie's been different lately, if this has been on his mind.

The shop is fairly quiet but I can't get any craft work done. Mrs Ruskin, the author who wrote the blog article and ordered the competition prizes comes in.

'I'm back for more,' she says. 'Your prizes were a huge success; I've been asked to make more available.' I show her some of the new ideas and thank her for the article.

'It's wonderful that you've had such a positive response from my blog post, you deserve it; I love what you do here. This is my new favourite shop.' She notices we've put her books on the front display and picks up her latest and smiles. 'Writers struggle to get their books noticed. It always helps when independent book shops make an effort to promote local and independent authors.' Eddie is always good about that. 'This one's doing well so far, I'm happy with it.'

I need to read her books. I used to read a lot; I don't have the time anymore, which is ironic since I'm working in a book shop. I tell her about Lily's dresses and show her the photos. She loves the idea of them; hopefully I'll have Lily's latest creations in before she returns to collect her orders. She notices when I swipe past the photos of my paintings.

'You like fine art too?' she asks. I show her my paintings properly. 'I'm going to have to commission you for my next book cover, aren't I?' Wow, I hope so, I'd love that; translating a story into art.

I keep thinking of that idea after she leaves. I could do that for any book in truth; a visual interpretation of an existing story. Inspiration could be endless.

The afternoon is steady and I'm relieved when four o'clock arrives. I close up and head home. Hopefully Eddie will be pleased with the day's takings. I pull into the drive and it's chaotic. All the shed tools are still out and there's rubble outside the door. What's Eddie been doing?

I get out the car and Eddie pokes his head around the washhouse door frame with a grin and I laugh. His face is covered in dirt and dust.

'This seemed like a good idea at the time,' he says. There's a gaping hole in the wall where the bell mounting used to be. 'I had this hunch. I was obviously wrong but I had to find out. That note about Edgeworth ringing a bell? I thought it was a cryptic clue because I remembered Oliver's tobacco tin, where he found the note behind the bell. Do you remember?' I can't think. It was a light bluey-grey beaten-up tin if I remember. I shake my head. 'It was Edgeworth tobacco; that was the brand.'

Oh. I can see why he thought that then. The tin was found on the mount ledge under the bell sink. He obviously didn't find anything. My mind automatically goes where I don't want it to. Did Oliver's parents find the painting when they removed the bell? I'm going to have to ask Caleb outright tomorrow.

'I never realised it would make this much mess or take this much effort,' Eddie says, trying to fit the wooden supports back. 'I have some plaster out there somewhere but probably not enough. I might need to improvise.' I tell him I'll make dinner. Bless him, what a discovery that would have been if he was right. It might have been a clue but then we must be out with our timing because if the painting was taken with George Kimber while the wood was hidden, then the note in the tin wouldn't have made sense. Besides, he would have had to remove the bell before placing the painting there.

I get changed after dinner and help Eddie. I clean the sandstone shelves and flooring with a bleach solution while Eddie repairs the wall. The pig-skin pink shows through in places; it would be cool to sandblast it all back to its original state. Ideally the walls could do with a fresh coat of paint too. Eddie had already brushed them all down so that they're free of cobwebs and flakes. By nightfall the place looks clean even if the driveway is cluttered. I'll help put things back in tomorrow after my trip to Durdar.

***

You would think I would have slept well after such a tiring day but I didn't. I don't know what Caleb expects of me today and I worried all night. Would I let him down again? Will he expect more of me that I can offer? Will I stumble over my words and come across as a stammering monkey? Thoughts were plaguing me all night. I was up early and had a shower and I'm now having a clothes crisis. It's a hot day and I doubt we'll go anywhere, so I don't need to be too smart. I don't fancy wearing jeans in this heat either so I opt for denim shorts and a thin white embroidered top.

There are country lanes all the way to Caleb's house and it takes nearly an hour to get there. I eventually pull up at a small row of semi-detached houses in the tiny village. Caleb opens the front door before I get out of the car. No time to psyche myself up, I take a deep breath then get out the car, smiling. He looks good in three-quarter length jeans, a Harley-Davidson t-shirt and baseball boots. His fringe hangs over one eye.

I'm introduced to his mother, Sue, and Daisy, the Border collie whose tail whips my shins so hard I'm worried that my legs will bruise. Caleb puts the kettle on while Sue sits opposite me with an e-cigarette, doing a crossword.

'Oliver insists I bring you over for a bite to eat at lunchtime so you can see the bell,' Caleb says. That's cool. I stop myself asking if he knows about the sketch.

'Modern day Anatonia?' Sue says, interrupting without looking up.

'Try Turkey,' Caleb replies in an instant. I'm impressed.

'I hate geography,' Sue says.

'Have you done any more paintings lately?' Caleb asks.

'Opposite of imagine?' Sue says before I can answer. I smile and shake my head.

'Mum? Do you have to?'

'Four letters.'

Caleb grimaces, shakes his head then smiles, motioning me up, with two mugs in his hand.

'We're going in the sitting room,' he says.

'Starts with K.'

'Try "know".'

'No need to be rude.'

'I'm not, I mean the word, "Know". With a K.'

'Oh. That works.'

'Come on,' Caleb says to me, walking out the kitchen into the hallway, 'before she asks again.' I laugh.

'Sorry about that. She's got her problems, she means well she just doesn't do company.' I know that feeling but I hope I don't come over that awkwardly.

We talk without bringing up the letter he wrote. Looks like it might be an eternal taboo. Daisy joins us. She sits on the floor in front of Caleb opposite me with her tongue out, watching me. I find myself looking her in the eye more than Caleb as I talk. I tell him about Eddie deciphering the note incorrectly and explaining his thought process with the tobacco tin.

'Oh. I never thought of that either,' he says. 'We should mention it to Oliver. I haven't told him about the wood. It might be best that we don't.' I'm relieved; I just hope I don't accidently mention it now.

Oliver lives about a five-minute walk from Caleb; over the road and up a dirt track. The farmhouse is typically Cumbrian, much like Eddie's with barns and stables either side of the main living area. I notice the wishing-well in the centre of the yard. The bell hangs from a terracotta roof with a round bricked wall. At the bottom are pebbles and what must be hundreds of pennies and two-pence pieces.

'Most people have a copper jar but we have a wishing well,' Caleb says. 'Oliver empties it every Christmas and donates it to the local children's charity. It's mainly family and friends but we get the odd hiker that contributes when they pass.' I go to my bag and open my purse and find some pennies. I flick each one so that they hit the bell. It makes a solid sound, different to how I thought it would. The bell must weigh half a ton.

'What did you wish for?' Caleb asks. Now that would be telling. I poke the side of my nose twice as Oliver comes outside. Saved by the bell.

'Well, well, well,' he says. Funny. 'There's your old sink. She shines up nice, don't she?' It's hard to think that it was once used as a washing basin. It's wonderful that's it's been put to such positive use.

We go inside the house. From the porch I was expecting to walk in to utter chaos but the house is clean and tidy and quite modern. There's a distinct smell of dog but also of cooking. 'Some proper Cumbrian lamb,' Oliver says, ladle in one hand, tea towel in the other. Good job I'm omnivorous. We all eat sitting at the breakfast bar on stools. The kitchen is big; there's a large wooden dining table as you come in but I suspect they're used to eating here.

'Kayleigh's grandfather had a theory about the note they received asking if Edgeworth rang a bell,' Caleb says to Oliver. They've obviously discussed it.

'Aye, the tobacco tin, I reckon,' Oliver says, filling his fork. I look up, has he spoken to Eddie?

'Yes. How did you work that one out?'

'I thought it too. The mention of the bell had me thinking. Can't be though, the architect took it with him to Mardale. It don't add up.'

'Eddie cleared out the washhouse and dismantled the old bell mounting in case it was hidden there,' Caleb says.

'Smart thinking. I take it he found nowt?' I shake my head and smile. The lamb takes some swallowing. I'm trying to be polite but my mouth is filling with unswallowable meat and I've no idea what to do. I have no tissue and no drink. I take a fork of mash that I drown in as much gravy as possible to wet my mouth as they talk.

'My old man let that place go. He did have a good look for the wood but I don't think he found any art. The bell was his pride. I don't think anybody lived there for seven or eight years before he sold the place. Though the Edgeworths took care of the garden and kept the grounds from overgrowing.' I manage to swallow a big lump of lamb but I can feel it linger in my throat. I repeat the gravy soak several times before my mouth finally clears. I hope they haven't noticed my struggle.

'Maybe the Edgeworth guy found something after all?' Caleb says.

'Aye, most likely.'

I survive my meal and thank Oliver. Thankfully my insides can't speak; they would be less complimentary. I notice that the tobacco tin is on show in the cabinet behind me, next to the table. It does say Edgeworth on it. It's easy to make that connection but is it too much of a coincidence?

I managed to endure the visit to Oliver without mentioning selling out to the French.

'Fancy seeing some more ruins?' Caleb says. 'High Head Castle isn't far from here. Few people know about it.' Good idea. We drive along country lanes for fifteen minutes and finally pull over by a dirt track.

'We go the rest of the way by foot,' he says. If there are nettles, I'm screwed.

I manage to avoid the nettles and brambles on the way to the castle. There are KEEP OUT signs everywhere warning of danger, but Caleb ignores them and wanders in. I stop. There's an eerie feel to the property as we approach and I notice there's silence. I hear no birds or animals and there aren't any main roads nearby either. The place looks more like an abandoned manor than a castle even though it does have a mediaeval pele tower. Huge sandstone gargoyles stand on the columns in the courtyard. I take pictures. The place is massive; I need to look up the history.

'I've been here a few times. My grandad wanted to buy it at one time. It was for sale for only about a hundred thousand but it's a Grade 2 listed building so it would have to be restored to its original state. English Heritage offered a grant of half-a-million but it would take two or three million to get it habitable.' I can believe that. The walls get taller as I walk nearer. I'm nervous to get too close as it looks unstable. I bet this place was some lunatic asylum. It's got that horror movie look to it; I wouldn't come here at night.

'It was destroyed by fire about sixty years ago. A famous astronomer lived here at the time, I think.' I can't believe this place was just used as a home; it must have had about thirty bedrooms. I joke that the butler did it.

'In the kitchen, with a paraffin lamp,' he adds.

I take more photos and venture a little nearer. The building has no roof and grass grows from inside. There must be a groundsman here though as the grass is short. Some of the stonework looks loose as if it might crumble so the danger notices are probably valid. As much as I'm fascinated by the place I'm also a bit frightened by it. Maybe it's the silence. From where I stand I see red and grey with the dark green of the wooded area behind the house and the yellowed green of the dry grass. There's no life though, in any of it. If I were to paint this I would have to turn back to the time of the fire that destroyed it. It's a totally different feel to Mornas. The longer I stay the more agitated I feel and yet I don't want to ruin the moment for Caleb.

'It seems alien for our generation to realise that territorial wars have been fought for centuries. We take peace for granted. Cumbria is littered with castles and halls. People lived in constant fear of invasion.' I love it when he gets philosophical; we're kindred spirits in that sense. I ask if he has ambitions or goals.

'Not really. I just want to enjoy life and get by.' Seems like everyone I know. We get shoved into adulthood with no vision, only the expectations of society. 'I'm lucky, the family are comfortable enough not to insist I get a full-time job but I will have to eventually. I can't live at home all my life.' I ask what he enjoys.

'I like my music, I guess. I'm not artistic or creative; I envy you, your passion fascinates me. I wish I had it. You're the landscape garden, I'm the still life.' I smile at the metaphor. There's a poet in him, I know that much. I tell him that I disagree, but don't elaborate. He's full of surprises and consistently fails to let me down. He's no still life; he is, at least, the waterfall.

I wish I could think of something to say that could inspire him to find his own path in life. I get the feeling that he's delaying his youth for as long as possible, waiting for the inevitable deep-end to rise up and swallow him.

'I'm thirsty now,' he says. It's hot, I would welcome a drink. We head back along the lane and I'm almost at the car when a stray nettle brushes my leg above my ankle. I curse and hop. I knew it. Caleb finds it funny and I fake a scowl. Great, now I have a rash.

We find a pub on the main road and pull in. We both order fruit juice and take a window table. I get a message from Lily to say she's back home safely. She wants to come up at the weekend to see me and bring her latest creations for the shop. I message back quickly to say I'm with Caleb and that it's okay for the weekend.

'It's cool that friendships have formed from the mystery of that sketch. Little did the artist know the impact it would have on the future all those years ago,' Caleb says. I've been thinking that too lately. My leg is still itching and I have to resist the urge to scratch it. I note his use of the word friendship rather than relationship and become aware of my own confusion at this situation. What do I have here? Is this a date or are we just friends spending time with each other? I don't know what I want it to be but it's a terrifying thought.

We talk for an hour or so. Caleb talks a lot but hardly speaks about himself, only his memories, bands he likes or his DJing. I'm processing it all as he speaks. I'm looking for any passion, any spark of something that paints a picture of who he is. I listen, fully aware of not coming over as self-absorbed. I like him. I like that he's kind. I like that he's polite to everybody and friendly. I like his stories. I like his voice, his eyes, his smile and the way he struggles with his fringe, yet remains loyal to it. Yet all the time I'm thinking, could I be with somebody like this? Could I bring colour to his soul? Does the waterfall have a rainbow?

He enjoys DJing but wouldn't want to do it as a career. He plays guitar but not well. I suggest lessons and lots of practice. If he's dedicated he could make a career of it. He dismisses it, stating that it's not a viable career option and he would never be able to live off it. How could someone who shines so bright be so colourless?

We head back to his house in the late afternoon. I drop the pressure as I don't want to come over as bossy. As we pull in, his neighbour, an elderly woman, lights up when she sees Caleb. She comes to the drive and thanks him for mowing her lawn. Her front garden looks immaculate; she obviously loves it and appreciates Caleb's help. I suggest he makes that a career.

'That's what my folks want me to do, or work on the farm, but that's definitely not what I want.' I leave it before he gets agitated with me. It's sad though, it sounds like his family give encouragement and are happy to let him live with them. I realise he needs a muse and not another mother figure. It's no wonder he was enjoying the mystery; I wronged him more than I realised by keeping things back from him. I change the subject and question what we might be able to do to track down the descendants of Brandon Edgeworth.

'I guess we need to find out where he was buried,' he says.

In the kitchen, Caleb puts the kettle on. I don't know where his mother has gone. I try to find some records of Brandon's death on my phone. If he was already old in the seventies he probably died in the eighties or early nineties. I'm surprised I can't find anything considering he has a rare name and lived locally. We know that he had family. Caleb checks the ancestry site as he is more familiar with that and looks for any mention of Brandon.

'Only one mention of a Brandon Edgeworth. Looks like a family tree connection. Claire Radcliffe, not sure if it's connected… Wait.' I look up; Caleb's face is almost totally obscured by his fringe. 'Was John Robinson's wife called Beverley?' She was. 'Beverley Edgeworth.'

Caleb passes me his phone. The outside of the family tree doesn't go as far as the Robinson's but does follow the Edgeworth family into Radcliffe. Brandon had two sisters, Sarah and Beverley. I try to work out the timing. Yes, Beverley and John would have been similar ages. It makes sense; they were neighbours, maybe childhood sweethearts. No wonder the Edgeworths looked after the property.

'Should I leave a message for Claire Radcliffe?' I hand back the phone. Claire will be two generations down but must have had some connection. She has family but no grandchildren so she's probably in her forties. Brandon would have been her great-uncle but she might know something. Caleb leaves a message to say that we're trying to track descendants of Brandon Edgeworth. 'I should have thought of this before, I keep missing the obvious. I'd make a useless detective.' He berates himself a lot. It's usually a symptom of social anxiety; it hasn't occurred to me that he could also have issues. Being a DJ, it never crossed my mind, but I suppose a DJ has the perfect excuse not to socialise. He can shut himself away in the booth and be in his own space. Why didn't I notice this before? If I mention it I could make things uncomfortable for him, so I don't. I tell him not to be so hard on himself.

'It just gets frustrating sometimes, being dumb.' I roll my eyes. I don't want to get drawn into the sympathy trap but I genuinely believe he thinks that. I change the subject again and ask where his mum is. 'It's Monday; that means she'll be at the supermarket. She lives her life by routine; you can set your clock by it. She'll have left at four and she'll be back around quarter to six.' I look up at the wall clock and it's just gone five o'clock. Eddie will be shutting up shop soon; I probably shouldn't leave it too long before heading back. I feel guilty that I've not helped out today and Eddie's going to be tired. I've enjoyed today though; it's been nice spending time with Caleb even if I do feel helpless.

'Are you going to stay for a while?' he asks, as if I've been thinking out loud. Maybe he's learning to read me. He probably feels helpless too, only I know what I want from life, I know the direction I'm heading. He's standing still, on a mountain of potential, looking for somewhere to go. I tell him that I'll need to head back. He smiles, as if he knew he read me. 'It's been nice today. We need to do this again; you know, more than every two months.' I laugh. I know Lily's coming at the weekend so I suggest evening video calls again and for him to come round one evening next week and I'll show him the Edgeworth house. 'Yes, good idea!' he says. I'm relived he still wants to see me after last week.

We head out to my car. I'm nervous. I hate saying goodbyes at the best of times but I don't know what this is between us yet. He hugs me before I get in the car and I avoid eye contact. I get in the driver's seat and wind down the window and he leans in, his arm resting on the roof.

'It's like a TARDIS this. Looks tiny on the outside but there's more room inside,' he says. I guess so. It's perfect for me; it's small, slow and easy to park. My heart races, knowing that this is an opportunity I have to let the heart win. I lean over and press my lips to his, just gently, and hold them for a couple of seconds before pulling away. He looks stunned. I smile and tell him that I'll see him next week.

CHAPTER 28

In the weeks that followed my accident with the razor – or as everybody called it, my attempted suicide – the pain and panic of those minutes replayed on an endless loop in my head. I couldn't stop it. Every time I closed my eyes the sight of the towel turning red and the stinging pain and panic would return. It woke me every time I fell asleep. I tried staying awake every night to avoid my subconscious torturing me but that made it worse. I became trapped in my memory and the trauma wouldn't reason with all the advice I was getting.

I was assigned a counsellor. I had psychiatrists and social workers visiting me every few days. I'd break down. The crippling pain in my gut at the thought of dying made me sick. I could hardly eat or drink. I ended up back in hospital twice to be rehydrated. It wasn't about *Four* anymore. I hated myself for loving him and I hated him for not loving me. After a while I hated that I'd survived. If I'd woken in hell, it wouldn't have been as bad as waking in hospital. Nothing I could do made any difference. I couldn't face school and thankfully nobody pressured me to. Lily was a rock. She came to see me armed with paints and fabrics, sometimes she wouldn't even speak, just let us create. Everything I did was abstract. How many shades of red and black could I find? I once made a beautiful sketch of *Four's* face, the best sketch I had ever drawn, just so I could paint over it in red, orange and black like dirty flames. Lily understood.

After a while I just felt numb. I would have frequent

flashbacks that came from nowhere and would be powerful enough to make me sick. I spent most of my time in my room or entertaining Jared and Rosie. I found it hard to talk to Mum or communicate anything above the trivial and she began disapproving of everything I did or said – or didn't do. When I went back to school I quickly grew a backbone. Shelley Watson would sneer and taunt me in front of her friends and then try to talk with me when she was alone. I told her once, in front of her disciples, when she was taunting me about the failure of my suicide attempt, that considering I had nothing to lose, I might not fail at murder and if she wanted to know how far she had to push me, then to go ahead. I'm not sure if I ever would have but at the time life was already a jail sentence, so I had little to lose. I even fantasised about it on my darkest nights.

Mum kept *Five* quiet at first, understandably. It had only been three months after my accident and I was still recovering. I saw my counsellor once a week but still had nightmares and flashbacks. I still had pent-up anger and was still a social recluse. I only felt safe with my art. Mum had known *Five* for a while, I had met him too, he ran a well-being clinic and had helped Mum sort herself out after she had drugs problems with *Three*. I didn't know at the time and certainly didn't know they had started a relationship. I found out about it on my fifteenth birthday. They sat me down to tell me and talk to me together with my counsellor. They agreed they weren't going to rush things. He wasn't going to move in, not for a long time at least. Mum would make sure he had no one-to-one contact with me. They still thought *Four* had manipulated me in personal contact, which was never true. I was the hunter.

At first I was okay with it. I thought I could handle it and I guess I did initially. I didn't ask any questions and Mum hardly mentioned him. She spent time with him during the week. I would sometimes babysit while they went out for a meal, or whatever. The weekends were devoted to Jared and Rosie, and she spent the rest of her time arguing with me. Or was it the other way round?

The day I saw *Four* with his young girlfriend hit me like a train. She looked like me. She was my height, with short brown hair and my face shape. She looked young too and I pictured her in the same way as I had so often pictured myself with him. I couldn't take it. I wasn't prepared. I ran up to him screaming, calling him every profanity I could think of, in floods of tears. He tried restraining me. The woman ran off; I don't know if she was scared or went to get help. I was trying to kick him, punch him, I was wild and out of control. He tried holding me away. From the corner of my eye I could see *Five* approaching; he had driven past and recognised me. As he approached, I screamed at *Four* to get off me and leave me alone.

***

For two nights in a row I've woken up with the same nightmare. I'm in my car and I make the brave move to kiss Caleb but when I open my eyes I see *Four*, his disappointed eyes staring back at me. Both times I've woken up screaming and then spent over an hour crying myself to sleep. Every time I get close to loving myself again something triggers a reminder of how evil I am. I didn't expect to be so easily triggered after all this time.

'You look tired,' Eddie says as we drive in to Penrith. I must have yawned a dozen times since we got in the car. I apologise and blame the heat. In all the time I've been here I think it's rained twice. Before we reach the shop my phone pings with a message from Caleb.

Morning beautiful, I've had a message from Claire Radcliffe. She knows of Brandon but doesn't remember him. His youngest son, David, is still alive and lives in an elderly housing project in Penrith, so she doesn't think we'd get much information from him.

She wants to know our connection to him. Need to know what to reply x

'I think I remember David,' Eddie says, as we pull up to the shop. 'My parents would have known him better. We need to be careful here, Brandon would also be Colleen's great uncle. Claire and Colleen would be second cousins. They'll be aware of each other, especially if their grandparents were neighbours at that time.' That's a good point; we promised Colleen we would drop our investigation. It might be something that Caleb has to do on his own, independently. I message Caleb back to explain why we need to think it out before replying.

The shop is quiet in the morning so I get a chance to focus on my orders, even though my mind is everywhere else. Maybe Caleb can say that he's fascinated by the abandoned house near Thackthwaite and was looking in to the history of it. It's not connected to the mystery then. We would need to find a way to bring the painting into the conversation later. I ask Eddie.

'Yes. That's a good idea. That angle will work.' I message Caleb who immediately texts back:

Excellent. I have the perfect excuse to come over and explore the Edgeworth house now x

By late afternoon tiredness overwhelms me, my eyes sting and all I want to do is sleep. I ask Eddie if I can go for a walk in the hope it will wake me up. I'm half way up a steep hill towards the beacon when I hear a car beep at me. My initial panic recedes as I recognise the car. It's Polly.

'Hey, I thought it was you. Where are you off to? Need a lift?'

I tell her that I'm trying to stay awake. I also tell her about Claire Radcliffe and my dilemma with Colleen.

'I know a Claire Radcliffe. She's a teacher at our school. I wonder if it's the same one.' It's not a common name, there can't be too many in the Penrith area. 'She teaches art too.' That's interesting. Maybe Polly could talk to her instead of Caleb; it might seem more credible then and won't upset Colleen. I suggest it to her.

'I could test the water at least,' she says. That will make things easier.

I thank her and tell her that I'm okay to continue walking around the block and she drives on. I'm out of breath by the time I reach the top of the hill but it's worth it, I enjoy the view. I walk past our favourite chip-eating place and stop to look out at the Lakeland Fells. I'm regretting the kiss now. I don't know what to expect from my relationship with Caleb and I still don't understand why I kissed him. Maybe it was guilt for making the excuse to leave. I'm undecided about building a relationship; part of me feels like running away and shutting off all contact. I tell myself I don't need him, I don't love him, but it's all words.

I get back to the shop as Eddie's cashing up. Considering the tiredness, I guess I've been productive. We stop on our way back to get a microwave meal, neither of us up for cooking tonight. Eddie and I spent all yesterday evening getting his stuff back in the washhouse so the driveway is finally clear when we pull in. The washhouse has never looked so tidy and organised.

I should try to settle for an early night but I'm terrified of my subconscious waking me again. It was hard enough having Polly's face on the windscreen in my nightmares, it's been nearly two years since the flashbacks of *Four* disturbed my sleep and I've been off the medication for a year. I fear them. I've always considered it karmic retribution for my sins. I don't want to tell Caleb about my past but neither do I want my relationship to destroy my future. I hate myself for feeling this weak when I know I have so much strength.

Caleb video messages me, distracting me from my self-loathing. I tell him about my encounter with Polly.

'I hope it's the same person,' he says. 'It'll save me having to explain too much.' I guess he wasn't looking forward to the pretence. 'So, when can I come and see this house?' he asks. It would have to be tomorrow or Monday night because Lily is over at the weekend. I explain in the hope he suggests Monday.

'Tomorrow will be great. I'll come round about half six, shall I? It will give you time to get home and eat.' I'm going to be so nervous all day but I smile and agree. Tomorrow it is.

CHAPTER 29

Eddie locks the shop door mid-morning as Niagara Falls has descended on Penrith. We could see the grey clouds forming as we drove into town and we've heard distant rumbles of thunder all morning. For nearly an hour the rain has been torrential. The drains can't cope so the water banks up against the side of the shop and waves lap about twelve inches to the door. A tiny gap is letting in water and Eddie has towels down. He's worried. If anybody opened the door the water would cause devastation in here. We both look out the window to watch nature's theatre. The thunder is deafening; the storm is directly overhead. It makes you wonder how the clouds can hold so much water - it must be like a river in the air.

We can hear sirens all around us; I assume fire engines coming to pump out the floodwaters.

'At least you won't need to water the garden tonight,' Eddie says. True, if the plants haven't all been washed away by the storm. It might be impossible to get to the Edgeworth house tonight now. Maybe I should cancel Caleb's visit. And, as if the universe can read my thoughts, the rain stops. Typical.

I'm itching to go outside and inspect the damage in the town but we're trapped until the waters recede. It takes half an hour for the door to clear. Eddie eventually braves it enough to reopen the shop. There's still a flood outside but it doesn't threaten the shop anymore. I venture out to get us a barm cake from the bakers. The sun is shining now and there's that strong smell of summer rain. I can feel the humidity on my skin. There are still floods in the centre of town and the traffic is slow to move through it. The waves lap onto the pavement; there will be many soggy shoes today. I can't imagine what it looked like thirty minutes ago.

When I get back to the shop Polly is inside talking to Eddie.

'I was right about Claire,' Polly says as I enter. 'She knows of Brandon Edgeworth, he's a family legend, but she never met him. Claire's been tracing her ancestry online recently. She mentioned that she's had contact this week from somebody curious about Brandon's old house.' Oops. She's going to suspect a conspiracy now. 'She's nice, you'll like her. I told her you live in Thackthwaite and were researching the area and also told her you were a talented young artist.' I'm probably blushing but hope it's not obvious. Maybe Claire could come round for a visit, though she's probably seen the Edgeworth house. I suggest it anyway.

'Good idea. I'll tell her you offered.'

After Polly leaves, I work on my orders. I've hardly had time to make shop stock so Eddie's ordered hand-made literary crafts in from an online store. I think Lily will help out over the weekend. The afternoon is quiet, though I'm aware of butterflies in my stomach all afternoon, knowing Caleb's coming over. I regret that kiss now; I was an idiot. Luckily the nightmare didn't wake me last night but it took ages before my mind let me sleep for fear it.

We get back and I have a freshen-up while Eddie cooks. So much for not watering the garden - it looks like the storm missed Thackthwaite; the soil is dry. I'm just finishing my food when Caleb's car pulls up. I'm shaking and feel nauseous; how on earth do people cope in a relationship? I watch him get out the car and realise he doesn't know whether to knock on the barn or the house. Eddie leaves his seat and knocks on the window, waving him towards the house, then opens the door.

'Sorry, we're just finishing our dinner,' he says. I smile and wave, finishing my last mouthful before saying hello. At least I avoid the awkward hug. I point to the chair next to me on the table. Caleb looks up to see my collage where the wooden sketch once hung.

'That's amazing,' he says, leaning in to have a closer look. 'You're honouring the space with its story.' That was the idea. I tell Caleb about Polly's visit and he laughs.

'Claire never got back to me, I wondered if I'd scared her off. I'm curious about the house though.'

Before we head to the Edgeworth house we water the garden. Caleb carries a full watering can with ease and I notice the tone in his arm muscles briefly before looking away in case he catches me. He waters each plant with care and checks the soil with the back of his hand then pulls up some weeds along the edge without speaking. He looks around and eventually finds a small piece of slate and uses it to dig two holes at the end of the bed before carefully digging around two plants and replacing them in the new holes.

'They were a little too crowded; you can tell these flowers are open less here,' he says. He's right. I hadn't noticed. There's more symmetry to the flowerbed now too. Caleb returns to the washhouse to get more water for the replanted flowers. It feels awkward to join him so I wait, picking what I hope are weeds from the back of the garden. I can't fathom him out. It's as if he loves gardening but won't consider it as a career just because it's what his family encourages him to do. Is he just being stubborn?

We return to the house to wash our hands and get a drink before finally setting off for the Edgeworth house. I catch Eddie's eye as I close the door and he winks. Awkward. The old road is overgrown with weeds and nettles.

'This is awesome,' Caleb says as we reach the house. He ignores the danger signs and leaps into the building. 'What a waste. Look at that view.' Matterdale looks beautiful but not the usual rich colours of mid-summer, there's more gold and yellow than you'd expect because of the parched grazing fields. He's right, it is a waste. The house would need to be rebuilt entirely. 'It wouldn't surprise me if a painting is hidden here.' Eddie did look; I can't see how it would have survived if it was here. Caleb disappears into the spider room, there's no way I'm following. The danger signs should show the eight-legged monsters.

I wait outside, hearing the occasional curse and ouch and I shout out to be careful. God knows what he's doing; I hear knocking and banging as if he's moving furniture. He eventually emerges with dust and cobwebs in his hair and on his shoulders. I laugh.

'There's no way anything's hidden in there other than vermin and spiders.' I don't trust him enough not to try and scare me if he knows of my arachnophobia so I laugh. 'I found this though.' Caleb holds out what looks like a cast-iron model airplane, maybe a Spitfire. It looks old and tarnished but it would probably clean up well. We spend another half an hour here and I brave more of the house. There's no upstairs but you can see where the stairs were; you can walk up the first six steps but the rest have fallen into the floor. Most of the upper floorboards have rotted away so they frame the downstairs walling. I take lots of photographs. The chaos caused by forty years of neglect has claimed the house. The tree, growing through where the kitchen used to be, is a testament to the hardiness of nature.

We return to the house, neither of us mentioning the kiss or anything about our relationship. It suits me, I think. I need to work up courage before I ask him into the barn, maybe one day. I'm still unsure of whether I want a relationship; I'm more excited about seeing Lily tomorrow. I don't want to give Caleb the wrong signals or false hope. I open the door to the house and let Caleb inside. As he walks past me I involuntarily scream and back away. He turns to me with horror in his eyes. There's a huge spider on his back; it must be the size of a tennis ball. I can't bring myself to speak at first and I'm terrified he might get closer so I point and he sees the movement on his shoulder. He throws off his t-shirt in a second and shakes it. The offending creature scurries away from the house towards the garden. I feel pathetic and hate myself for it. The only way to cover my shame is to laugh and I tell him they usually don't get to me but that was a monster.

'Same,' he says, shuddering and shaking the t-shirt again. His torso is tanned; he must have been sunbathing or gardening shirtless. I look away. I'm glad the spider ran in the opposite direction of the barn. Just knowing it's nearby is bad enough. Caleb made no effort to kill it. I'm not sure I would have given it such freedom. I hope it finds its way home.

Eddie comes out to see what the commotion was about. Ground, swallow me, please. I give him a stare as if to say, *Don't you dare*. He laughs.

'Come on, I've just made a fresh brew of coffee and some fruit bread,' he says, but before I relax, he points at Caleb. 'And put some clothes on, will you?' At least I'm not the only one feeling awkward. Caleb grimaces at me after Eddie turns to enter the house and puts on his t-shirt.

'I bet you did that deliberately,' he says quietly to me as we make our way into the house. I don't know whether to laugh or hide.

'There's definitely no painting hiding in that house,' Caleb says to Eddie.

'No. We went ourselves a while back; I can't see how it can be hiding in that rubble. Our best bet was the washhouse, but we've had everything out of there lately. I think it's been removed. Maybe it was chucked out with the builder's rubble when my parents did this place up.'

'Sad to think that.'

After half an hour, Caleb surprises me with an excuse to leave. I know I'm not the best host but the evening has been relaxed as well. Maybe he was expecting more private time.

Maybe he considers me a fourteen-year-old passing him by my father for approval. Frigid. I guess I am. I walk with him to the car.

'I'm glad I got to see round that house. I'd love to rebuild it. Makes you think about Beverley Edgeworth and John Robinson. I bet they sneaked out in private, avoiding their family.' I laugh but instantly my mind goes there, retracing their romantic journey. As he opens the car door with one hand he reaches for mine with his other, taking me by surprise. 'You should come and see me again next week,' he says. I nod, and then he leans in to kiss me. This time it's a proper kiss that lasts fifteen seconds and feels like fifteen minutes. He gives my hand a little squeeze as he releases the kiss and gets into the car. I dread to think of the colour in my cheeks and hope Eddie's not watching. I can't believe I feel like this at eighteen.

I wave as Caleb pulls away then head for my barn. I've certainly got plenty of details for Lily tomorrow. I feel giddy and inspired. I place a canvas on the easel without thinking and get my paints together. I don't even know what to paint yet but I must do something. It's been too long. I flick through my phone; I have so much inspiration but I'm drawn towards the Edgeworth house - the chaos and beauty juxtaposed in one scene. I feel it. I'm broken because of my past and yet there's beauty in this feeling inside, my passion for my art and my fear of being wrong by doing what feels right.

I'm so focussed. I don't sketch; I see invisible lines where the pencil must be. The house is etched into my memory; dark shadows inside the walls on a backdrop of greens and golden yellows of the fells surrounding Matterdale Valley. The tree in the foreground emerging from inside the building, too big for the frame, has its own dominance over the painting. Nature is in love with the chaos. Inside the shadow, on the edge of the entrance to the spider room, I add a deep red, which breathes life into that area of the picture. It represents Caleb and the first time in my life that somebody chose to kiss me.

CHAPTER 30

Lily's train's late so Eddie and I wait in his car outside the station. I'm tired again but it's my fault. I didn't stop painting until nearly five in the morning and was too hyper to sleep when I did settle. I don't mind; the painting turned out better than I hoped. Eddie loved it when he came in this morning, wondering why I was late. That never happens. Thankfully the shop wasn't too busy today so I could work at my own pace.

We see the train approaching so I leave Eddie to greet Lily. She has a huge suitcase with her, that she drops on seeing me and gives me a big hug.

'I missed you, Kayleigh babe, I have so much to tell you,' she says. My eyes well and I return the hug tightly. For all the emotions I'm discovering with Caleb, what I have with Lily is special. I'm always relaxed with her, she knows me better than anybody. She knows my past and yet still stays loyal to me and our friendship. I miss her more than anyone; I can easily imagine life without Caleb but not Lily.

'I know it looks like I'm staying for a month,' she says, pointing to her suitcase. 'I've just made so much stock for the shop. It might need an iron though now.'

Eddie leaves the car and comes over as we exit the station to take the suitcase. He's such a gentleman.

'I'm fine,' Lily says, smacking his hand away. 'I'm younger and more agile than you.' Eddie laughs.

'At least let me lift it in the boot then,' he says, taking the case from her with ten yards still to go.

'Men!' Lily says, with a smile. 'Thank you.'

I tell Lily about my painting and late night without mentioning Caleb.

'Cool. Look forward to seeing it; you'll have to show me the Edgeworth house too.'

'Hungry?' Eddie says as we fasten our seatbelts.

'Starving,' Lily says, without hesitation.

'Fish and chips it is then.' Well, it is Friday.

We collect our meal and Eddie drives to our favourite place to eat them. I catch Lily up to date on the situation with Claire Radcliffe.

'Art teacher? The universe is speaking,' she says. I ask how Marcus is.

'He's good now. I think we've patched things up. I got to see your sketch, Eddie.'

'Oh. He hasn't sold it already then?'

'No. He's put it in his library room. Pride of place.'

'I'm pleased. He must have been genuine then. I was half-expecting to see it on the news as some lost treasure worth millions.'

'Shame about the painting though,' she says. 'Didier was saying that there's been many local legends about it. Even one that Didier's grandmother had an affair with an artist at the time and that it was his grandfather who gave the paintings away.'

'Oh. That's interesting. No wonder Didier wants to piece the story together.'

'Yeah. Later in life she recognised the man from Vincent van Gogh's painting of Paul-Eugéne Milliet so then started rumours that it was Milliet and Van Gogh that had visited that day.'

'Oh. No wonder they were keen to find the painting. Did he get the wood sketch authenticated?'

'Yes, he's getting that done at the moment.'

'Does he think it was Van Gogh that came with Milliet?'

'There's a gap in his letters to his brother, Theo, around the date but no mention at all of the outing. Lots of theories though. Some think they had a relationship that they kept to themselves and that's the real reason the picture was titled *The Lover*.'

'I guess he wouldn't have confessed that in his letters.'

'No. Didier himself doesn't think it was Van Gogh but whoever it was liked Didier's grandmother's art at the time. He thinks she was smitten until she realised he'd vandalised the garden.'

'I guess we'll never know. It's a shame though. Maybe I'll take up Didier's offer for a visit some time.'

'I think he'd like that. He was full of praise for you, and for Kayleigh; he loved her paintings.' More praise. I like the feeling of pride that surges through my body when that happens but it's like I dampen it down with guilt and disbelief. I know I have a talent but there are millions of artists out there I'd consider better than me. How could I be good when I can only do one painting a month? Some of these artists spend a lifetime doing nothing but painting. I would love to do that but it will never happen.

Eddie drives back to Thackthwaite as Lily tells of the rest of her trip to France and how she fell in love with the ancient town of Arles. It sounds so romantic. She has these experiences and memories that will stay with her forever, regardless of whether she stays with Marcus, and all because I got curious one day.

Back home, Lily is immediately drawn to my new paining, studying it in detail.

'This is amazing. It almost seems surreal, with the tree growing from inside, people wouldn't think it was a real place.' I guess so. 'I'm looking for the Kayleighism.' She giggles. I tell her it's there.

After a minute or two she says, 'It's the reddish streak here. Blood or passion?' Wow. I'm stunned. She looks over her shoulder at me, one raised eyebrow, awaiting my response. Oh God. I'm so bad at lying. I tell her Caleb came round yesterday evening.

'I knew it! Details. Now!'

I laugh.

I tell her about my evening and about my day out with Caleb last week. I tell her about the kiss, the nightmares, and the latest kiss and explain the red streak and when I look up, she's in tears. I apologise.

'No. No, don't apologise. It's… it's beautiful.' Oh. 'You don't understand how happy I am for you. I wanted you to experience this… this real emotion. After everything you've been through. Finally; something honest.' She leans over to hug me. I feel a bit of an idiot but understand why she feels this way. She dragged me out of hell in my darkest days. I hug her back and try to stop myself from becoming emotional. I remind her that I'm a bad person.

'If you say that again, I swear I will kill you myself!' she says with conviction but I don't loosen my embrace. 'You're a good person who made one mistake, out of fear and insecurity and you've paid the price emotionally all these years. If you were a bad person you wouldn't feel guilt or responsibility. You're the most beautiful soul I've ever met and it's not just me who sees that, it's everyone that ever meets you.' I think that's stretching it too far. I don't even like being around people, except Lily and family. I have to psyche myself up to spend a few hours with my own boyfriend. Eventually she loosens her grip. 'Come on, I'll show you what I made.'

Lily shuffles across the floor on her knees to the suitcase. First she pulls out another vintage dress and bonnet, Bronte-style with floral patterns and lace hems; it's beautiful. Then she pulls out a patchwork quilt that looks like a bookcase. She opens it out on the floor - the edges are dark and inside the shelves are yellow and she's somehow managed to stitch it together to look like there are many coloured books on each shelf. It must have taken ages.

'I'll never get the money for the time I put in to it, I just enjoyed making it.' I reckon it must be worth a hundred and fifty pounds at least, probably a lot more. 'I made these though.' Lily pulls out a pile of square cushion covers based on the quilt design, as if they're zoomed in to one of the shelves only with smaller strips of fabric. They should sell well, they look amazing. How did she find the time to do them all?

'I rewarded myself with an hour's procrastination for every two hour's revision, then spent all this week, though I've been working on the quilt for months.' Oh, to have that discipline. 'I've made these as well,' she says, pulling out a pile of what look like fabric and leather book sleeves. 'They're tablet covers for e-Books. Look.' Lily shows me her own tablet. What a clever idea. She's stitched in pockets inside too; I dread to think how much it cost to make them. 'I bought a sheet of moldable fabric and made templates then glued the fabric, stitching the edges. Now I've perfected it I can make them cheaply.' They look so cool; Eddie's going to love these.

After a drink we water the garden; the glorious summer evening commands our company so we go for a walk. I show Lily the Edgeworth house but we don't brave the spider room. Lily's fascinated and takes plenty of photos.

'Why would anybody leave this place to rot?' It's sad, like a forgotten beauty waiting to be rediscovered. 'I'll probably make an art piece of this too.'

I feel energised so we head for Kayleigh's Corner as it's a while since I've been. I often get the feeling Lily struggles between her need for socialising and her love of the countryside. She could live six months as a party animal and the other six months as a hermit. She's an extreme ambivert.

'One day you'll buy this land,' she says. I'd love that. I've never seen the river dry before, I'm used to the rush of the water under the bridge. It's been a harsh summer for the flora. The edges of the lower leaves are brown and curling up; you would think it was late September instead of early July. Not that this tranquil heaven has lost any of its beauty. I'd be tempted to walk to the top of Mell Fell if it wasn't so late.

'I wonder what the classic artists would make of this,' Lily says. I've often thought that. It's a remote section of the Lakeland countryside, away from the tourist areas, a hidden gem. 'France is so different. There's arable farming, vineyards and different types of trees. The landscape is generally flat unless you head to the southeast. It seems organised and landscaped. There's none of this entropic beauty where nature is set free to adapt to its surroundings.' She's right. I think Bernard, Gauguin and Van Gogh would fall in love with this place.

We head back to the barn as the sun bids its farewell behind the mountains. Lily is helping me in the shop tomorrow so we need to head to bed at a reasonable hour but we have Sunday off. I've pulled the base bed out again for myself ready. Our phones ping almost in unison as we get into bed.

'How about that?' Lily says. 'Caleb, per chance?' I nod. He's sent me a goodnight message, as has become the custom this past week or so. I'm assuming Marcus does the same with Lily. 'Marcus says hi. He wants to know if you've painted any masterpieces lately.' I shake my head but Lily's having none of it. 'I'm telling him you've drawn more ruins but this time it's called *Desire;* for reasons.' Oh God. He's going to ask questions. I cringe. 'You're too cute, Kayleigh babe. No I've just said you have and that they're better than ever.' Hopefully the low light hides my blushes.

***

I've never heard a crack like it. The ferocity of the punch snapped *Four's* neck back and he landed on the ground with a thud, his grip on me eased in an instant. I knew it was serious and I was hysterical. *Five* didn't know whether to console me or tend to *Four*. Blood was oozing from *Four's* mouth and the back of his head and his jaw was distorted and out of line with his face. The owner of the house came outside, already on the phone to the emergency services. She ushered me inside the house but I couldn't stop screaming. What had *Five* done? What had *I* done?

The police wanted a medical officer to examine me in case I was hurt. I wasn't, though he noticed the bruise marks on my wrists. He kept asking me what happened but I couldn't stop crying. They wanted me to go to hospital but I refused. Eventually a senior officer took me to the station with a liaison woman and eventually my counsellor came. I didn't want to see Mum or Dad; I couldn't bring myself to and I don't think they knew what to do with me for a while. I was left alone with the counsellor, who didn't say much. Or maybe she did and I was too distraught to hear. After another hour or so Eddie came in with another police officer. He was in the area to see Dad. I ran and hugged him like there was nobody else in the world and he held me tightly until I stopped sobbing. He looked so worried. The policeman pulled up the chair for me and told me that *Four* had died from his injury. The shockwave hit me instantly and I don't know what happened after that. I woke up in hospital. At first I thought it was a dream; I felt calm and peaceful but that was the drugs. My memory returned but I felt too numb to fight. I had no energy left at all but I do remember feeling extreme jealousy. I was alive and I wanted to be dead.

The trauma of that day and the sadness and guilt that followed plagued my nightmares for months. It's rare that my subconscious tortures me with that memory now, but it has tonight. Lily woke me because she thought I was having a seizure. I woke and screamed and she held me. I cried and apologised but she just came down to my level and spooned me, holding me tightly, telling me to sleep again. I feel safe in her arms. I don't feel I could let Caleb get this close to me. Yet I could stay like this forever with Lily. Am I still a mess? Am I still that person I was?

No. I don't think so. I want to be alive. I'm very much alive.

CHAPTER 31

The morning comes quickly. We're both sluggish before our coffee but neither of us mentions the nightmare. Lily runs an iron over her stock while I cook us breakfast. I love the quilt; I would buy it myself but I know if I suggest it then Lily will give it to me without taking money for it. I call Eddie over before we leave.

'These are excellent, Lily,' he says. 'I think they should all sell quickly where they're so unique. We need to work out a price for everything.' He studies the quilt intensely. 'I've never seen anything like this before. We'll find a way to display this even if it means juggling the shop around a bit.' I agree, it would add to the ambience of the shop; it could be worth making a display model and taking orders.

'I didn't know whether to sell the cushion covers as covers or buy the cushions and sell them as a whole,' Lily says.

'Maybe both,' says Eddie. 'I'll see if we can buy some inners even if we have four of them and allow customers to interchange them.' Good idea.

Lily helps set up the shop all morning and during the quieter times we work in the craft room and manage to create paper flowers and notebooks for the shop again. We take a late lunch and go via Lily's favourite fabric shop. There's new material in stock, some of which have random letters in various calligraphic fonts. She spends a fortune; I suggest paying for it as she'll use it for stock but she's way too stubborn.

When we get back to the shop, something's missing.

'Where is it?' Lily asks.

'Sold it,' Eddie says with a smile, handing her the full one-hundred and fifty pounds for the quilt. 'They bought four cushions as well.' Wow. I thought it might sell quickly, I didn't expect it would sell that quickly. Lily places a twenty pound note on the counter.

'You have to take something for it. It's business,' she says.

'Not this time,' Eddie says, walking past her to rearrange the shop to display the dresses. 'Future quilts, but not this one. We probably sold it too cheaply anyway; it's hard to know what price to put on it. At least you know there's a demand.'

'Okay, but pizza is on me tonight!' Lily says. Eddie raises his eyebrows and shakes his head. 'No arguing, I'd rather starve than let you pay for it,' she says. Eddie's not going to win this one.

There's a good atmosphere in the shop all afternoon, not just between the three of us but the customers too. By the end of the afternoon there are only two of Lily's cushion covers left.

'I think it's safe to say your patchwork is going to be popular,' Eddie says.

'That's so cool. I hoped it would be. The cushions were an afterthought having made the quilt.'

We close the shop and head for the pizza restaurant. Normally we'd take it home to re-heat but there's a table available so decide to eat it while it's fresh.

'Marcus likes Italian food but said he's never enjoyed the food while in Italy.'

'Really?' Eddie says, taking his third slice in the time I've eaten one.

'They took a day trip into Italy, just so they could sample an Italian restaurant. They found one at a resort about fifteen miles inside. It looked nice on the outside but the food came back lukewarm and the pasta was too soft and even the garlic bread was stale.'

'Travesty! I hope they complained.'

'For all the good it did. Didier has been to Rome several times and said that he's yet to find a decent Italian.'

'I wonder if the Americans think that about our fish and chips. Let's face it, most of our traditional chip-shop chips are soggy and greasy. They're used to crispy dry fries over there.' I guess so. I think I'll need to take up jogging to work off these big meals lately. I enjoy them though.

We get back to Thackthwaite and I put the kettle on in the barn while Lily inspects her new fabrics. After a few minutes, Eddie knocks.

'I know who our mystery visitor was now,' he says. 'David Edgeworth has sent me a letter.'

'Brandon's son?' Lily asks.

'Yes.' Eddie hands me the letter and Lily reads it over my shoulder.

Dear Mr Halsey,

I tried to visit you twice but you were out. I am old and my sight isn't good. It's too dangerous for me to drive on the narrow country lanes. I am Brandon Edgeworth's son, David. I hear from my family that you are looking into the history of the French artwork and of my father's house. I hope I can help. I speak little of what I know to my family as my aunt's family have suffered so much because of it. I am also unsure if what I know is still relevant.

My father told me that a man named George Kimber, who once lived in your house, had befriended Brandon's father. George had been given some artwork while working in France and many years later had a visit from people in France to reclaim them. George rightfully refused but his son was beaten up badly at some point. I believe George gave a painting to my grandfather to look after because George's family had been told the painting had been destroyed. He could quite rightly claim that he didn't have it and George's son genuinely had no knowledge of where it was.

The French never returned and eventually George died. My grandfather, being an honourable man, didn't want to keep the painting, nor sell it. He regularly worked with Roland Robinson on the farm (and later his daughter married Roland's son). During that time he hid the painting on the grounds of the property, creating a false wall in the bell room. He wrapped the painting in tin foil and cloth.

After Roland died – shortly after another visit from the French - my grandfather felt it would be wise never to mention the painting. Many years later he told Brandon that one day it would be a nice find for the owners. Nothing was ever mentioned again until the family were contacted in the drought of 1984 about Mardale, the village that lies under Haweswater, where the French believed the painting had been destroyed.

I had forgotten about the tales my father told me until my cousin informed me that you had found a wooden sketch and were trying to look into its history. My aunt's family have lived in fear of another visit and felt that the artwork had cursed their family.

I don't know if you or any of the farm's previous owners ever found the painting but if not, I would check the bell room. I understand that your granddaughter went to France and met people out there who had interest in the artwork. Be careful. As much as generations will have passed since the darker days of the mystery, they were still curious 100 years later.

I wish you well. My cousin's family liked you so I trust their intuition. They do not know that I have made contact with you. I would rather they didn't.

Best wishes,

David Edgeworth.

'Wow,' Lily says. 'Where's the bell room?'

'I think he means the washhouse. It used to have an upturned bell in there that they used as a sink,' Eddie says. 'So it was dangerous for him to visit because of the driving and not because of any danger from the French.' That makes sense, I never thought of that.

We walk over to the washhouse. The walls are stone and have been painted several times. Eddie knocks the walls with the end of a screwdriver in case any stone sounds hollow.

'I've taken apart the bell mount recently so I know it's not there,' he says. He clears some of his garden tools aside and looks under the sandstone shelves. 'Actually,' he says, knocking the wall, 'I think the wall is out further here.' Lily and I bend down and she shines the torch from her phone at the wall. He could be right. 'We would need to remove the shelves. I can't see another way we could find out otherwise. I just don't want to break them.' Each shelf is a huge rectangle of sandstone. They would weigh a lot. They each have cement between them and there are four brick mounts; one at each end and two more evenly spaced between.

Eddie taps between each section. 'There's definitely some kind of different wall here because this isn't stone. I just assumed that was deliberate because of the mounting for the shelf but I think this section is different still. Listen.' The far end section, at the back of the shelving, does sound different to the other two sections.

'Maybe you only need to take out this end,' Lily says, attempting to lift the huge slab to see if there's any give.

'That's what I'm thinking,' Eddie says.

He wedges the screwdriver under the slab on the right hand side and hits it with a hammer. There's no rise at the front so he tries the back, under the shelf and there's a little rise so he tries the same on the other side of the slab and the same happens.

'We might be able to slide the slab forward if we can loosen the front. The cement here between the slabs isn't that thick, it's already crumbling.' I can see what he's thinking, though it will take a lot of muscle to move it I would think. 'Leave it with me and I'll give you a shout if I'm getting somewhere.'

Lily and I return to the barn and I put the kettle back on.

'This is exciting. I'm not sure if I should tell Marcus,' Lily says.

I don't think so yet, as much as it should be okay. I think we'll need to know if it's there first and, if so, get it authenticated. I suggest we hold back for now. I have the same dilemma with Caleb and I don't think he'll forgive me if I keep him out the loop again. I make a coffee and take a cup out for Eddie, who's smacking a chisel with a mallet, sweat beading on his forehead. I tell him to slow down and pace himself.

'It's a vendetta now,' he says. Even so, I don't like the thought of him hurting himself.

Lily lays out her new fabrics and sketches ideas, but we're both too hyper to focus properly.

'I can't believe my quilt sold on the first day,' she says. 'I need to start thinking about this more seriously.' I remind her she needs to think about university first. As much as it's great to have her creations, I'd feel guilty if she prioritises them over university. 'Yeah, I know, but I have two months until I have to go, assuming I get in.' She will, she doesn't know the meaning of failure, unless it's relationships.

Eddie knocks, asking for our help.

'I've wedged two claw hammers behind the slab. If you can prise them upward while I take the weight at the front, we might be able to release the slab.'

Lily and I stand either side of Eddie and push forward on the hammers after Eddie's count to three. There's a tiny movement forward and Eddie heaves his weight under the sandstone. There's some give but it's not as much as we need. We try a number of times and eventually it gets easier. The slab is about an inch away from the wall. We look down using a torch from the phone. It's hard to tell what's there but there's definitely space. There's no doubt that the wall comes forward.

After half an hour or so we've slid the slab forward by three or four inches and can see the edge of the new wall. Eddie's can just about lean over the shelf.

'You know, there's something in here,' he says. I can hardly contain my excitement. Lily climbs on top of the shelf to the left of the exposed hole and looks in.

'Yes, there is!' she says, excited. She attempts to get hold of it while Eddie tries the other end. I can hear their fingers rocking something loose. 'I've got it. If you can get your end we might be able to ease it up.'

'I've got it I think.' There's a thud. 'Nope. Nearly.' He tries again. 'Yup, this time, if we can raise it even an inch I'll be able to get it with my other hand.' My feet are on springs; I'm jumping like a lamb.

'Yes,' Lily says. 'I've got it, I can reach it.' Lily grabs it with the other hand. There's no doubt from the shape that we've found what we're looking for.

Eddie and Lily ease the object out between them, up and over the shelves. It's wrapped in a woven cloth.

'Let's take it in to the house,' Eddie says. I've never seen such a look of excitement on Lily's face, nor have I felt it. The light is starting to fade so we put the lights on in the house and I quickly clear the table. Lily starts to video and I remind her not to livestream it.

'I had to stop myself,' she says.

Eddie carefully pulls at the corners of the fabric.

'It seems dry so I guess that's a good sign.' It's wrapped well; he has to turn it over to uncover more. As he opens more out it starts to reveal metal. Tin foil.

'We really have found it,' Lily says.

'I'm nervous now in case I cause any damage; this has been hidden for over eighty years,' Eddie says.

The foil has been preserved well. Eddie finds some edges and gradually pulls it back. It starts to tear, so he uses both hands to guide the direction as cleanly as possible. The more he does, the more is uncovered. I realise it's the back of the painting. Excess canvass is pinned to the back stretchers which appear quite thick. The painting obviously isn't framed but must have been quite heavy. Eventually the back is exposed enough for him to turn it over.

'Oh my God!' Lily says, partly watching the scene unfold from her phone. It's unmistakably a painting of the Mornas fortress. It's been preserved well apart from the bottom left corner, which looks as if it's been scuffed rather than exposed. The colours are darker than mine, or maybe the sky is a little too blue, making the fortress appear more silhouetted against the skyline. The artist definitely used the wood sketch to base the painting on. The same initials are on the bottom right corner.

I feel an adrenaline rush like I've never felt before. Eddie is silent, staring wide-eyed.

'What now?' Lily asks. 'How much, if anything, do we tell people? What about Marcus and Didier?'

'We need to get it authenticated and we need advice before telling anyone. I'm even reluctant to tell Polly, despite the fact that she probably has the best connections,' Eddie says, still staring at the painting. 'All these years we've lived here. I wish my parents were here right now to see this.' I note that Lily captures him saying that on video; I don't think he noticed.

I take a closer look at the painting. The brushwork is quite heavy, the perspective is good but there are limited dynamics to the colours so the end result is blocky. I would have said the artist was an enthusiastic amateur, but who am I to say? I guess I prefer my own painting, given the choice of the two. If it is Milliet, it would make sense since he was a soldier by profession.

'The main question is, do we keep it?' Eddie says.

'You're going to need a bigger wall space if you're putting it alongside Kayleigh's collage.'

'You're right,' Eddie says, looking around the room. 'It would need to be a focal point.'

'Depends what it's worth. If Didier was prepared to pay twenty thousand euros for the sketch, imagine what he would pay for the painting?' It's a proper scruples dilemma. It really would mean selling out if it was a money decision but there's also a point when it becomes too much money to think about. If it's worth hundreds of thousands then Eddie will have to make sure the place was completely secure. It might even mean buying new doors and windows.

'I'll phone your father and see what he suggests. I know he made some investigations on the sketch independently of Polly so he might be able to help.'

Lily and I remain staring at the picture. She's put her phone away now but I'm glad she captured the discovery on video as it will help authenticate the find, should there be any legal problems.

'You realise this could be front page news? Not only in the art world but probably the daily newspapers too,' she says. She's probably right. 'I would even suggest doing it as it will help make your name as an artist too.' No. Even if that's true I don't think it would be the right thing to do. For a start it might open an investigation into Roland Robinson's death and maybe implicate Didier's family. It could cause stress for Colleen and her family too.

'I wonder if there are any more paintings. There are two more sections to that wall,' Lily says. We'll have to look tomorrow. Eddie finishes his call; it sounds like Dad's excited about it too.

'Your father will make contact with the people he spoke to about the sketch on Monday. He won't mention anything to Polly yet.' Monday seems so far away now. 'He wants some photos and an idea of its size. Maybe you can send them to him, Kayleigh.'

I take photos with my phone but I need to use the flash so the colours come out a bit brighter than they appear to the eye. Dad doesn't hide his enthusiasm when he messages back to acknowledge them. It's going to be so hard to keep this a secret. I'm supposed to have a day off tomorrow to take Lily out for the day but I'm dying to know if there's anything else in the washhouse. I suggest that Lily and I man the shop after all tomorrow so that Eddie can check.

'That might be an idea if I can loosen them enough. Would you mind?'

I look at Lily.

'I don't mind at all!'

We help Eddie re-cover the painting before we head to the barn. It seems quite heavy considering there's no frame, though the wooden stretchers are thick. We put it in one of the spare rooms, out of the way, in case we have a surprise visit from Caleb – or even Claire Radcliffe.

'I doubt I'll sleep tonight,' Lily says as we get ourselves ready for bed. I watch the video she made of our uncovering the mystery and get nostalgic butterflies inside even though the memory is little over an hour old. I doubt I'll sleep either.

'This could just be the start of it if the myths are right. Imagine what it would feel like to uncover a genuine Van Gogh?' I dread to think. 'You'll never be able to keep that out of the news.' That's true.

We talk into the early hours and its daylight before we finally sleep. The morning comes too soon and even the coffee does little to wake us. I don't mind, the adrenaline will probably get us through the day.

We're on tenterhooks all day in the shop. I phone Eddie regularly but there's no answer. As much as I want him to uncover more I don't want him to overdo it and come home to him lying on the floor. So part of me is excited and the other part uneasy. I spend the day at the counter dealing with customers and taking orders while Lily works in the craft room. She's perfected my style perfectly for the paper flowers and adds her own stamp by carving little triangles into the petals at the end to give a more authentic shape. I think they look better than mine.

The day drags but at least we can close at four, it being a Sunday. We sell the remainder of Lily's cushion covers after lunch. That's all of her patchwork sold in one weekend.

'I know what I'll be doing the rest of the summer,' she says. There's a proper community revolving around the shop lately. Many of the regulars are writers or involved in the industry in some way. I post photos we took of Lily's patchwork on our social media page, stating that they all sold out over the weekend and to expect more soon. Positive comments follow all afternoon.

When four o'clock arrives we shut up shop and head back to Thackthwaite.

'I hope Eddie's okay,' Lily says. The anticipation would be more bearable if there wasn't that niggle about Eddie.

We pull into the driveway. There's no sign of Eddie but he's obviously moved a lot of garden tools outside. We get out of the car and go into the washhouse. All of the shelves have been moved forward a few inches. We run to the house. There's nobody downstairs; I call out for Eddie and run to the bottom of the stairway.

Eddie comes out of the spare room and smiles when he sees me. I feel the relief surge through me. I ask if he's okay.

'My back aches but nothing a long hot bath and some painkillers can't cure, I'm sure.' He comes downstairs and I follow him to the kitchen and put the kettle on. 'I managed to get the slabs out and look behind but there's no paintings there, I'm sure of it. I think Edgeworth would have just built out the entire lower wall so that it wasn't obvious. Clever really.' In some ways I'm glad, as much as it would have been the discovery of the century. At least it makes things less complicated.

'At least we know,' Lily says.

'It was worth doing; it's taken me all day. I've no idea how to get all the shelves back again.'

Lily and I go back out to the washhouse. Lily looks behind the two new sections with her phone light.

'Eddie's right, there's nothing here. Maybe Didier can put that myth to bed now. At least he was right about there being a painting. We may never know who was with Milliet that day.'

CHAPTER 32

Mum phones while I'm having my breakfast with Lily. It takes a lot of willpower not to mention why I'm hyper.

'Hiya, are you doing anything today?' she asks. I tell her that Lily's here and that I'm dropping her off at the station at noon. 'Ah. I could do with seeing you; I was going to come up this morning. What if we bring Lily back with us?' I quickly explain to Lily.

'That works out better for me anyway with my big case,' Lily says. I tell Mum it's okay. Eddie is going to have to do the shop without me for most of the day. I've been thinking about Mum a lot in the past few months. I haven't kept in touch as much as I should have done. I message Jared and Rosie regularly but not so much Mum, I've just been so busy. I tell Eddie of the new plans.

'That's fine. I don't think it will be too busy today. It might be worth you putting all the tools back in the shed and closing the door though. The less questions the better right now.' He's right.

We pack the garden tools away after Eddie leaves then chill for an hour or so, speculating on what the day will bring.

'I feel a bit awkward with your mum coming to see you. Maybe I should stay upstairs?' I'd feel guilty if she did that. We see the car pull into the driveway while we're deliberating. 'I'll go upstairs anyway; maybe make an excuse to use the toilet and come and get me if it's okay.'

It's nice to see Mum. I go outside to greet her and *Seven.*

She looks smart. Healthy. Her makeup looks perfect, she's still pretty for someone who will be turning forty this year. I never thought I'd miss her but within two minutes of her being here I realise that I do. A lot. I put the kettle on and mention to Mum that Lily wasn't sure whether to stay upstairs to give us space.

'No, it's fine. I just wanted to tell you my news face-to-face rather than on messenger. She doesn't have to stay upstairs.'

I don't bother with our code. I call up to Lily and ask if she wants a cuppa and beckon her downstairs.

I make us all and drink Mum and *Seven* sit on my two-seater sofa while Lily sits at my desk and I pull up a chair from the dining table. *Seven* compliments me on my paintings.

'I thought it was important to come and talk to you about some decisions we've made,' *Seven* says, leading the conversation. I look over at Mum and she's smiling. 'I've asked your mother to marry me and she's accepted.' I'm stunned. I'm not sure what to say so I just stare, even though I know he must be waiting for my reaction. 'I know we've been together less than a year but we've become very close and we've ironed out old problems we both had; a result of past relationships and bad habits.' I look at Mum and she's nodding.

'I know how I can be, Kayleigh. I've made terrible mistakes in the past. I've become the person I'm with and inherited their faults too. When the relationship ends I close myself off, not having trust or faith in myself, and it's made me colder. For the first time since being with your father I'm aware of who I am. I have a relationship I want to make work and I've found someone who equally wants to make it work. It's a good feeling.' I try to stop my eyes filling. Part of me wants to scream at her and the other part wants to hug her and say, it's okay, I want you to be happy and I'm happy for you. Instead, nothing comes out and I see her smile crumble. I look over to Lily and realise all eyes are on me.

'I want to do this for you too, Kayleigh,' *Seven* says. 'Not all men leave. I know how your mother can be. I know how she's been in the past and I also know she's tried to protect you, and made a pig's ear of it along the way. I realise she's been damaged too and carried the guilt of your own traumas. You're happy with life now and that makes her happy too. Communication is the key to making all relationships work and that's what I'm going to make damn sure happens. We won't let our relationship become like the others.' Now my eyes well. I nod and see Mum's smile return. She comes over to hug me. Even that's strange, I needed those hugs when I was younger; why couldn't she have done it then?

I feel bad for Lily; she must be feeling awkward now. I eventually tell Mum that I'm pleased for her as she unfolds her embrace. I'm trying desperately hard not to let my tears consume me. I've wanted this for so long. I wanted Mum to be happy; I've wanted to believe that not all men leave. I wanted that hug, the honesty and reassurance from Mum. I look over at Lily and smile in the hope that it helps.

'I haven't told Jared and Rosie yet. I wanted to tell you first,' Mum says. I think they'll be okay. Jared seems to have warmed to *Seven* lately. I feel oddly numb; she has a habit of doing this to me lately. I'm not used to her company being a positive experience. For so many years I've harboured resentment and even now I'm fighting my cynicism: why couldn't this have happened earlier? If Mum was capable of being the person she appears to have become then why didn't that happen years ago? Maybe she really didn't know how to talk to me. I guess people really can change.

Within six months of me moving out, Dad has a girlfriend, Mum's getting married and I've had my first kiss. What would have happened had I stayed with Mum? Then there's the shop's success and solving a string of mysteries over a hundred years old. Was I holding everyone back?

'Are you okay?' Mum asks, sitting back with *Seven* and

squeezing his hand. I want to ask questions and I want to talk about the past but what good would that do? Am I still looking for the broken pieces or is this the closure I need to put the past to rest? *Seven* was right, I am happy. If that helps make Mum happy, I don't want to ruin that. I slowly start to feel the numbness fade and the excitement return. I smile and tell her that I am.

I bring Lily into the conversation, telling Mum about her patchwork sales and that lightens the atmosphere. I take the mugs through to the kitchen and put the kettle back on to be alone with my thoughts while they talk but before the kettle boils I'm joined by *Seven*.

'I told her you'd be okay. She's been worried sick for over a week about telling you. You're not a child anymore.' I tell him the truth; that I've always wanted this for her, I just find it hard to let go of the past and what she put me through. 'She really was protecting you. Nobody lived up to the standards she set herself to become the father figure she wanted you kids to have. Her biggest mistake was not talking to you about it, not telling you the things she found out about them: their addictions and obsessions or that they abused her. She thought you were too young. She was wrong.' Abuse? That never crossed my mind, not once. 'Your mother regrets that now. She regrets not encouraging you and she regrets the breakdown in communication with you. She wanted to be your friend but you saw her as an enemy. She didn't want you to leave. It broke her heart when you did but she understands now that that's the best thing she ever did for you. To let you go.'

I pour out the drinks, trying not to let the tears fall again. Not tears of sadness but tears of relief. I don't want to appear pathetic, I hate that *Seven* knows about my past but Mum must have spoken in depth about it. He's helped her understand what happened. Maybe talking about it is unnecessary after all. Maybe all that's needed to be said has been said without words.

Maybe *Seven* has said it all for me. I was wrong about him; it takes a strong man to love Mum unconditionally the way he does.

***

Dad phones shortly after I get to the shop. Mum and *Seven* took Lily back after we had some lunch; I was going to stay home but didn't fancy being alone with my thoughts too long. Besides, I was curious to find out if Eddie had heard from Dad. I serve customers while Eddie's on the phone though have half my mind on their conversation and accidently give the wrong change.

'Your father's spoken to an art dealer who's interested in the story and has spoken to an expert in nineteenth century French art at Lancaster University. He wants me to take it down this evening,' Eddie says. I tell him that's fine and if he wants to go sooner then I'll be happy to man the shop for the rest of the day. 'Oh, that will be even better, if you don't mind?' I laugh and usher him away.

The shop is fairly quiet for the rest of the afternoon. I stay behind the counter, ripping book pages between serving customers. It's strangely therapeutic even if I do still feel guilty for ripping them. I've barely thought about Caleb in the past few days, let alone spoken to him. I'm a bad girlfriend. I leave a quick message to say Lily's gone home now. He messages back instantly asking when I'm coming to see him again. Soon, I say. I can't commit myself right now. I add value to my one word statement with a happy-face emoji in the hope that will placate him. I think it works, he emoji's me right back.

It's strange coming home without Eddie being here but I use his kitchen to cook myself dinner. I haven't cooked in the barn for months. I have breakfast and the occasional lunch there, that's all. My brain can't decide what to think about most;

the mystery, Mum's wedding, Caleb? To top it all I want to paint again. It's a pressure valve for emotional overload. I scroll through my phone looking through my pictures and come across the table photograph with Eddie and Rosanna with the cupboard in the background. That spark ignites the fireworks in my mind.

I finish my food and run to the barn. I feel it. I see what I want to create vividly in my head. I remember the videos I watched about painting people and how to achieve skin tone and texture. I look at my phone and see the photo as if it were on canvas. Rosanna's laughter lines and the twinkle in her eye, the way she lovingly holds her coffee cup, Eddie's distinguished features and focussed stare. He's listening to Rosanna, relaxed, oblivious to my presence. The cupboard listens, absorbing their tales as if it's storing new history, like it once did. For decades it was silenced, behind plaster, waiting to be discovered, protecting the secret within. I'm watching; I'm listening to its secrets. People will look at this painting and see two people sharing memories but right at the centre, in the heart of my painting, is the real storyteller. Its memories are older, darker and speak louder.

Eddie knocks when he gets back.

'Hey, sorry I'm late. I went for a meal with your father… Oh wow!' he says, as he sees my painting. It's not finished yet but already from across the room you can tell who the subjects are. 'You never cease to amaze me, Kayleigh.' I tell him he scrubs up well in oil. 'I'll leave you to it, I'm tired now. Don't forget to sleep!' We'll see.

As the night goes on, I add more depth. There's less colour than in my previous paintings and more shade but the darker colours are varied. I think of Vincent van Gogh's painting *The Potato Eaters* but with more luminance, more joy, and less-weathered faces. The cupboard is intriguing; it looks more like a door in the wall. I try to give it as much detail as I can, using a fine brush to give texture, character and wear to the woodwork. It needs green to balance the colours so I create an olive green and blend it to the shadows creating a slight bevel as if the door is open, just slightly. It's listening. The result is perfect. I stare at the painting for five minutes, losing myself in the image. It's exactly as I imagined it.

CHAPTER 33

It's been raining all week, just as all the kids break up from school. Typical. The shop is quiet, not that I mind; I have to deal less with people and it gives me more time to make stock. I've finally caught up with my orders. Caleb has been messaging me most nights but I've not seen him yet. He suggested the cinema tonight. I've never been on a cinema date in my eighteen-and-a-half years.

Eddie's been on the phone for twenty minutes. I'm assuming it's to the art dealer or specialist because he's going in to a lot of detail, including Didier's story and the Robinson history. I hear him explain about the wooden sketch and olive tree, the letters, notes, photographs, the tobacco tin and even Lily's video of our discovery. I guess the value of the painting would lie more in its history than its artistic value, so provenance is probably more important than possession. My guess is that the painting is worth a lot more to Didier than it is to anybody else.

'I think we should close up early,' Eddie says, looking at his watch. It's three o'clock and it's been quiet all day. 'We need to go to Lancaster University.' I'm up for that, I'm sure Caleb will forgive me. I can hopefully explain why afterwards and make it look as if everything happened in the past twenty-four hours. That way he might not have to know I've held back on him again.

Eddie considers going back to the house for my collage but knows we'll hit rush hour so we head down the motorway to Lancaster. I've often seen the building as we've passed; it's an intriguing green and orange with towered halls around it. Eddie thinks it's ugly, but I like it. We make it down inside the hour and head for the Lancaster Institute of Contemporary Arts building, a fascinating white architectural structure with plenty of glass. Inside it's bright and modern and even the smell triggers creativity. I have a feeling I'll be questioning my career choices again later.

We're introduced to Professor Peter Brady and led down a hallway and upstairs to the fine art's department. I try to take in the work on the walls; my stomach grips me with excitement to see all this passion and talent. I can't help but compare my work but much of what I see is abstract, albeit excellent. We walk down a corridor and into a room with a strict No Admittance sign on the door. Brady punches in a numeric combination to unlock the door before letting us in. Inside is a short blonde-haired woman in a suit. She greets us before introducing herself as Susan Mallick, a doctor of nineteenth-century fine arts.

'Thank you for coming so quickly,' she says, 'I have to travel back to London tonight.' We're led to another room with a further security level; it's darker and has artificial light and a table in the middle. Brady uncovers the painting carefully wearing gloves, while Dr Mallick speaks.

'The tales you tell me are fascinating about its discovery and history. I would love to see the collection of letters and photographs that you have too.'

'I nearly went home for the evidence that we have but it would have added another few hours, so we left from the shop,' Eddie says.

'No matter right now but it will help later. I've had a good look at the painting. I would like to have it looked at by a forensic expert but I can tell you my opinion based on my knowledge. From the materials used and matching the signature and wear on the painting I would say that this is indeed late nineteenth century and I have every reason to believe it is the work of

Paul-Eugéne Milliet. He wasn't a prominent figure in the art world; his legacy is known because of Vincent van Gogh's famous portrait of him. He's documented well in the letters Van Gogh sent to his brother, Theo. If the sketch was dated the thirtieth of September that would fit in with Milliet's known movements at the time.'

'Didier Bernard would be pleased to hear that,' Eddie says.

'The painting itself, though quaint, lacks the texture and depth of colour of the renowned painters of the time. The brush strokes are how we would expect an enthusiastic student to paint, focussing on the edges and filling in blocks of colour in the centre; there's little variance to the colour blending which means it lacks character. He's set out to paint what he saw and that's all.'

'I suppose its value lies in its history. I haven't told Mr Bernard about it yet, but I would imagine it would be worth more to him than to us. It's a matter of whether we decide to keep it.'

'Yes and no,' Dr Mallick says. 'There will be collectors who would be interested in this. It's an old painting that has been preserved well. There's little weathering to it. Slight damage to the corner here but that wouldn't affect its value. There have been no extremes in temperature change, it hasn't been affected by damp and hasn't been exposed to much light so for a painting this old it's in a good condition. I can't put a value on it but yes, it would be worth more to Mr Bernard than to anybody else, together with the wooden sketch and letters. It's quite a story, but only half the story.' Dr Mallick looks over to Professor Brady and he pulls out another painting. We watch him uncover it.

'This on the other hand…' she says. The painting is of a house, a garden, and an orchard of what looks like apples and oranges, full of colour, full of life, and swirls. 'This is a different story.'

I start to shake. What is this?

'This painting fitted neatly inside Milliet's painting. At first I was confused by the thick stretchers - it looked like a double stretcher - and then I realised there were two paintings. We carefully managed to separate them; the only damage is to the stretchers.' Oh my God! I lean in to the table. I think I'm going to pass out.

'Are you okay?' Eddie asks.

I try to breathe. I don't want to disgrace myself. I nod, probably unconvincingly and Dr Mallick laughs.

'She recognises it,' she says. I nod again.

'Again, we need to get forensic assessment and proper evaluation, but I suspect, and have no reason to believe otherwise, that you might have uncovered an undocumented Vincent van Gogh.'

'Oh lord!' Eddie says, leaning a hand on the table. Now I'm worried that he might pass out.

'Some of the painting has imprinted itself to the underside of Milliet's and there's a little bit of damage to the impasto texture but it's not been enough to spoil the painting at all. In fact it's been pretty well preserved. The canvas fibres will need to be removed carefully. This is an exceptional piece, painted at the most prolific time in his career as he was developing the style that has become synonymous with his post-impressionist reputation.'

I take a closer look. I don't recognise the house but then I wouldn't since the original was destroyed in the war. The colours are vibrant, as if each leaf, each flower and each fruit are individual souls, dancing for the artist. My heart pounds with excitement and awe.

'What now?' Eddie says. 'Do we tell Mr Bernard? Where would I stand legally? Am I the official owner or does it belong to his estate, the Robinsons or Mr Bernard?'

'It was discovered on your property, it wasn't documented

as stolen so I would assume you have ownership, but I can set you up with a legal adviser. I would advise keeping it quiet for now but if we can authenticate it then this is going to be global news and the story is going to be told everywhere. You need to prepare yourself for that.'

'I could take both back with me now and not say a word to anyone though, surely?'

'Yes. Yes, you could. I wouldn't advise it and I would make sure that you keep your house secure and pray you don't have a fire because you'll never be able to insure this with a standard household insurer.' Eddie laughs.

'No. I'd be too terrified to ever sleep or cook. Can you help? I wouldn't know what to do or who to contact and I know everyone will cost, which is likely to force me to sell it anyway.'

'We need to get everything verified. One thing you could do for me is to document the find and your story as much as you can and send me as much photographic and video evidence as you can. I would love to visit your property myself at some time.'

'I can do that, and you would be more than welcome.'

'We'll take it from there. You can never put a price on it but there is likely to be a lot of interest. It could possibly go for seven or even eight figures. It would be to your conscience what happens from there.'

'I understand. I do feel I need to prime Mr Bernard about it. I can see the Robinson's opening an investigation into Roland's death.'

'Do nothing for forty-eight hours. Professor Brady has agreed to keep the paintings here overnight. I wouldn't want to take them with me to London but I know of the people to contact for its authenticity. If the department covers costs for now and I get a proper quote that you can agree to initially then we can get the painting couriered down to them safely.'

'Yes, that's fine.'

I ask if I can take a photograph of it.

'I've taken some already. I'll forward them to you.'

I can't believe it. I stare as hard as I can, trying to take as in as much as possible while Eddie signs some forms and they work out some phrasing by way of a keeper's agreement and ownership.

'To think those paintings were there all that time,' Eddie says as we leave the inner room and Professor Brady locks it.

'It's the sort of thing you can only dream about. Let's hope we can get it authenticated properly. There's no official provenance but the evidence you can supply would be valuable as Vincent van Gogh didn't make reference to the visit or the painting in his letters, so the story will have to hold strong.'

'Most of the evidence is with Mr Bernard now but I have photographs of everything and my granddaughter made a collage documenting everything. She even painted both the fortress and the house depicted in the new painting.'

'I'd be interested to see those too. Anything you can send me the better.'

We're shown out of the building and thank Professor Brady and Dr Mallick before we head to the car. I'm shaking; I need a coffee or a piece of cake. Anything.

'I don't think I can drive back right now. I need to calm my nerves and think,' Eddie says. I don't blame him. He phones Dad to see if he's already left for Penrith and thankfully he hasn't so we drive there as he only lives twenty minutes or so away. We can bring him back to Penrith with us later. We need that coffee and Dad needs to know the news.

CHAPTER 34

'Ladies!' Didier Bernard says as we leave the airport and he kisses us on both cheeks. Lily looks for Marcus. 'Don't worry, he'll be back at the house by the time we get there; he couldn't make it in time so told me to go ahead so that you wouldn't be waiting around.' He greets Eddie too. 'Good to see you, glad you could come.'

It's been the most surreal five days of my life, trying to keep the biggest secret in the world and carry on as if everything is normal. It was a relief to finally tell Lily. Eddie phoned Didier on Monday night and we only booked our flight yesterday. Didier doesn't know the reason for our visit yet. It made sense for Lily to come along; she jumped at the chance. Polly agreed to man the shop for a couple of days as she has some time on her hands now the summer holidays are here.

'Thanks for picking us up,' Eddie says. 'Sorry for arranging a quick meeting; I need a favour so thought it would be better to come to you this time. I can see the sketch as well.'

'That's no problem. A favour?'

'Yes. I'll make it worth your while. I'll explain in the house.'

'There she is,' Eddie says as we see the fortress appear closer to Mornas. I'm not sure he'll be able to make it up the hill but it would be good for Eddie to see it after all this time. We've booked to stay at Marcus's parent's hotel overnight though we have to fly back tomorrow evening. There might be time tomorrow morning. 'It's an iconic landmark.'

'Indeed it is. It has a dark history too,' Didier says.

We turn off the motorway and make the short journey to Didier's house; Eddie hardly takes his eyes off the fortress. As we turn into the driveway to the house, Didier points out the olive tree. Time has repaired it but you can still see a slight indent into the shape of the trunk. The tree looks old now.

Marcus comes outside as we pull up and throws his arms around Lily when she gets out the car. We follow Didier into the house and sit in the huge music sitting room. I look at the paintings by Didier's great-grandmother. They're so detailed; I wouldn't have called her a copyist. I think there was some extreme prejudice going on and I wonder how Berthe Morisot faired so well; she must have got lucky.

'They are magnificent, aren't they?' Didier says. The paintings are on large canvasses. 'It took her weeks to make one painting.' I can see why. I wouldn't say they were painted with passion but with plenty of love, even though the subject is passionate.

A woman brings in a silver tray with freshly brewed coffee, which Didier pours, letting Eddie speak.

'You were right about the paintings,' he says. Didier looks up, pausing his coffee flow mid-cup.

'Paintings?'

Eddie explains about the letter from David Edgeworth and how we found Milliet's painting in the washhouse. Didier is animated; he claps his hands, rolling back on the sofa. 'That's fantastic news,' he says. 'Was it in good condition?'

'Surprisingly well kept. It couldn't have been hidden in a better place.' I show him a photo on my phone and he studies it for a while, showing it to Marcus before handing it back to me.

'You have made an old man very happy. Where is the painting now?'

'It's in London. We're getting it authenticated but we met with a specialist at Lancaster University, who suspects that it is genuine despite lack of provenance. This is part of the favour I need from you.'

'You said paintings?'

'Yes. While they were examining the painting they were confused by the double thickness of the stretchers, the wooden frame the canvas was pinned to. They realised that there were two paintings.' I show the photograph sent to Eddie by Dr Mallick.

'Oh my word!' Didier says. 'Is this what I think it is?'

'It's being tested by forensic experts but it's very likely to be a genuine Van Gogh.' Didier leaps up from the sofa. I think we're all shocked at first but I realise he's smiling.

'Incredible. Incredible. My great-grandmother was right.'

'This is going to be a major story if confirmed; I think we all need to prepare ourselves. I have a worry for you though.'

'My father?'

'The Robinson family have lived in fear of your family for decades. Roland Robinson was beaten up badly and later took his own life shortly after a visit from French visitors asking about the paintings. A later visit, in 1984, suggested that he was murdered. There's bound to be an investigation.' Didier's smile falters and he paces a couple of times before sitting back down. 'I have a plan, but I'm going to need your help in order for us to authenticate the paintings.'

'What do you need?'

***

Lily is emotional as we say our goodbyes at the airport.

'I promise to come to England as soon as the tourist season is over,' Marcus says, releasing Lily from a tight hug, 'even if it means staying with you at university.'

'Thanks for bringing us down,' Eddie says, shaking his hand. We go inside the airport building and Lily waves at Marcus until he's out of sight.

'I'm aching now,' Eddie says as we finally take our seats on the plane. I'm not surprised. 'I'm glad I got to see the fortress at last though.' I'm pleased he saw it. Marcus drove us to the mediaeval church so that Eddie only had to walk the final hundred metres or so.

'Yeah, it's a shame we missed the tour, you would have enjoyed it,' Lily says. It's been an enjoyable visit. Marcus, Lily and I went for a walk yesterday afternoon while Eddie and Didier talked. Marcus knows so much about the local history; both world wars impacted on this region heavily, and even though it's sparsely populated, it was occupied with much resistance from the towns and cities of the region.

'I can't believe I have the wooden sketch back in my possession again. Albeit temporarily.' Didier agreed to let him bring it back with us, together with the relevant letters from his great-grandfather so we can send them for authentication.

I try to keep my head clear and don't dare to look forward to what might happen if the story holds true. I know if I ever have serious money that I'd do good things with it. I would still paint, make crafts and read books. Eddie said he would still keep the shop open, he would just employ staff for it; even if it makes a loss as he loves it and loves the social interactions it brings.

'Mornas will never be the same again if it turns out to be a genuine Van Gogh,' Lily says.

'I think that's what Didier wants,' Eddie says. 'Maybe he's bored of the quiet life now. I can see him getting thousands of visitors.'

I'm lost in my thoughts as we start our descent to Manchester. Caleb wasn't happy at me bailing on him twice but trusts me enough to know there's a genuine reason. I didn't tell him exactly what was going on but I did explain that it was connected to the mystery and that we're keeping quiet until we can legally say. I think he's guessed we've found a painting but

I doubt he's guessed the truth.

Eddie drives us to Dad's to so that he can take the wooden sketch and letters to Professor Brady in the morning and we drop Lily off en route. She's done well to keep this all a secret too considering how hyper she is. I follow her into her house while Eddie waits in the car as she's made some more patchwork cushions for the shop.

'I really hope they can verify the paintings. I can't breathe!' she says. I know the feeling. 'Thanks for letting me come with you.' She hugs me goodbye as I leave. I always feel empty after I've seen her.

We don't stay long at Dad's; just long enough to update him on the trip and leave him Didier's sketch and letters.

'There must be a serious rumble in the art world about this. You can't see these investigators not having a gossip,' Dad says. I can imagine how it would be.

'I wish they'd hurry up,' Eddie says with a laugh. 'My nerves are shredded with it now.'

Eddie is joyful as we head back to Penrith, listening to eighties music on the radio as we go.

'I've done my bit. I'll switch off now until we know,' he says. 'I have a mental plan of action and the rest we'll improvise. You've been excellent, Kayleigh, you've played your part well too. If we navigate this properly I can make sure everyone benefits.' He's obviously given it all a lot of thought. 'Do you remember what a lie-in is?' I laugh. I have vague memories. I tell him that I'll work the shop in the morning so he can have one tomorrow. He laughs. 'I'll return the favour on Saturday so that you can then.' Sounds like a plan.

I settle to bed soon after we get in. I lie awake in the quiet and comfort of my barn, replaying the last few days in my head. I'm happy with myself for surviving all the social pressures recently but no matter how much I do, the social anxiety never leaves. I think people mistake it for lack of confidence. I'm forever told it gets easier with time and experience, and yes, confidence does, but not anxiety. Every day is a struggle. I'm happy with life, I'm happy with what I create and I'm so grateful to be in the position I am with my career and finances, but whether I'll ever be happy with me, I don't know. It's odd having such a passion and desire for life and yet at the same time wishing I was on a private island with a cat. And maybe Lily.

CHAPTER 35

'Finally!' Caleb says as I get out the car. I'm only two weeks late, he's so impatient. I ran out of excuses to delay our cinema date any longer. 'You look stunning,' I don't think so. I barely had time to have a shower and put any make-up on so must look a mess. I knew he was weird.

We don't go inside the house. He motions to his car, which I realise he would have to manoeuvre past mine so I motion him back to my car.

'I won't fit in that thing,' he says. Cheeky sod. I sit back in the driver's seat and switch on the engine and wave him in. He stands defiant with his arms crossed so I start backing up and he rolls his eyes and shakes his head. Fair enough, I wave goodbye and start to pull away, revving the engine and he starts a sprint towards the car. Yes. I win!

'If we crash and I lose my legs, I'm suing your arse!' he says. I wasn't going to let him win this one. I'm now terrified of crashing so drive like an angel into town.

'Are you going to tell me your secret yet?' he asks. I can't and tonight wouldn't be right anyway. I want to switch off for a few hours. He doesn't push it, thankfully. We get to the cinema complex and he tells me he's paying for the tickets. I don't argue, I go to the shop and buy a big tub of popcorn and two drinks and wait for him, pinching the popcorn between my finger and thumb while holding the drinks, praying I don't drop it. Luckily I don't have to wait too long. Caleb laughs, pretending to walk on before turning around to take his drink.

'Hope you're hungry,' he says. 'There's no way I'm eating them.' I never thought of that; I just assumed he would like them. I joke that he'll be wearing them if he doesn't help me eat them. 'You're such a lady.'

He does help me; even if I do eat more. I try to switch off during the film but I can't. I'm wondering how Lily's doing, about how to tell Caleb the truth, whether he'll be angry at me when he finds out, and if any experts can authenticate the painting. I think Caleb's noticed that I'm distracted.

'Are you okay?' he asks. I smile and nod and look up at the screen again to hide my embarrassment. I can't concentrate but then I never really did have the attention span to watch films. It's just nice being out in good company.

We head to his house after the film and he asks me inside as I pull up in his driveway but I say no. It's late and I was up early. He leans in to kiss me before he gets out the car. It's the most passionate kiss we've had and lasts for an eternity. As much as it's nice and releases butterflies, I get anxious too and, as his hand runs from my shoulders across my chest, I get that cue to gently release the kiss. I smile and tell him it's been nice to see him again.

'Yeah, I've enjoyed tonight. We will have to do this more often,' he says with a smile. I remember those words from the last visit. I'm a bad girlfriend, I know. He leaves the car and I wave goodbye as I pull away. I'm shaking and I don't know if it's excitement or extreme anxiety. I really don't know what I want. I enjoy his companionship and I know he's hot. I just don't know if I want more, I don't know if I want him touching me and I don't know if I want to touch him. Is this a hangover from my mum's relationships? Do I distrust men? Or is this me defending my love of *Four*? I don't think so. I hated him when he died. I think. I don't know.

What I crave isn't sexual. It's companionship, it's tenderness and being able to share my passions and ideas with someone.

Lily once joked that the boys think I'm not girlfriend material, whatever that means. Maybe that's right. Luckily for me I love cats, so that's my future sorted if all else fails. Caleb must be so confused.

***

'It's a beautiful drive here,' Dr Mallick says, greeting us at Thackthwaite.

'It is, I wouldn't want to live anywhere else in the world,' Eddie says. 'Come on in, we're about to tuck into some freshly made bread for lunch if you'd care to join us.'

'That sounds wonderful, thank you.' Dr Mallick follows us inside. 'So full of character too, this farm. I love the solid oak beams.'

'From ships,' Eddie says. 'Many from around the time of the Spanish Armada.'

She spies my collage. We'd already sent her a photograph of it but it looks better in real life.

'That's a clever idea. I'd be interested to see your paintings, Kayleigh.' I smile and agree but panic inside. I've never had a professional look at my work before. We sit down to eat and Eddie explains again about the discovery of the wooden sketch. He points to the cupboard and explains about the plaster. Dr Mallick occasionally writes notes onto a small pad then takes photographs of the cupboard open and closed. Eddie uses it to keep utensils in.

After lunch we show her the washhouse. The shelves are still out, exposing the fake wall underneath. She already has David Edgeworth's letter.

'I need to get a builder to put the shelves back again, I haven't had time. It was easier to prise them away from the wall.'

'I'd be tempted to leave them out and put a glass panel behind, maybe with lights to make a feature of it, especially if the painting is authenticated.' She takes more photographs. Eddie explains about the upturned bell used for the sink and how Oliver Hutton has made it into a wishing well.

'This house has so much character,' she says. Eddie smiles and I like that he's proud of it, and so he should be.

We take her into the barn and I show her my paintings. I explain my thoughts behind each one and she looks at them carefully. She turns to my new painting and instantly recognises Eddie.

'Looks like you're immortalised too,' she says with a laugh. She understands my thinking before I have to tell her. 'They're all excellent, Kayleigh, but this one is extra special. Your eyes are drawn to the cupboard even though it's seemingly insignificant. It demands to be seen, even though the people in the painting are the subject.'

'Didier Bernard told her she paints like a poet,' Eddie says. I still don't know how to react to praise, how can I feel so ashamed at feeling pride? Dr Mallick's praise means more to me than solving the mystery did.

'He's right. She does. And these painting need to be seen.'

We return to the house for another drink. 'Sorry the authentication takes so long,' Dr Mallick says. 'They're even testing the canvas and comparing it to other canvasses Vincent van Gogh used around the time. They can tell within the weave and fibres if it's likely to have come from the same stretch and who manufactured it. For something as big as this, they need to be one hundred percent sure.'

'I guess so. Were there any fingerprints?'

'I'm not sure but the painting has been handled in its time. The main problem is that Vincent van Gogh's letters to Theo don't document a visit to Mornas, but there is a gap and he was spending time with Milliet during that week and Milliet was known to travel by coaches, which were horse-drawn in those days. They'll need to review the whole story. Another reason that I'm here is so that I can add my own personal judgement.'

'I appreciate it.'

'Ironically, the fact that Kayleigh is such a good painter also poses more questions to be answered in case it's an elaborate hoax.' Oh. I never thought of that. Eddie laughs. 'Don't worry,' says Dr Mallick. 'Now I've seen the setup for myself I'll argue your case.'

'Do you think you have enough information without talking to the Robinsons and Edgeworths?'

'I hope so. I don't fancy visiting the Robinsons but I do understand if this breaks, they're going to want an investigation.'

'I know. I've spoken to Mr Bernard and we have a plan, which will hopefully give them some closure.'

Dr Mallick stays for another hour or so and asks questions about my art, my shop crafts and my career aspirations. I get carried away with my enthusiasm and ideas and realise I must be coming over like a four-year-old talking about her favourite toy. I stop myself, apologising.

'Don't be silly, sweetheart. It's good that you're passionate; passion is what makes great artists. I have two sons; my eldest can read music and play beautiful piano pieces, my youngest son can't read music, he taught himself to play but he writes beautiful pieces. My eldest son can't write. Practice can make perfect but passion comes from within. The greatest artists all share that secret ingredient no amount of practice can ever teach you. All great artists are passionate.' Wow.

Dr Mallick sets off to leave mid-afternoon and Eddie goes into town to relieve Polly, who's been looking after the shop a lot lately. I go back to the barn and look at my paintings. I am passionate, but I don't have an ego so I don't know if my work is good or bad. I'm pleased with them and proud of myself but wouldn't know if other people would like them. Dr Mallick's praise shocked me. I was expecting to be labelled an enthusiastic amateur. Was she just being kind because she was trying to work out if I had painted an elaborate hoax, or did she mean it?

CHAPTER 36

I've been avoiding Caleb all week and the guilt is keeping me awake at nights. I've got a problem and I don't know who to talk to about it. How is it that I enjoy his company, can recognise that he's hot but have no desire to engage in a physical relationship? I even enjoy his kiss. I guess some would call me frigid but it's not just inhibition or being prudish, I just don't have any desires that way. I want to love and I want to be loved, I don't care if that's male or female. I just… I'm confused. I'm tired. I think these past few weeks are taking their toll. The waiting and anticipation is wearing; it's the ultimate in excitement and anxiety, especially knowing that if the painting is authenticated, I'm going to have my fifteen minutes of fame whether I like it or not.

The shop has been busy too. I've been keeping up with my custom orders but not been able to experiment with new ideas. I'm manning the shop myself today as Eddie has more meetings. He's struggling too and I worry for his health. He needs a holiday but at least we're in a better position now to employ staff, even if it is part-time. Eddie posted an advert last week and there's been a steady response.

Mrs Ruskin comes in and is full of smiles, as always.

'I haven't shown my face in here for a while because I'm finishing off my latest novel, I've come to see what new delights you have in.' I show her some of the new things that Eddie has bought in and Lily's cushion covers. We sold four of them at the weekend but there are still six left. 'These are a must!' she says, grabbing all six. 'I've recently decorated our sitting room and it's book-themed, look.' She shows me her photos, even the pictures on the wall are fantasy book-art. I'm impressed. I tell her about Lily's quilt and show her a photograph of the one that sold. 'That's incredible. Could she make me one?' I give her Lily's email address so that she can discuss colours and price. I remind her that I'd still be happy to have a go at her book cover.

'Yes, I haven't forgotten, don't worry,' she says. She leaves happy and I quickly message Lily to prepare her for the email. I've done my good deed for the day.

Eddie phones at three o'clock and tells me to shut the shop at four and head home. Dr Mallick wants to see us. That dreaded knot in my stomach returns; does she need more information? Does she think I faked the whole thing after all?

I do as I'm told and head back to Thackthwaite, half-expecting to see a police van in the driveway, but as I pull in there's only Eddie's car. Maybe Dr Mallick is late.

'They're due here at five; I've just been tidying up quickly as I only got home myself just before I called you.' They?

The kettle has just boiled when a car pulls into the driveway. I stay in the kitchen while Eddie greets our guests. Dr Mallick enters with a dark-haired man in a suit with a briefcase. He looks like a lawyer or M15 secret agent.

'Hello again,' she says. 'This is Charles Cavendish from the Society of Fine Art Dealers in London.'

'Hello,' he says, softly. He looks awkward.

They sit down and I bring through the coffee tray while Dr Mallick tells Cavendish the tale of the wooden sketch's recovery, pointing to the cupboard.

'There have been several meetings this week and we have the forensic report back,' she says as Eddie pours the coffee. 'The lack of documentation meant that we had to be extra thorough with the authentication process. There have been several forgeries over the years and one such picture was deemed a forgery because of lack of mentions in Vincent's letters to his brother.' Cavendish pulls out some papers from his briefcase as Dr Mallick speaks. 'However, it was decided by a unanimous verdict that the painting you found is indeed a genuine Vincent van Gogh.'

'Oh my...' Eddie squeezes my hand. I feel the smile grow too big for my face.

'All the evidence you've documented, together with records shown of a letter by Milliet before he went back to Africa, where he details a trip through Provence with Van Gogh to paint the vineyards, corroborate your story. They decided the painting was indeed genuine.'

'The Bernard family were so sure from the start.'

'We're going to hold back on any publicity for seventy-two hours to give you time to think about what you do and prepare anybody that needs to know. We want to hold a press conference and it would be nice if you could be there.'

'Yes, that's fine. I need to make contact with the Robinson family. I've already discussed what I plan to do. I will sell it. But I want to do things right.'

Eddie talks with Cavendish about what to expect and how to sell it, and fees, and percentages, and... I zone out. I'm so excited I can't stop smiling. It's surreal. I daren't even pour out another coffee as I think my hands would be too shaky. I'm high on adrenaline.

'I take it the Milliet painting was verified as well?' Eddie asks Dr Mallick.

'Yes, it was,' she says with a smile.

I message Lily quickly and tell her not to mention it yet to Marcus until Eddie's told Didier. She messages back an expletive-laden reply of sheer joy. My smile grows even wider. I could get used to this feeling; it's pure euphoria. I can't believe that all this started from a random question about the cupboard, seven months ago. It's funny how a seemingly insignificant moment in your life can be life-changing, beyond imagination.

Right now I just want to bathe in this feeling and try to hold on to what it feels like.

***

The press release is tomorrow in London so we have to get this done today. I'm braving the worst anxiety ever because I know it's the right thing to do. I've been smiling in my sleep, what little of it I've had, but now I have to be serious. We're waiting for Colleen and Harry in Greystoke. They weren't happy when we made contact again and Eddie explained that there's going to be a news story that they need to be aware of.

'I'm going to have to be careful not to land David Edgeworth in it,' Eddie says. It will be hard not to. Colleen comes in with her husband and an older woman. We stand up to greet them and Colleen introduces her mother Lucille, John Robinson's daughter.

'I'm assuming this is about the artworks? The mystery you told us you were going to leave?' Colleen says, even before Harry gets back to our table with drinks.

'Yes,' Eddie admits. 'And we did, until the mystery landed back on our doorstep. While clearing out the washhouse we uncovered a false wall under the shelves. Inside was a painting.' Their faces are expressionless. 'We got advice from Lancaster University, who put us in touch with specialists. They found another painting embedded into the frame of the painting we found. After a long verification process, which included talking to the family in France, they've confirmed that the painting is a genuine Vincent van Gogh.'

'Goodness me. Well, that explains why the French were desperate then,' Lucille says.

'I've met the family in France. They still live in the house. The owner, Didier Bernard, was aware that his great-grandfather tried to reclaim the paintings but he was unaware, and saddened, by the hurt they caused. I understand there's no love lost between him and his ancestors.'

'You're as bad as them,' Colleen says. 'My great-grandfather died because of them and you're selling out.'

'I wanted to talk to you before you found out about it on the news. I have a letter here from Mr Bernard. It's an apology for the behaviour of his grandfather and an explanation about what he knew and the myths of his ancestors. He also waivers any cut in anything made from it, which I had previously offered for his help in verifying it, and asked me to give it to your family. I don't know how much the painting will raise and there are many fees and costs but five percent net of expenses will come to you and I'm personally matching that too. It won't make up for the hurt and the fear, but I hope that, together with this letter, it will bring closure for your family.' Both Lucille and Colleen are in tears and Colleen shakes her head. It's heart-breaking and I want to hug them but I'm scared that I'll make things worse.

'Do you even have a right to sell it? Should it not be our property?'

'When you sell the house the buyer assumes ownership of everything, including what's left in it. We looked into it. Your family sold the house to the Hutton's who then sold it to our family. I just felt I had a moral obligation to tell you and make the offer to you. I have no need for the money as such but I do have plans for it, good plans, and most will be given away anyway. I love that house; I would never want to move.'

'All these years I've wanted to know the truth about what really happened,' Lucille says. 'I don't know if I care about the truth now.'

'I wish I could make this easier for you but I can't prevent the truth from being true nor can I undo the past.'

'I respect you telling me and I respect your offer, but this doesn't feel like justice,' Colleen says.

'I know. This was never going to be about justice. The perpetrators are long gone; they didn't gain anything in the end. Had the painting been lost under Haweswater you would still never have achieved justice or any have answers. This way you have something, including recognition from the family that their ancestors behaved in a despicable manner. Nobody will ever know the truth about Roland. If he took his own life or had an accident at the hands of the visitors, we'll never know. Maybe if there turns out to be a heaven, he can tell you. At least you can tell him that eighty years later you had closure.'

We're all quiet for a while as if we're lost in our own thoughts.

'When the story breaks, I don't want my family involved,' Lucille says. 'I don't want to be dealing with reporters. There's no reason for the dark past to be resurrected.'

'I'm in London for a press meeting tomorrow. I'll insist on that. I can't promise that reporters won't look into the previous ownership of the house. All I can do is make sure we don't mention it ourselves.'

'I don't value your promises, Mr Halsey, but I hope you can respect our wishes.'

They stand up and get ready to leave, so we do likewise. Eddie offers a handshake, which only Harry accepts but they do thank us for telling them. We sit back down again to give them time to go.

'I knew that would be tough. Thank you for coming with me; I hoped that you being here would help soften the blow. I'm not sure anything would have made a difference in the end. David Edgeworth will no doubt find out before the news breaks now.' I give him a hug outside the car before we set off home. They were mean to him but I understand why; I would have probably reacted the same way.

The mood lightens again as we head back, probably out of relief. I don't think anybody really knows what will happen from here; I'm dreading it, yet so excited about what we've achieved. The only thing I know for sure is that life won't be the same again.

CHAPTER 37

I've never been at a proper auction before. The place is heaving with men in suits, many with designer moustaches and beards. It's hot and extremely loud, everybody talking at the same time with raised voices. I've had a whirlwind three months; everything has been thrown at me, good and bad. The week after the press conference was insane; we had requests for interviews, public-relations companies offering us deals for exclusive interviews, of which we had many. I was on live television four times. I can't watch them as I cringe, I think I look so awkward, even though people told me I didn't and that I came across well. Eddie has played his part too - he's a star - and Didier has had a chance to tell his family stories, even admitting that his ancestors had tried bullying tactics to find out where the paintings went. Thankfully, the Robinson family seem to have been left alone.

Eddie and I are on a small balcony section overlooking the auction room. Vincent van Gogh's painting, now named, *The Orchard of Mornas,* stands framed beside the auctioneer.

The auctioneer calms the room, explaining about the painting before opening the floor. The bidding starts and it's manic, I can't keep up with what's being said at first. I feel the adrenaline surge again and I swear I hear *one million.* My heart races; I couldn't dare think of what the painting's true value would be. I spoke to Caleb last night on messenger and he warned me what it could be like - he's been to auctions for both livestock and antiquities before and could only imagine the chaos today.

I guess it is chaos but there's a civility to it as well, many people on phones as the auction progresses. I've only seen Caleb a few times but we talk every day; I think he understands my frame of mind over our relationship. We don't talk about the physical side but he has tried. I change the subject and he doesn't push.

Five million and I start to shake. Maybe it's the heat in the room too. I lean on the balcony rail; the bidding slows but the figures rise steeply. *Ten million.* I look at Eddie and he pulls a face at me as if he's in disbelief as well. I tried not to think too hard about the money; I hoped it would make a million but didn't think beyond that. I'm fighting the adrenaline and heat and breathe deeper, trying to take in oxygen. *Fifteen million* and there are three, maybe four people bidding now but it continues with nods and hand signals and the rest of the room hushes as it continues. I start to feel nauseas and hope Eddie isn't feeling the same. *Twenty million.* I'm not getting oxygen; I don't know what's happening to me. I breathe heavily and I don't think Eddie's noticed. The sounds become a blur. I tremble and reach towards Eddie but I don't think I make it. I hear a raised voice and I can't make out what was said, but as the hammer comes down, everything goes black.

Then there is the brightest of lights. I feel an excruciating pain in my head and behind my eyes and it takes a few minutes to realise that I'm in hospital. I want to cry, scream… or die. I catch sight of a familiar face silhouetted by the light above me. My grandad. And all I can do is smile.

'Hey,' Eddie says gently. 'You passed out and hit your head on the floor.' That explains the pain. I feel so stupid and embarrassed. 'Don't worry, the cameras caught you.' Oh, just great. I feel disorientated still and my head pounds. I can't believe I overdosed on adrenaline. I ask how much the painting sold for.

'Twenty-six million,' he says. Wow.

***

Jared reminds me of my fame and infamous collapse last week. They've all been following the stories over the past few months. Jared and Rosie were proud of me until my monumental fail, now I think they get picked on because of it. I tell them people will forget about it soon, and anyway, how many eleven-year-olds have half a million in their account? Admittedly they can't touch it until they're twenty-one or in their second year at university. Eddie was clever with that one.

Mum hands me a cuppa and joins me on the sofa with her husband-to-be.

'You're a celebrity. I keep getting asked for your autograph,' she says. It's so surreal. I tell her that I want to go and live in the Outer Hebrides now, with a cat, and endless art supplies. She laughs.

'You could afford that now.' She's right, I could. I don't know what I'm going to do with the two million pounds Eddie gave me from the sale. Eventually I'll buy my own place, for now that's not even important. Just knowing I'm secure enables me to think and plan and if I want to invest in art projects over the years, I can. There is one thing I do want to do right now with the money.

'You've been a superstar,' *Seven* says. 'I'm so proud that I even know you.' I think that's a compliment. Mum nods in agreement, which I think might be an admission that she feels the same.

'Thank you, Matthew,' I say. 'I'm glad you found Mum and I'm happy you're planning to stay. That's why I want to pay for the wedding.'

'Aw, sweetheart, no, you shouldn't feel it's your responsibility. We're saving and planning and it would be wrong to...'

'Shush!' I say to Mum. 'Let me speak. I have a speech in my head.' She laughs.

'I've had a rotten time leading up to this year. I know it was largely my own fault and I know Mum's made mistakes. It's only since I've been away I've been able to be philosophical about it. I get it now. I have so many regrets and some of the guilt I'll carry with me forever. I've had no trust in men because I've thought they're spineless and walk away rather than fight to make their relationships work. I thought you were the same. I was waiting for it, I could see the signs. But instead you did the right thing and Mum's better for it and Jared and Rosie are happy. Nothing would make me happier than for you to be with Mum. Put your savings towards a honeymoon and I'll come and take care of Jared and Rosie while you're away. But let me pay for the wedding; even if it's in two or even five years from now. When you're ready, let me pay. Okay?'

Matthew reaches out for Mum's hand and they look at each other. I look down. I want them to accept this. It's a fresh start for me. I did so much that impacted on so many people and I feel it's my responsibility to make amends. A person died because of my obsession with him, another had a suspended sentence for involuntary manslaughter, lost his job and wanted nothing more to do with us. I've lived with the trauma, the guilt, the flashbacks and nightmares for years. I've wished death upon myself and nearly succeeded. I'm the luckiest person alive right now. There's so much good I want to do and this is where it starts.

I look up to see them both on the edge of tears; I don't want that either, unless they're tears of joy.

'Okay. But you're going to have to help your mother choose the dresses and all that cosmetic and frilly stuff, because there's no way I'll be any help there.' I laugh.

'I'll even pick out the suits if you like,' I say.

They both reach to hug me in turn. I feel huge relief. I'll

probably help them out financially afterwards but the wedding is symbolic for so many reasons. It's important for Mum to know that I love her, that I forgive her, and that I'm sorry.

CHAPTER 38

I'm back in the spotlight again. We invited the media for the open day and they've arrived from all over the world. My twenty-first birthday should be a day to remember for very different reasons to my eighteenth. It's taken two years for Didier Bernard to rebuild the old smithy. Eddie paid for it and it looks magnificent. It's now the Vincent van Gogh *Orchard of Mornas* museum.

Eddie gave Didier Milliet's painting as payment for lending him the letters and wooden sketch, which are now on display together with my paintings, the photographs of the find and the letters from Gerard Bernard. The stories of Van Gogh's stay here and the discovery of the painting are told on ornate boards beside the paintings. There are the photographs from Thackthwaite and my paintings have their own story told beside each one. In the middle of the centre wall is the original *Orchard of Mornas* by Vincent van Gogh.

Didier Bernard had put together a consortium of investors to bid for the painting. Apparently thirty million was their limit. Eddie had told Didier before the auction that he would love to make a museum in Mornas with the money and that it would be the best result for everyone if the painting could come home to Mornas. It's been a three million pound project for Eddie and Didier over the past two years. And now my paintings are in a museum, alongside a Vincent van Gogh.

I look over at the scene before me as the press gather outside. The euphoric feeling is back, the pride, the feeling of accomplishment - and the anxiety of course.

'Don't pass out this time!' Jared says. Cheeky monkey. That won't help. Lily holds my hand and we walk to the back of the big hall. Two of Emily Bernard's huge canvas paintings hang behind us. She was as integral to the story as anyone; it's only fair that her work should be honoured too.

'Thousands, maybe millions, are going to see your work now,' Lily says. It's an amazing thought. The fact that people would even consider my work to be worthy of showing is incredible. Apparently, Didier mentioned to Eddie even before we found the paintings, that he was going to try to get my work exhibited. Eddie's intuition was right about him and they're becoming good friends.

'I'm so lucky,' I say. I know my paintings help make the story; I don't expect the elitist art critiques to mention my work any more than I'd expect them to mention the wooden flooring or the high rounded windows. There are two other windows, one on either side of the room. One is small and if you rest your chin on the sill you see the exact view and frame size of Milliet's painting of the fortress. The other small window overlooks the orchard, not exactly from the viewpoint of Vincent van Gogh's painting, but it's still a beautiful view. I'm tempted to paint it one day.

Security open the doors to the press for the first time. There's a brief speech by the curator of the official Van Gogh Museum and then the journalists are free to roam. I'm asked hundreds of questions by scores of journalists, who all seem to like my work. The painting of *The Cupboard* with Eddie and Rosanna seems to generate the most attention.

I'm asked to sign postcards of my paintings. Among the things for sale in the shop are postcards of all the works on display and a book was also written of the story, which included all my works connected to the discovery. I'm asked to date many of the postcards too.

'What's the chance of that being up for auction online by tonight?' Lily whispers after the latest request. I nudge her with my foot and smile. Even after these years of relative celebrity I still have to psyche myself up, I still dissect each encounter in my head, often cringing.

We survive the day but I'm exhausted. The museum opens to the public tomorrow so it's much of the same. We all walk into the village; it's not too far and French winters don't bite this far south but we can see the clouds close by.

'Look,' Rosie says, pointing to a rainbow forming beside the cliff. Lily and I immediately reach for our phones to snap a shot. It looks majestic. I'm inspired.

I'm pleased that Mum and Matthew came down with Jared and Rosie. They haven't had their honeymoon yet, despite getting married last September. The day is still fresh in my memory; everything went so well, I was possibly over-emotional but so happy for them. Dad and Polly are coming down tomorrow. Polly now lives with Dad; they moved to Lancaster together last year.

Matthew managed to trace *Five* for me without telling Mum and took me to him so that I could apologise in person and I gave him a cheque for fifty thousand pounds. I know it is little compensation for his own trauma but I never got to say sorry, or thank you. He hugged and thanked me. I haven't had any nightmares since; maybe that was the closure I needed.

I still lie awake at night thinking of the lives that have changed because of that secret trip to Mornas that Van Gogh and Milliet took that day. It changed the lives of many families, for good and bad, and one hundred and thirty years later it has changed the path of history for so many people. Who knows what Lily and I might achieve in the future, who knows how many lives we can change? How many people will meet here and start families? What compelled me to ask about that cupboard? Would we have ever found the painting? Would anybody?

***

'Are you disappointed Caleb couldn't come?' Lily asks as we get ready for bed. We stay in the same room as we did on our first visit here together. It's been fully refurbished over the past year or so, courtesy of Eddie, and Lily, who donated some of her half million that Eddie gave her. All the rooms display her textile art now too. The hotel also has a proper restaurant. I enjoyed my birthday meal; it was fit for royalty.

'I knew he couldn't come. It's difficult for him with his exams right now.' I persuaded him to take up horticulture at college and he's doing well and enjoying it. 'Besides, I'm not sure if his new girlfriend would approve.'

'I guess she finds it hard to accept that his best friend is a girl.'

'They all do. I feel bad for him, but I can't fault his loyalty to me. She seems nice though, I have high hopes for her.'

Lily cuddles up to me and turns the light off.

'It's hard for people to understand my asexuality. It's hard enough to understand it myself. It makes you wonder how many people there are like me, who don't realise that it's okay and that we aren't freaks. I'm never sure if I was always this way or it's a result of my past.'

'I guess,' she says. 'It's also hard to build confidence. I dated so many guys and they always ended it when they realised I was holding back on the physical side. That's why Marcus has been so good for me; the long distance relationship gave us a chance to talk about it and theorise it. I'm looking forward to living down here after I finish university.'

I'll miss her when she moves down here. She's going to help run the hotel and work part time in the museum. I'm glad she's stuck it out at university though; it must have been tempting to quit with the money she had. I'm happy for her and Marcus.

'We both got lucky,' I say softly. 'It's nice to know that not all men leave. I'm glad I can put that myth to bed.'

'Aw,' she says, cuddling me tighter. 'I'm ever yours, whatever they do.' I smile.

I'm tired now. It's been a good day. I've had the best three years of my life and I'm the luckiest person alive. If Vincent van Gogh knew the legacy he would leave behind he would have died a happy man. Some people never have the opportunities or the lucky breaks, but it doesn't mean they can't create them for others. I owe him.

I feel myself drifting, content and aware of Lily beside me.

'You always were,' I whisper. 'Goodnight, Lilypops.'

'Goodnight, Kayleigh babe.'

*** _ ***

ACKNOWLEDGEMENTS

I'm eternally grateful for all the help and support from my family, who all played their role in some part: Kyle, Harley, Jake, Annette and Hannah and especially to Marilyn, without whom it would have been impossible to find the time and space.

Special thanks also to my wonderful editor Alison Williams and to Emma Pritchard for giving me faith in my own ideas. Also thank you to Catherine Cousins at 2QT Publishing for helping me through the labyrinth of admin in order to get the book out.

Finally thank you also to my researchers and beta readers: Dr Emm Johnson, Steven Greening, Caitlin Lynagh, Sarah Loftus, and Laura Hulse.

NOTES FROM THE AUTHOR

At the age of fourteen I moved to a farmhouse in Matterdale with my mother and sister. We discovered a wages cupboard behind the plaster in the main room. I remember the excitement of that discovery and the disappointment when all it contained was horsehair and dust. Still, I've fantasised about it many times since. The beauty of being an author is that I can bring the fantasy to life.

I grew up in the Penrith area of England and fondly consider it as home, even though I live in Lancashire now. I hope to return one day – maybe I can open Eddie's shop. Maybe I can make Penrith a *writing town.*

Asexuality is a topic I've planned to write about for a while. I wanted to reject the myth that asexuals are cold and incapable of love. They are not. They are passionate and have a need to love and be loved. They can still have crushes and engage in long-term relationships – often with the same gender. Some often have children; they just don't enjoy the physical aspects of a relationship or have that desire for fulfilment. Kayleigh is typical of many.

As I write this, a remarkable film is about to be released based on the life of Vincent van Gogh. *Loving Vincent* was animated by paintings made by a team of artists in his unique style. I was never an artist – indeed I was so bad that it was crossed off my list of options for O Levels, but I have always loved and appreciated art. I am inspired by the passion and creativity in an artist as much as I am in their vision. I enjoyed researching and entering the mind of a painter in writing *Unwinding Time*.

I always enjoy engaging with readers and other authors. Feel free to send photos of your artwork too. I will happily feature it on my Pinterest and Tumblr. Check my website for further details: **www.jamesstoddah.com**

Facebook: /JamesStoddah
Twitter: @JamesStoddah
Pinterest: JamesStoddah
Also **on Tumblr, G+, Goodreads, Amazon** and **DeviantArt**